MW01384580

IPDOWN ROSES

IPDOWN ROSES

a novel by

William C. Holden III

PHOENIX PUBLISHING
West Kennebunk, Maine

Library of Congress Cataloging-in-Publication Data

Holden, William C., 1942-
Ipdown roses : a novel / by William C. Holden III.
p. cm.
ISBN 0-914659-81-2 (alk. paper)
I. Title.
PS3558.0347754I63 1997
813'.54—dc21 97-32027
CIP

Printed in the United States of America

For

Florence Dieckhoff Holden

Forever alive in my heart

"Let no man deceive himself. If any man among you seemeth to be wise in this world, let him become a fool, that he may be wise."

CORINTHIANS I 3.18

"Nor thieves, nor covetous, nor drunkards, nor revilers, nor extortioners, shall inherit the kingdom of God."

CORINTHIANS I 6.10

"The night is far spent, the day is at hand: let us therefore cast off the works of darkness, and let us put on the armour of light."

ROMANS 13.12

Author's Note

CHARLES WINGATE disappeared without a trace in April of 1994 on a trip to Germany, little more than three months after writing the preface to the manuscript which follows, and one month after writing his "Postscript Two" on March 11, shortly after returning from the hospital; recovered from the savage attack by the boy he took under his wing.

William C. Holden III

Dunkerque Chamonix 1847 - 1940

Preface

AT ONE TIME, I thought it all started with yellow roses. Long-stemmed. One dozen. I was wrong. I know that now. Only now.

I put mine in water. A vase made of clay. It was long after Laura came into my life, and long, long after it all started.

Hector watched me, standing with his hands on his hips, as I walked to our old pick-up with its falling-off rusted tailgate, a reclamation project from the town dump in Dayton, the town here. He watched as I looked to the barn and then the old corn field with the aged, broken-down harrow sitting in the middle, alone, like something I don't know.

I asked again, as I opened the truck door. Do you want to come with me to Boston. To the cemetery. No answer. He turned and walked away. Started to walk away.

"I'm goin' to see Laura," I hollered.

Then he cried.

No. I would not be sitting down to write about any of this were it not for Hector. He watched over my boat when I was away from St. Martin and, in return, I helped him with his English and entry into the States. Hector is probably a mulatto (I think), born in Santo Domingo or Dominica (he thinks), almost eleven years ago, in 1983. He still only barely speaks English and understands even less of it when he hears it spoken. But that doesn't prevent him from being an excellent hand, a budding caretaker and equipment mechanic here at Finnsheep Farm, despite his age and one arm. One natural arm. He uses the prosthesis and hook on his left as adroitly as I use my good arms. And he can be a very hard worker. Not just lately with his job here and the work he has done on my boat over the past year, but also in his goal to better himself by learning to read and write.

Laura was actually the one who found him for me. When I needed a boat boy. A little young. But that's okay. He's a quick learner and conscientious. Usually. And very strong.

It is mostly, I think, for him that I intend to set forth the events which have so pre-occupied me over the past year and occupied others for much longer periods. I will write and Hector will read and copy my tellings. My hope is that with hard work, he can enter fourth grade this fall here at the Dayton public school. That will put him, agewise, almost two years older than his classmates. That will be difficult for him, I'm sure. But, he is short for his age and maybe will be able to fit himself in with the other students in his class before he begins to shoot up. Let's hope so. (He is shaking his head, "yes.") Maybe a future Edison or Einstein.

This story or saga about which I intend to write does not have a happy ending, at least in many respects. In other respects it does. To a degree. And I have frequently reflected on how I came to get involved. Involved at all.

In a sense I owe it all to my grandfather. In a sense I do. He worked for Elmont & Thornton. He wasn't a senior partner or even a partner, that was only for Elmonts and Thorntons. But it was because he let me come with him to his office on Christmas Eve Day when I was ten that I met Elmont "Buzzie" Thornton IV, same age as me. We became friends and went to Swarthmore College together eight years after that, in 1960. So you see, if not for my grandfather, I never would have met Buzzie Thornton, and things would have been simple. But I did and they aren't or weren't. I will tell you what I know. Which is not everything.

My name is Chuck. Charles Wingate to be precise. I am not a writer, so please bear with me as I set down what has happened, what I know and what I still don't know. Know and don't know. There is much of both.

I think back, knowing that my crazy college roommate and friend, Buzzie, had been listed among the dead for almost ten years. But I also thought sometimes that he could show up tomorrow. I knew I loved Laura. Laura Reo. I knew that Dunkerque Chamonix died in 1940 at the age of ninety-three, bent over his dying coal stove in an alcove at the top of St. Paul's Cathedral's steeple in London.

And, I knew that Buzzie Thornton harbored a secret, or half a secret, he thought. For, when we met in New York for lunch about fourteen years ago, he told me that he believed his life might be in danger as a result of some things he had discovered. Not all by accident. Not any.

A telegram from Santa Fe, New Mexico, told of Buzzie's death in 1983 at the age of forty-one. He told me some time before that that he was about to complete the unraveling of the long hidden story. And that it related to an old side-wheel steamer, S.S. *Claxdow*, which had sunk in a late fall gale, a hurricane, more than one hundred years before while en route from Hamburg to Halifax; the year after valuable cargo was discovered missing from the HMS *Truro* in the same region. Cargo insured by the family firm of Elmont and Thornton, founded by Buzzie's several times great-grandfather in 1780.

Eleven years after the first news of his death, as I sit here and write of Buzzie's "secret," there are few missing pieces. I know what Buzzie discovered about his ex-wife, Jubilee Chosen. And I recently uncovered something he did not know in 1983. I know about Conswella Van Ogtrop and what she learned in the little tavern in Cuxhaven at the mouth of the Elbe River before she set sail for Halifax. And I know some other things.

But there are things, I mean, people who remain somewhat of a mystery to me. Though less mysteries they are now, than just plain mysterious. The old man, Dunkerque Chamonix. And Fury Ipdown. And, of course, Igamuche.

The keys to a lot of things were found in Cuxhaven, Germany, and in old boxes of records, many 100-200 years old and stored most all those years at 10 Hanover Street in New York City; and in a book. A book which sits next to me as I write. A book entitled *Child of the Island Glen*, written in 1872; the same year the S.S. *Claxdow* sunk en route from Hamburg to Halifax.

I do not believe that I, rather we, would have solved Buzzie Thornton's mystery without Conswella, the parrot Guyane, or the book, *Child of the Island Glen*. Only with that help did I come to understand more about the old man, Dunkerque Chamonix. I am going to write what I know. What I know now. For, who knows, before I am done, there could be more to report.

I hope not.

I remember how I used to lie awake some nights, trying to make sense of Buzzie Thornton's words to me. Was it all just another Buzzie Thornton crazyism or was he indeed close to something as he claimed. I wondered. Strange.

But, possibly the strangest events of all surround or surrounded a man I have never met. A man who as a fourteen-year-old boy survived the August 1945 Atomic Bomb attack on the city of Nagasaki. A boy named Aki. Now missing and presumed dead. But, wanted for murders committed in 1973 and 1993.

Some of what follows I recorded as events unfolded. Other parts were written after the fact. Hence there may be some jumping around as I attempt to tie everything together for myself as well as for Hector.

For the parrot, Guyane. Born 1869, Buenos Aires, Argentina. Died 1988, Radstadt, Austria.

For my uncle, Didier Mollard, and for the old man who died in tears in 1940. At the age of ninety-three. In London's St. Paul's Cathedral.

For the block of marble, solo sailor, Conswella Van Ogtrop, and her Grandfather Luther. With gratitude to her father, Frederick, who bravely lived twenty-six years without a face and saved our lives.

And, of course, for you Elmont Thornton IV, and you Fury Ipdown, your burps and hair plugs.

And, lest I forget a man wronged. For you John.

Here's to you and a gold pocket watch with a shattered face, brought to light 128 years too late.

Charles "Chuck" Wingate
Finnsheep Farm
Dayton, Maine

New Year's Day
January 1, 1994

Contents

PART I

PART II

PART III

Part I

1

"It's All Right"

THE WIND SHIFTED from the southwest, clocking around to the north, northeast, which was good, for she could broad reach or run down from St. John's along the eastern coast of Newfoundland, the sixty miles past Witless Bay, Burnt Cove, Cappahayden and Cape Ballard, until she reached Cape Race. From there, due west twenty-five miles to Trepassey Bay and then due north five miles into Mutton Bay, where she would anchor her boat, *Weitra*, with bow and stern anchors, and go ashore to start her search, six miles away on the shore. There was no secure anchorage near the shore, none closer in Mutton Bay. She would have to make the six-mile trek from her boat with her pack and whatever she thought she might need for however long it took, so that she could minimize back and forth trips between the site and the boat.

Despite its latitude, Newfoundland has a temperate marine climate. Winters are usually not severe, with a normal or average temperature of 32°F or 0°C. Nevertheless, she reflected on the weather and hoped that she would be long gone before the first snow flew.

She set anchors in Mutton Bay on the southern tip of Newfoundland under a full moon and clear sky at 2300 hours or 11:00 P.M. on the night of September 12, 1993, packed her bag for the hike next morning, studied the replica of a 122-year-old map, stretched, did 100 sit-ups, 50 push-ups, dove off the boat into the icy waters for a short swim, climbed back aboard, doused the kerosene lamp and turned in for the night. She told herself that she wasn't tired, which wasn't true, and that the real work was not the miles she had just covered, but the search which was to begin the next day, and that was true.

Two miles to the west of Mutton Bay, just past the tip of Powles Point in Trepassey Harbour, the vessel *Ocean Loon* was set to anchor in a secluded cove, two hours after Conswella Van Ogtrop had doused the kerosene lamp on her boat at anchor in Mutton Bay.

And high on the hill overlooking a peninsula to the west, Trepassey Bay, Trepassey Harbour and Mutton Bay to the east, three miles off the old Route 10 running from St. Stephens to Trepassey, a campfire burned down, and three people huddled round it, drinking hot coffee just before climbing into their sleeping bags. The weather was bringing in a cold front and they rubbed their hands over the coals to keep them warm.

"We will have company," said the rotund man, oily, black plastered-down hair combed straight back, the stub of a Cuban cigar hanging from his lips.

"Stupid fool," said the other man, a dim wit.

She polished the lenses of her binoculars, placed the binoculars and the polishing cloth in the leather case, snapped it shut and said, "It is all right."

"All right?" asked the rotund fat man, both smiling and frowning at the woman. "It's not all right," he said, putting his hands on his fat knees, fat legs apart at the knees.

"I said it is all right," the woman said softly.

"Are you crazy?" asked the second man, the dim wit.

"You. Shut up," she said, sticking her finger into his chest. "Let them do the work for us."

The rotund man looked at her, smiled without a frown and began to laugh. "I think you are right," he said, now laughing louder. "I think she is right," he said again, slapping the second man on the back, the dim wit.

"I'm always right," she said, dumping the remains of her coffee out of her cup with a large, expansive swinging motion of her arm. "I'm always right," she said again. She went to bed. The two men sat for ten more minutes and then they went to bed.

That night, a front came across St. Mary's Bay to the west, passing over southern Newfoundland, dropping a foot of snow. The next morning Conswella Van Ogtrop finished packing her knapsack aboard *Weitra* at anchor in Mutton Bay, climbed into her dinghy and rowed ashore.

The captain of *Ocean Loon*, anchored two miles away, rowed ashore and watched, waiting to follow.

The three people camped on the hill to the north, off the old Route 10, overlooking the peninsula, sat and drank coffee and waited and watched. Watched through their binoculars. The binoculars trained on the old oak tree far down the hill near the shore where the now snow-covered knoll met the ocean at the tip of the peninsula's point.

Five people. Three, plus one, plus one. One already presumed, pronounced dead years before. Another to be dead in three days.

Her skull split open with an axe.

In room 113 of Grasslands Hospital in White Plains, New York, a man admitted near comatose on August 10, one month before, lay with a drain in his mouth, a plastic tube and needle in his arm, one hundred stitches across his bandaged throat, his severed esophagus sewn up, his voice box silenced. The man tried to roll over in his bed, but his hands and arms were strapped. He fumbled and undid the straps on his right arm, which then undid the straps on his left arm and pulled the tube and needle from his arm and the drain from his mouth, and he tried to roll out of the bed, then fell back in a state of exhaustion.

He tried again and this time he rolled out of bed, pulled on his shirt and trousers and he was gone. In the direction of New York's JFK Airport.

And then in search of a man at that moment at the helm of a trawler, the *Glory Be*.

2

Candles and Dowdy Dresses

LAURA HELD THE "Soap and Candles" booklet in front of her as she simultaneously watched the boiling pot of tallow on the old wood cookstove, read about purifying tallow, and counted the dry wicks which she had just brought in from the sunshine. She was proud of the booklet, which she had written, proud of the 500 candles which now hung from the beams of her country kitchen, all the multi-colored candles molded, dipped or rolled by Laura to be boxed and shipped to customers in time for the holidays; and she was proud that she had been able to make all of the candles from pig fat rather than the hard fat of beef or mutton. To the best of her knowledge, no candlemaker sold candles of pig fat tallow except for "Right and Ready Reo-Candles and Soap, Inc." And she liked the name of her little business. "Right and Ready Reo," she said to herself with a smile as she stirred the perfectly clean fat as it boiled. Little Laura Reo, the oft spectacle-clad, sinewy, blue-eyed librarian turned entrepreneur, playing her own little jokes with the name of her business. She smiled again, and was glad that she was using pork fat for tallow unlike all other candlemakers who used beef fat because it was the cheap route, not usable for lard. At least she thought so. Hoped so. It was her first year in the candle business, so she couldn't be totally sure.

As she took off her spectacles and began to read her little booklet, "Soap and Candles," she focused on the instructions she had carefully written for the new reader. "Always add lye to COLD water, never to hot water, because the chemical action heats the cold water to the boiling point. It also produces harsh fumes which are harmful if breathed deeply." Laura knew that beginners could easily make that mistake and that in certain conditions, certain circumstances, in a tightly closed room it might even be fatal. That is why she wrote the warning on every tenth page of her booklet, her first little publishing venture in her first little entrepreneurial effort. "Fatal, fatal, fatal, potentially fatal," she said to herself as she began dipping cotton wicks into the pork tallow, building up layers; layers for the additional 200 candles she wanted to have ready for the holiday customers.

But Laura was sure that no one would ever use hot water with lye to make candles, not anyone who read her booklet. And she was glad of that, glad to give warnings every tenth page, because Laura Reo was "a very caring, loving person for whom being nice and helpful to people is my foremost joy in life," she said aloud to herself. "Except for Perfect."

"Perfect" was Laura's seven-year-old pet, 1000 pound pig. The light of her life. Better than a husband. And Laura's best friend. Perfect was that for Laura Reo.

"You needn't contribute if you don't wish to," she said, clicking her red flats together, smiling behind her wire-rimmed glasses, blue eyes squinting in the sun, hair pulled back in a bun and, I noticed, the dress on her svelte figure as close to dowdy as they come; obviously plucked eyebrows not seeming to fit with the rest of her demeanor. Her truck behind her, its engine still running.

"Come in," I said.

"I really can't. I've a dozen more stops to make."

I wrote out a check to the Library Fund Drive, and convinced her to stay for a cup of tea, as I am a voracious reader and was new to the town, always spending much of what little free time I had in libraries and bookstores, wherever I happened to be.

"You look like a librarian," I said with a smile.

"I hope so," she said, and "Is that good or bad?"

We both laughed.

That was my introduction to Laura Reo and her dowdy dresses. But I began to feel and sense a strange moth to light-like attraction. I found myself stopping at the library quite frequently not too long thereafter. And that led to lunches. Then dinners. Then more time together, though both of us careful to respect the desire for independence which we had in common, mindful of the need for solitary time which we both treasured, Laura occasionally disappearing on her week-long trips to "nomadic hideaways." But none of that prevented us from enjoying our times together, of which there were many.

I remember the evening we graduated from friends to lovers. Laura sat up, pulled her knees to her chin and glared at me, a hint in her twinkling eyes and smile. "You put up with me only because you like having Perfect around, isn't that true, Charles?"

"I must confess to that," I said, just as Perfect let out with a resounding volley of snorts from the barnyard and I confessed silently that "dowdy" might describe only her dresses.

"I knew it," she said, and, as she hit me with a pillow, "so does Perfect," the two of us laughing again as we had come to do so often together.

3

Fireplaces, Wagon Wheels and the Southern Cross

HE SMILED TO himself as he watched the crooked wheel go round; eyes fixed, staring without moving; reins in the hands of the crusty cowpoke sitting next to him; nothing but tumbleweed as far as the eye could see in any direction. He did not move his eyes from the Conestoga wagon's crooked wheel for almost an hour as he thought and thought and thought and sat and sat and sat. This was his dream boondoggle vacation. A 200-mile journey in an old Conestoga wagon across the Kansas plains, sleeping under the stars at night, cooking on a campfire, dreaming up one crazy stunt after another. July 1980.

It was his latest stunt that had finally precipitated a unanimous vote of the senior partners of the 200-year-old firm of Elmont & Thornton, Investments and Insurance, to relegate him to sorting and reviewing. But he didn't care. Rather, he was glad of it. It gave him more time to study what he had found and to pursue clues and leads. "They all think I'm nuts," he reflected to himself when his father and grandfather told him of the senior partners' decision to ". . . lighten your workload."

It was not because he had elected Swarthmore rather than Princeton, where all the Thorntons and Elmonts had gone since the War of the Roses, that the senior partners thought him to be crazy, although they universally believed that that was an early warning sign. There was the blown Bethlehem steel stock trade, blown because he failed to simply keep his eyes on the wall as trades flashed across. It cost the firm a small fortune. And his reason for missing it. Chasing a fly with a wastebasket full of water, across his office. And the broken window. If his employer needed any proof that the man was not going to make it, the fly incident did it. But they had stuck with him through a seemingly unending series of more stunts and capers.

He was fascinated by log cabins. Always had been, since he was a kid and had gotten his first set of Lincoln Logs. Finally he decided to build one. He designed it and drew the plans himself, complete with stone fireplace.

For some reason, which he could not explain, he decided to start with the fireplace first. He worked on it during his lunch hour, every day, at first. Bringing stones in bowling ball bags, and cement in Tupperware containers to the site. It was only when he began to disappear for hours at a time and the fireplace was almost complete that his project was discovered, by a building maintenance man at 10 Hanover Street in New York City. The maintenance man discovered it quite by accident. But there it was, on the roof of the fifteen story building in the heart of the financial district, and surrounded by skyscrapers. A huge fieldstone fireplace and four stakes in galvanized pails filled with sand marking the four corners of the about to be built log cabin. One of the senior partners asked how he intended to get the logs to the roof. "Helicopter." None of the partners smiled. They just looked at each other. The fireplace and galvanized pails with the stakes were gone the next day amid a flurry of workmen with sledge hammers.

He continued to stare at the crooked wagon wheel. And he smiled to himself when he thought of the day after the fireplace was discovered, the day it came down. For that was the day that his name had been removed from the internal distribution list for all important Elmont & Thornton reports and memos. "Good," he said to himself as he inspected the wagon wheel's spokes, rim and hub. His eyes now moving from hub to spoke to rim, then along the rim to the next spoke, then down that spoke to the hub, then across to and up the next spoke to the rim and so on until he had covered the full wheel and complement of spokes ten times; then he did it one more time, "For good measure," he said aloud. The cowpoke driver ignored the man who had been sitting next to him without saying a word or moving his head or eyes for almost an hour.

The man who had been "inspecting" the wagon wheel pulled a photo, given to him the month before, from his wallet. A picture of a man taken at a family picnic in 1952, twenty-eight years before. A man he had never met. He shrugged his shoulders and returned the picture to his wallet. He began to think about "Jubs." He had met her the year he graduated from Swarthmore, 1964. November. The day before Thanksgiving. He had been working at Elmont & Thornton for almost six months since taking the month off after graduation to design a shoe sole that gum wouldn't stick to. She interviewed for his unadvertised secretary's job, and was quiet, reserved and, he thought, very, very pretty. He hired her. He, the ugly, with his giraffe-like neck, monstrous ears and nose and near non-existent chin. Less than one year later, Jubilee Chosen asked him to marry her.

Blond Jubs with her lusty green eyes, long lashes and thick eyebrows, drove a broken-down VW bug and owned a total of eight dresses and three pairs of shoes when she met him for the first time. Six months after their marriage she went on a spending spree and an eating spree. She talked him into buying her a new mink coat and a Jaguar. She began to shop at Saks Fifth Avenue, and her nose went in the air. And she was no longer quiet or reserved, ordering him around, he soon to cease to listen, ear plugs securely in place. And Jubs Jubilee began to eat. A petite 110 pounds her first day on the job as his secretary, she gradually and steadily ballooned to 170 not long after their marriage. In the heat of an argument one evening, he told her she looked liked she stuck an air pump nozzle in her mouth every morning. She smacked him.

"Dork," he said aloud, staring again at the wagon wheel. The crusty cowpoke glanced at him and then turned his head and eyes back to the open spaces ahead.

But he hadn't divorced Jubilee Chosen just then, and neither did she him. She had plans for him. What she did not know was that he also had plans.

I have just decided. I will be on "Island Time" shortly. Just decided. January here in Maine is not for me. Head south. Soon. No more thinking of the past crap. But, you know something? I have been away from my boat for more than two months. The whole damn, floating thing is now running amuck with — you guessed it — cockroaches, I'm sure. They used to be called "waterbugs." That should make it easier for me as they crawl across my face at night. Well, not much easier. They really freak-out Hector.

He was glad to be on the trail, in a Conestoga, just like a pioneer; and away from the bullshit world of New York, investments and insurance. He turned his head from the wagon wheel, looked at the vast expanse of the trail ahead, turned to the cowpoke with the reins, smiled, and said "What you thinking about, cowboy?"

"The Dow Average, Sonny. And my IBM stock."

"Christ," he said, under his breath.

He lay next to the campfire in his sleeping bag looking up at the stars. "Summer in the Southwest," he said to himself. He found Arcturus, in Bootes, "Bootes the Kite," with the bright orange star Arcturus as its tail. His eyes went down to the southern horizon, looking for Alpha Centauri, the most famous star in the southern constellation, Centauris. But he could not see it. It is never above the horizon at latitudes higher than 25°N, visible only from positions south of latitude 25°N, approximately at and south of Miami, certainly not in Kansas. He knew that, and tried scanning the southern horizon while standing on his head to see if he could spot the star that way. No luck. He thought about the Southern Cross which, like Alpha Centauri, is visible only from locations farther south than latitude 25°N. He wanted to see the Southern Cross again. He had only seen it on his honeymoon in St. Martin and the times he took vacations back there later.

He decided he didn't want to stand on his head anymore. He went to the Conestoga wagon where the cowpoke was snoring, withdrew his briefcase from his trunk and sat down by the fire and began to design an ocean-going motor-sailor. He had never been on a sailboat.

"It would be a nice way to see the Southern Cross," he thought to himself, sketching with his pen.

4

Aboard the Glory Be

WHILE THE trawler *Glory Be* rolled side-to-side in St. Mary's Bay in the early morning of September 15, 1993, the queasy man watched through field glasses and thought back. Of the five people ashore, some one mile away, he knew one woman well, very well indeed; the two men with her, he knew them both; one quite well, the other not so well, but both of them slimeballs, he said to himself as he set the field glasses down and inched the *Glory Be* in closer, one-quarter mile toward the lee of the shore and calmer water, but careful to remain far enough offshore, slowly running a course as if trawling, fishing, so as not to arouse any suspicion, be noticed as anything other than a fishing boat by anyone who might be watching him, but no one was. Not anymore. He had taken care of that. He looked below at the slumped figure and smiled.

The two men and the woman lay back, just up the knoll from shore. They had come together. He had watched through his glasses as they had pitched their camp three days before high on the ridge. He wished she had come alone. The two slimeballs were nothing but trouble. He would do it his way, by himself, from here on. He was linked far too closely with them already. The salvage company out of Grand Cayman was one thing; *Glory Be* was a legitimate concern, though a money loser from day one, but the two casinos and diverted funds were another thing. He knew they were laundering money and that one was running guns and drugs and the other was his dim wit henchman. Both of them, together with a third man, now fugitives on the run, arrest warrants over their heads.

But, he thought, why should he care now. "I no longer work for Elmont & Thornton. I was fired. Remember?" Knowing that that solved nothing.

He popped the cork on a bottle of rice wine, put *Glory Be* into reverse, hurled the anchor through the air and waited for the old fisherman's anchor to grab bottom, which it did; he clumsily set the "hook," tied off the rode around a forward deck cleat and sat down hard on the bowsprit. He got up, went aft, then below.

Fire in his eyes, blood on his hands, he watched through the window. The coordinates were correct. He watched the digging. *Glory Be* drifted closer to shore, anchor dragging. He reset the anchor. He saw a man climb from and lift a box out of the hole and set it down by the hole. He watched through his binoculars as the man seemed to do a war dance, jumping and shouting, raising his hat in the air as a woman popped open the box. He had never seen either of them before. But, he could see it all happening clearly and wondered if they had found what he knew was more than the money in the bottom of the hole. He would wait briefly and then bring *Glory Be* to shore, anchor in the lee of the point and then row to the sight of the hole and surprise them. All of them.

The stench was too much now. He took one final look at the man propped against the forward bulkhead and snapped a picture of the body with its stitch-marked neck. "Family, Country, Love and Honor," he said. "*Bock's Car*." Then he spat.

He climbed back on deck and scanned the shore with his binoculars again. "Come on, come on," he said aloud before returning below.

When the old sandals had been placed on the dead man's feet, the captain of the *Glory Be* stuffed the body, face down under the starboard berth in the main cabin and again climbed back on deck.

He began to row ashore. He wondered what Fury Ipdown would have thought about him manning the *Glory Be*.

The seas tossed the dinghy about, and within 500 yards of the point he lifted his oars and sat in his dinghy, watching as the three figures approached the hole from the knoll above and to the east, the woman in the lead with what appeared to be a drawn bow.

He felt dizzy.

Death rose before his eyes, only moments before he blacked out; his dinghy to drift aimlessly, rolling with the waves, away from shore; oars now floating, in tandem, like toothpicks in a boiling stream.

That is all I can tell of him. All of what I now know. All of what I can surmise.

Siegfried and Anne flew the coop this morning. It was a good lesson for Hector in raising pigs. I say that now, but I sure was not feeling that way when the two piglets set tail across the barnyard and disappeared in the alfalfa field out near the pond, our two dogs chasing them at full speed, despite my orders to stop; the dogs making the pigs run even faster, the pigs squealing like death, a shiver running down my spine. But I settled down. "Piglets needed to get some air and space, anyway; root a bit and get fenced trained," I said to Hector as we pulled on our Wellies; I, my green ones, and Hector, Laura's old yellow ones. With the roses she had hand-painted on the boot tips.

5

Hurricane of November 1872

THE ONLY thought Dunkerque Chamonix had was to stay with the sidewheel steamer as he watched the crew of the S.S. *Claxdow* wrestle with the lifeboats, rain driving across the deck in sheets as the wind raced through the rat lines; and with the vessel now listing heavily to port, bodies slid over the deck, into the mountainous seas, the first lifeboat overturning as it hit the water, the second disappearing no more than fifty yards from the *Claxdow*.

There was no chance at all, he thought, in one of the lifeboats. His only chance was to stay below and hope that rescue would come before the mother ship sank.

"Abandon ship, abandon ship," yelled the captain as he fought his way into one of the lifeboats, pushing his way past women, children, men; anyone who got in his way. The captain's shouts were barely audible above the roar of the ocean and din of the wind. Twenty-five-year-old Dunkerque Chamonix huddled between the coal stove and settee on the starboard side of the galley, his body wedged tightly to keep from being thrown about.

"Don't go," he whispered to the two shaking figures nestled next to him. "You will surely die if you leave this ship."

"What if we stay?" asked the frightened woman holding her baby.

"It is our only chance," the man said, the parrot on his shoulder shivering, claws tightening as the vessel rolled.

"We will drown in the ship," quivered the woman, her shawl wrapped around the child, the hurt of a huge wave rocking the ship like a cannon shot and lifting the woman off the cabin sole, throwing her into the outstretched arms of Dunkerque Chamonix.

"Stay down. Stay down," he said.

"I must go. My baby must live."

"I know. I know," he said. "I have a five-month-old baby myself. Back in London."

"What is its name?" asked the woman. He did not answer.

"You will die out there if you go. There is a ship not far away that knows of our plight. We must wait for rescue," he whispered.

"Suppose this ship sinks before help arrives?" the woman implored, tears now streaming down her cheeks.

"Then we will die. But not before." The man put his arm around the woman and pulled her close to him. He hugged her and the baby tightly as the ship suddenly listed further to port and the words, "Abandon ship, abandon ship," and the vessel's captain trailed off into the night and disappeared. She did not know why she listened to the man huddled with his arm around her; why she did not seek the safety of a lifeboat as the captain ordered. She had only known this man since she boarded ship in Hamburg. But as she tried to struggle to her feet with the baby, he pulled her back down and held her more tightly. She was very afraid, very afraid for herself but more for the baby. But she listened to the man who would not let her go. And she was frightened when he kissed her on the forehead. But she did not go.

And well the woman should not have attempted to go. For all lifeboats went down that night 100 miles east of Halifax, Nova Scotia, in the hurricane of November 9, 1872. The S.S. *Claxdow* would be rocked for ten hours, its three survivors awaiting death every moment, awaiting a watery grave.

"We are just postponing the inevitable," she whispered after three hours, the vessel now pitching wildly, water rising to their knees as they now lay in the top berth of the bow.

"Just wait," the man said, his body shivering with hypothermia, his mind playing tricks on him, the woman and her baby huddled next to him in the only blankets, wet wool but warm blankets, he could find, his ice-blue feet and legs in the water.

They did wait. And at the end of the ninth hour, the ship was still afloat and they were still alive; the parrot riding, now clinging to the gimbaled, dying kerosene lamp, head under its wing, feathers ruffled and soaked with salt.

And with the seas flattening out, the wind down to a strong breeze and only the bow of S.S. *Claxdow* protruding from the water, the Canadian fishing vessel *Red* came alongside, sent two people below and pulled three semi-conscious bodies to safety; the S.S. *Claxdow* to disappear into the North Atlantic Ocean no more than ten minutes later.

While they waited for rescue or death, she terrified and he delirious with hypothermia, the man talked, sometimes coherently but often unintelligibly as the hours wore on. And he began to tell the woman stories of his past, and he withdrew a half sheet of paper from his vest pocket on which was a carefully drawn outline; the other half of the sheet of paper left behind in a Cuxhaven tavern. He gave her the half-sheet of paper from his vest pocket on which was drawn an outline of an unnamed peninsula with bays to the east and the west. And before he lapsed into unconsciousness, he showed her a newspaper article and photo of Abraham Lincoln which she placed back in his vest after writing five words on the back. "Child of the Island Glen."

The half sheet of paper with its drawn outline would be lost by the woman in the years ahead, but not before it was reproduced exactly in *Child of the Island Glen*.

The three survivors, having met less than six weeks before, knew little more than each other's names; the man and the woman with her baby to go their separate ways upon leaving the hospital in Halifax, never to meet again.

Dunkerque Chamonix would remember nothing.

The woman would remember everything.

The three-year-old parrot remembered everything he saw and heard; and was taught long before to tell nothing. His name was Guyane.

The woman's name was Sara Kellog.

6

A Locked Bottom Drawer

THERE WAS SO much to remember. So little he could remember. There had been his mother and father sending him off to boarding school in 1857 at the age of ten to "make a gentleman of you." The dusty headmaster with his fast-moving switch on young buttocks who told him he was destined to be a "n'er do well." His flight in the night in 1862. His crossing to America. The demeaning treatment from the immigration authorities. His call to his uncle which cleared the way. And then, at age eighteen, his first real job, with Elmont and Thornton, insurance brokers and investment bankers, in 1865. He had recorded it all. It was a crude diary. But it was his friend. To write in it at the end of each day was to talk to it, to someone.

And when Elmont Thornton IV found the diary in 1973, more than one hundred years later, buried in the locked bottom drawer of a file cabinet under more pictures of his father, grandfather, great-grandfather, and great-great-grandfather on the top floor of 10 Hanover Street in New York City, "Buzzie" forgot the fly, the crushed coffee cup and flattened eclair; and he decided that he was "fed up to the teeth" with pictures of ancestors on the wall, insurance actuarial calculations, bond quotes and bids, stock exchange "jerks" and "the whole fucking works." The fly was now probably biting someone on Wall Street, Buzzie thought to himself as he smiled and settled into his chair; his desk chair now back from his desk, Buzzie's feet up, his thoughts of missing the Bethlehem stock trade receding from his mind.

Elmont Buzzie Thornton IV read and read. He savored every page and entry in the diary from the start. He wondered about the man who had worked for Elmont and Thornton for six years, one hundred years before. The man who had a baby. The man who was dismissed from the firm, abruptly.

The man who was aboard the side-wheel steamer, S.S.

Claxdow, that went down in a hurricane in 1872 off the coast of Nova Scotia.

The man whom the Elmont and Thornton insurance and investment company records noted had "stolen, robbed, fraudulently obtained" more than $19 million in cargo from the HMS *Truro* the year before, in 1871, the theft of which nearly bankrupted the New York firm, and led to the suicide of Jonah Bellows, the man who underwrote the insurance policy on the *Truro*'s cargo for the Royal Bank of Scotland.

Buzzie Thornton decided that day in 1973 that he would go through the motions and collect his paycheck from "the family tit"; do as little as possible with insurance, stocks and "associated bullshit and bullshitters." Spend his time instead with the crude diary and its wonderful and exciting entries.

"I will figure out what really happened," he said to himself, a new and fresh eclair and cup of coffee next to his raised feet on the desk. "I will show this whole group of clowns."

He looked up to his Swarthmore diploma on the wall, next to the collage of ancestral Princeton diplomas, and again, smiled to himself. "You guys missed the boat," he thought to himself, and then, standing up, raising his arm, he swept the arm with pointed finger across the wall of portraits.

"Literally," he said, then hollered, "Literally." He lowered his arm and finger and dropped back into his chair.

"You guys missed the whole thing," he said again, as he pulled open the top drawer of his desk and lifted out a handful of fresh, raw carrots.

Wild purple irises seem fragile but more alive and more beautiful to me than purple ones grown in a garden. I see it in both the stem and leaves. And in the flower itself. When the ground thaws, I am going to transplant some of them from our back field here. Transplant them next to the gravestone. She would be pleased. I have not forgotten her. And I never will.

7

Chance Meeting at Mitsubishi

THEIR FIRST meeting was quite by accident, in 1972. Aki was busy running trial balances for Mitsubishi's balance sheet when the man walked past his desk and cracked a joke in broken Japanese. Aki had laughed and the man, with time to spare, asked Aki if he cared to join him for coffee. Aki poured two cups of coffee and the two of them struck up a conversation.

And it was in the same year that the Japanese man learned that the Englishman knew a woman by the name of Mandalay Mandarin, and he discovered it only by accident.

And the Englishman did not know that that revelation would eventually lead to the death of "Mandy" Mandalay Mandarin. And he did not know that the Japanese financial whiz had another side, a dark side. A side born in April 1942 when the city of Mandalay fell to the Japanese in Burma, Aki's two brothers killed by Chinese forces under the command of U.S. General Robert Creighton. A side which exploded on August 9, 1945, when the crew of the B-29 *Bock's Car* unleashed the plutonium bomb nicknamed "Fat Boy" on the city of Nagasaki. A side which began to develop long-term objectives for retribution during the two-year hospitalization in Sasebo. A side which received new food for growth everytime Aki had an attack of vertigo or looked at his scars in all the years that followed. And if he ever felt tired of his journey for retribution, he would take out his old photographs and newspaper articles and feel renewed in his quests.

"Two brothers. One sister. A father. A mother. 300,000 Americans. 2,000,000 dead Japanese. Family, Country, Love and Honor."

The day after Aki was introduced to the petite "Mandy" Mandalay Mandarin, in 1973, he went to the phone.

"Long-stemmed roses. Yellow," he said.

"How should the card read?"
"Ipdown Roses."

There is no accounting for a lot of things. Feelings, I mean. About people. I sat down and wrote a list today of all the people involved in one way or another. In the whole episode, or episodes. Why? I don't know for sure. I guess maybe it was because of so many cross-currents I felt and sensed; and a feeling that maybe no one was what they seemed to be; or that my feelings did not in some cases correspond to reality or my rational perception of things; in terms of for whom I should have what degree of positive or negative feelings. Based on what? I'm not sure of that either. But, I feel far less confusion now than I did, say, last year. Most of the time.

I've got to work on keeping my irrational feelings and thoughts in check.

Hector sometimes gives me the shivers. There is a cock fight going on in the barn right at this moment. I can hear it from my desk here in the farmhouse. And, judging by the sound of Hector's shouts, he is doing nothing to break it up. To the contrary. Oh, boy.

8

"Praise The Lord"

"SANDY GROUND Church of God." I stood at the side of the road looking in through the open doors, pews lining both sides of the aisle leading from the doors to the altar at the other end of the tiny church, the congregation singing Praise the Lord; the preacher bellowing forth, waving his hands and arms wildly, little girls and women in brightly-colored skirts and blouses and dresses of yellow, orange, pink, purple and green, singing from their seats; men in white shirts, black suits and neckties singing from their seats; all the members of the congregation of the Sandy Ground Church of God looking freshly washed and their clothes freshly pressed. Praise the Lord.

A native Antillian in black suit, white shirt and black tie, standing and singing next to the open doors, sang and glanced, glanced at me and sang and then glanced back. He stopped singing and walked out the doors and down the steps, glancing then staring at me as he walked directly toward the spot where I stood, he holding his Holy Bible.

"Are you Wingate?"

What in hell? I thought to myself, and "That's me. Why? How did you know me? My name?"

He turned his head from me and looked back to the open doors of the Church of God and said, still looking away, "I suggest you leave the island. Today." His eyes came back to mine. I had never seen the man before. "Today," he said again.

"Who are you?" I asked, clutching my bag of groceries.

The man looked into my bag of groceries, plucked out an orange as I stood transfixed, pulled a pocket knife from his pants, cut the orange in two, and began to suck on one half while squeezing the other half over the groceries in my open bag, eyes fixed on mine. He dropped the squeezed half into the bag. He started to walk back toward the Sandy Ground Church of God, stopped, turned and said in a deep, official and officious-sounding voice, standing straight up and down as a pin, as if at attention, "My name is, of course, Billy Waddie, Governor of Sint Maarten." And then, "There is a time to live and a time to die."

I almost filled my pants as I watched him disappear into the church and the doors were closed behind him.

Newfoundland, a peninsula, five people on shore; a mysterious boat, the *Glory Be*, offshore; a man named Elmont Thornton IV, with crazy ideas, vacationing in an old Conestoga wagon, in 1980; a sinking sidewheel steamer, the S.S. *Claxdow*, in 1872; three people, one a baby, to survive; me outside the Sandy Ground Church of God with a Billy Waddie, the then Governor of Sint Maarten early last year; $19 million missing from a ship named the HMS *Truro* in 1871. A man named Dunkerque Chamonix supposedly to blame.

I knew only some of that as I reflected and sighed and I pulled the wool blanket over my head, swatting mosquitoes on my boat one evening last year.

I thought back to the words I had heard as I walked away from the Sandy Ground Church of God that day. The words rang in my ears, "'There is a time to live and a time to die.'" I had heard that before. Twenty-nine years before. From someone else.

When I had returned to *Boogie to Go* from the church, Hector was busy varnishing the portside rail. He studied my face and, in his best broken English/Spanish words, asked me if anything was wrong.

"No," I said, "I don't know."

He scampered below decks and returned with a

Rolling Rock, ice cold, for me. "Roller Rook," he said smiling, as he handed it to me, hiding his prosthesis with its hook, behind his back, embarrassed of it, as he always was.

"Thanks," I said.

I am next going to roll the clock back from that day in 1993, to 1985, when I begin writing again, in order to catch up on something else that happened, somewhat unrelated. "What it is?" asked Hector just now.

"You'll have to wait and see," I said.

It's about two fishermen on the Pecos River.

"Fishes," says Hector.

Hector and I spent the day today going over care of the animals and fowl here at Finnsheep Farm. Dogs, sheep, goats, pigs, cows, chickens and turkeys. ("And the one goose," he just said.) I am helping him put together a daily, weekly, monthly and yearly care schedule and calendar for each type of creature we raise (including the goose!). It is more organized and formal than I do for myself, but it will be a great tool for Hector, putting it together and then following it to the letter. If he can do all that is required, he will definitely be ready for the fourth grade this fall. Who knows, maybe even fifth grade. (He just shook his head yes, again, with his huge smile, gleaming white teeth.) But we won't push it. An Edison maybe. No Einstein.

Now he wants to go fishing.

9

No Bodies Recovered

THE PECOS RIVER winds its way south from Lake Sumner through the Pecos Plains east of the Rocky Mountains, down toward the Texas border and the Carlsbad Caverns National Park, the river flowing into Texas's Red Bluff Lake and then crossing into Mexico. Largemouth bass, many of them certifiable "lunkers," prowl the cattails and the flowering lily pads in the backwaters and eddies near the river bank on the south end of Lake Sumner.

A roll cast with his fly rod set his homemade felt and beaver tail lure with three hooks going in different directions over a lily pad and into a calm spot just below the river bank about forty feet from his brightly colored canoe. He smacked and swatted his pants and shirt, craned his long neck, picked a mosquito off and sat back with his feet up, letting his lure rest on the water until the circles around it disappeared.

He took out his sketch book and began turning pages, quickly studying preliminary drawings. He stopped at his rendering of a disassembled Browning submachine gun, World War II vintage.

"What are you doing, partner?" asked his friend, who slowly paddled the canoe, a Camel dangling from his lips as the felt and beaver tailed lure was sucked under near the bank by a gaping mouth and a "whoosh."

"Fishin!" he hollered, dropping his sketch book and beginning to horse in the fish, the fish quickly diving deep into the lily pads, wrapping the gut leader hopelessly around the underwater stems, the leader snapping as the fisherman tugged on the rod.

"You lost 'em, Geronimo," said his new fishing buddy and companion traveler.

The man who lost the fish in the lily pads picked up his pen and sketch book, turned to a fresh page and said, "Tell me again exactly what you heard, what you learned. Tell me again. Try and remember exactly. Including the dates."

The friend leaned back on his elbows in the middle of the canoe, sighed, and began again for the "tenth time," he said, to tell of his visits in 1940, forty-five years before, when he was only twenty-five years old. Visits with the old man who lived in a small alcove near the top of London's St. Paul's Cathedral. With the ninety-three-year-old man who had fingered a yellowed newspaper article and photograph from 1865, the photo of Abraham Lincoln, the article about the assassination, the article with five words written on its reverse side, the words "Child of the Island Glen."

When he finished telling of his visits, he sat up in the brightly colored canoe and said, "That's it."

"Damn right that's it," said the fisherman with his pen and sketch pad. "Now, tell again about *Bock's Car* and then the reunion at the St. Moritz Hotel in New York. 1975, right?"

"That's right, the reunion, 1975. It was 1945 in *Bock's Car*. August."

"I know that much. But, I'm not clear. Not totally. Why are you so convinced the guy is out to find you and kill you?"

"Lots of reasons."

"Well," said the man with the pen and sketch pad, putting both into his fishing vest, "I've got lots of reasons to think Blowfish is out to kill me." He reeled in his fly rod.

Two hours later, the brightly colored pink and orange canoe was reportedly washed over the rapids of the Pecos River, five miles south of Lake Sumner just east of the Rocky Mountain Range on the northern edge of New

Mexico's Pecos Plains.

No bodies were recovered.

June 10, 1985. It was quite sometime thereafter that any of this came to my attention. And, even later before I became suspicious.

10

A Burned-Out Tavern

HE WAS SETTLED into a routine but, if you asked him, he would not say that he enjoyed it or did not. Each morning he would bike the three kilometers south along Strasse 39 to Altenwalde and place his food order for the day, and once each week, on Monday, he would bike the ten kilometers west along the Elbe to Otterndorf and place his beverage orders for the week and then bike back to Cuxhaven to arrive before 8:00 A.M. He was always on time.

Frederick Wenzel would not say that he was happy or not happy if you asked him. A short, broad-shouldered man with massive forearms and hands, he ran the tavern like a rooster ruling a hen house. There was always some rowdyism at "Die Haar auf der Hund," but seldom any trouble, for most of the patrons were regulars who knew that Frederick Wenzel would toss a rowdy out the front door and on to the cobblestones as you or I would flick a piece of dust from our cuff. And he was prone to a bit of boisterousness himself. Frederick Wenzel liked to raise a mug or two. And he treated everyone the same, fairly, unless they be Dutch. He hated the Dutch.

Frederick Wenzel ran the tavern much as his father had, his grandfather before that and his great-grandfather before him. Things sometimes got a bit out of hand during the war, particularly in late 1944 and early 1945 when most all of his fellow Germans knew that the Nazi cause was lost, and many of them would stop at their favorite watering hole at the mouth of the Elbe River and drink and eat and talk; talk about what the end of the war would bring to those of them who survived. And then the Allied occupation, troopships coming up the North Sea to Cuxhaven and the Elbe, some of them stopping briefly, others longer as they made their way up the Elbe to Hamburg.

The Americans and English and, later, the French did not concern Frederick Wenzel at all, though he could no longer run the tavern as he had before; a place where the patrons were mostly local Germans, men of the docks, many of whom had known each other for years and whose families had known each other for generations, working the docks of Cuxhaven, Altenwalde, Otterndorf and even Brunsbuttel across the Elbe to the east, coming before and during the war at the end of the day in work-boats. Things were different after the war. The soldiers, Americans and English and French were not old friends, to be sure, but they were not overly condescending nor dictatorial when they came to eat and drink. It was the Dutch.

Frederick Wenzel had never trusted the Dutch even as a boy. And now, who the hell did they think they were? Coming in, drinking, laughing, raising their mugs to the Allies, cheering them, hugging them, thanking them night after night, week after week for the "Liberation of Holland." Traitors, thought Frederick Wenzel. Damn traitors. And when the Dutch would get drunk, spit on the floor at Frederick Wenzel's feet, the Allied soldier patrons would do nothing. And when at midnight on July 4, 1945, six drunken Dutch "soldiers" raised their chairs and smashed the kerosene lamps, no one did anything to stop them.

The Haar auf der Hund burned to the ground that night of July 4, 1945, leaving only the old stone walls and charred floor and towering fireplace.

And when Frederick Wenzel walked through the ruins after the embers had died away three days later, he fell through the burned out floor and into the stone foundation; and he reached down to grab his twisted ankle and his fingers touched a damp piece of moldy paper saved from the fire by the cool of the cistern next to which the paper lay on the earth below the burned-out tavern above.

The German rebuilt the tavern himself, his own hands. It took Frederick Wenzel two years. But when he was done, his patrons were no longer soldiers. His old friends returned and the Hair of the Dog was once again the old Hair of the Dog.

"Vielleicht un Segnung." Maybe a blessing, he said to himself as he closed up after the first night, alone at the bar, raising his mug to the old piece of paper which he had touched with his hand as he grabbed for his ankle two years before, the old piece of paper now framed on the wall in back of the bar. He stared at it. "Vielleicht un Segnung." Maybe a blessing, he said again.

11

A Burned-Off Face

HIS FACE WAS so disfigured that he wondered again if it was he that his eyes caught in the reflection of the window's light. He rubbed his forehead and cheeks, his neck, feeling the pulpy-burned flesh, the hairless scalp. His fingers ran down his chest, then to his thighs, knees and calves. The feet were even worse. He threw himself on to his cot, put his head back and thought about crying. He did not. He thought about laughing. He did not. He was taught not to smile. By his father. And never to laugh. By his father. And he, in turn, unconsciously showed his daughter how not to laugh. How not to smile.

He closed his eyes and thought back ten years and saw the sunlight reflecting from the top of the crude, tin-roofed Quonset huts below as his helicopter blades began to stutter and shake. He saw the naked and the poor in the rice paddies stand up and look to the sky, the men pointing; the women and children stopping their work only momentarily, and then bending down again, hunched over, their feet in the dank, dark muddy water, working the rice plants into the mud with their swollen, tired fingers.

The blades of the helicopter stuttered, shook, stalled and stopped; the reflection of the International Red Cross insignia on the side of the helicopter grew on a tin roof below, the last thing he saw before the plunge into the riverbed.

He rolled over on his bunk, a bunk on which he had slept every night in the same dirty squalor, in the same dirty shack next to the same dirty muddy riverbed where the women and children worked their swollen fingers. The same dirty riverbed and rice paddies where he had lost his freedom and dignity and face in a fiery hell ten years before. He remembered thinking of his seven-year-old daughter as the helicopter's blades shook, stalled and stopped.

He tried to go to sleep as the bugs circled his head like

flies on carrion. He swatted his hand and pulled the blanket up over his head, leaving his feet exposed which were covered with welts in the morning.

He drank his coffee and accepted his new shirt and his new pants at first light. It was time to go. "No stay," said the Vietnamese guard. "Home. You go home."

He took off his torn tee shirt, ran the razor over his pulpy, scarred face and washed himself as best he could with the jug of water from the riverbed brought by Me Yong, the young Vietnamese woman. He put on his new shirt and his new pants and his old boots.

"Ich nicht gehe." I not go, he said

"You go," she said, smiling at him, rubbing his arm, then kissing his cheek, then on the lips. "I will see you again." He knew that she would not see him again.

"Nein."

"Yes."

"Nein."

"Yes, you must go," she said, running her hand and fingers down his back. "Someday we meet again."

"Aussehen zu mir." Look at me, he said.

"I look at you. I look at you. I love you."

"Ja, Me Yong. Ich ihr liebe auch." I love you, too. He smiled, kissed her on the lips for a long time.

"I love you, Frederick."

"Ich ihr liebe auch Me Yong," he said again.

They took him in his new shirt, pants and old shoes 700 kilometers, 420 miles through the jungles and riverbeds, his hands cuffed to his feet as they had been since 1967, ten years before, save the times Me Yong had stolen the key, released him, and they had made love. It was all he had to sustain him. That, and the image of his daughter he had left behind, he an indomitable spirit. "Indomitable spirit," he said to his guards, his eyes half glazed, after ten days with no more than a pint of water daily and the scum of killed snakes to nourish him. His father had called him that. "Indomitable Spirit." He thought of his father Luther Van Ogtrop. And, again, of his own daughter.

The guards took off his handcuffs and leg irons, grabbed him by the neck and pulled him from the back of the sodden truck. They poked their rifles to his back and pushed him onto the plane.

He was going home. Home to Austria. But he had resolved years before that he would never go home to Austria. Not as he was. The broken-down man was only forty-two. And his scarred and ruined face and body and mind would take him elsewhere. The airplane that day, bound from Ho Chi Min City to Bombay and thence to Vienna.

He disembarked in Bombay.

Bombay to New York City.

New York City to San Juan.

His layover in San Juan was long. But, he didn't care. He had thought it all through. He had had plenty of time. Ten years. A new life. Where no one he had ever known would see his faceless face. Starting over, he said to himself. "Beginnen wieder."

12

Boyhood Friends

THEY STARTED with steak and kidney pie, and smoked salmon from Nova Scotia. Both of them had a laugh, a good laugh, about the smoked salmon. Its source. "Cold there, smoked here," said Jersey Ipdown with a chuckle. Dunkerque Chamonix joined him in the joke, and raised his empty stein in the air, gestured with two fingers, as the waiter, having read the request long beforehand, thunked two fresh steins of ale on the table. The waiter smiled at the two amiable regulars, good tipping regulars. Guyane sat still on his owner's shoulder, head and beak high in the air, all-knowing.

"To us, Jersey Ipdown. To us and our fortune, well earned, and well deserved. We are both Horatio Algers."

"Aye, my friend, but we are only halfway there, Dunkerque," replied Jersey.

"Oh, but Dunkerque Chamonix sails tomorrow," said Dunkerque to his old boyhood friend, the boy with whom he had jumped the fence at boarding school, both in their pact to seek, find their fortunes and, as important, end the lashings, the pact of ten years before, in 1862.

"To Hell with the Eton School," said Dunkerque, raising his glass in the air, laughing aloud.

Guyane watched and listened.

The two young men drank, ate and laughed until the old tavern was near to closing.

"You have my map?" asked Jersey Ipdown, concerned, eyebrow arched, beer stein poised an inch from his mouth, Eton School tweed sport coat replaced by a rotting old, yellow oilskin.

"Aye," replied Dunkerque, forsaking his learned upbringing. "Aye, my friend. The map is with me." He withdrew it from his pocket.

"Dunkerque, my friend," said Jersey, leaning across the table in the old tavern in Cuxhaven, a twinkle in his eye, his hand grasping his friend's hand, "I have, I have . . ."

"You have, you have, what?" laughed Dunkerque Chamonix, "A woman for me tonight?"

"No. No. No. I have a concern." Jersey Ipdown's eyes stared at Dunkerque. "If something, God forbid, should happen to you; to the ship; on your passage; there must be another record of the path. The path to our glory. Our find."

Dunkerque Chamonix looked at his friend, raised his stein, took a large swallow, slammed the beer mug down and, said, laughing uncontrollably, "We shall hide it, the top half, here. Right here. Right here in this bloody tavern. I need it not. It is well etched in my head."

And they did hide the top half of the map which Dunkerque Chamonix had in his pocket. The torn off bottom to travel with Chamonix. They hid the top half under the boards of the floor, next to Jersey Ipdown's foot. A wide oak board. Jersey laughed, gulped his beer, and slammed his foot on the board.

"Two maps," said the parrot.

Dunkerque Chamonix turned his head and glared at his shoulder-grabbing friend. "No tell. No tell, or I'll break your neck, Guyane."

Guyane stuck his head under his wing.

The two men winked at each other.

The parrot withdrew his head and said, "Break your neck."

The men roared with laughter.

And Dunkerque Chamonix boarded the steamer next morning, bound for Nova Scotia. The side-wheel steamer.

S.S. *Claxdow*. On October 11, 1872.

And as he boarded the vessel, he was still abuzz from the night before. The night of beer, food and laughter.

A wonderful night it had been, indeed, with his friend at the old tavern.

Die Haar auf der Hund.

13

Fly and Glue

Dizzy and Gone

ELMONT THORNTON IV sat at his desk with one eye on the ticker tape as it sped across the screen on the wall, the other eye riveted on the fly prancing around the rim of his coffee cup; Elmont's eyes too close together, a characteristic seen in many of the Thorntons over the years, and one of several signs that a Thornton or two on the family tree had married a bit too close to the source. He could not let his mind and eye stray from the tape or he would miss the block of Bethlehem Steel stock as it traded. But the rotten fly was driving him nuts. He slowly pushed his chair back on its rollers, reached for the 600-page Standard and Poor's *Directory* behind him, raised it over his head with both arms and hands, and brought it crashing down on top of the styrofoam coffee cup. The fly sailed off, the coffee sprayed in all directions, and the cup flattened, just as the block of "Big Steel" stock flashed across and disappeared from the screen.

The fly circled and landed on Elmont Thornton's eclair. He raised his opened hand and slammed it down on the eclair, creme filling shooting like water from a hose, covering the papers on his desk; the fly now heading on a northwest course, buzzing toward the window. Elmont raced across the office and slammed the window closed before the fly-in-charge could find the opening leading to Hanover Street. He then dashed back to his office door and slammed it closed, trapping the buzzing insect in the room. "Gotcha now, you little bastard," mumbled the man with the long giraffe-like neck, small chin, big ears and nose and poorly hand-tied, red bow tie. He watched as the fly buzzed up and down against the closed glass of the window; watched it intently as he filled the wastebasket with water from the cooler and ran to the window. The basket slipped from his pitching arms as water splashed against the fly and the glass and the half-filled basket crashed through the window and plunged down fourteen stories to the pavement of

Hanover Street, as Captain Fly set a new, now southwest course towards Wall Street.

He knew his father and grandfather would be very angry with him for missing the Bethlehem Steel block trade, but he "didn't give a cat's ass" right then. "Buzzie IV," thirty-years-old and almost eight years with the firm in 1972, went back to his desk, sat down in his chair, gazed at the framed portraits of his father and grandfather and his own Swarthmore degree on the wall to his left, took a tube of glue from his suit coat pocket, removed the cap and shoved the nozzle of the tube up his nose, squeezing and sniffing, inhaling and floating; head back, eyes fixed on the flickering fluorescent tube, covered with years of gray dust hanging from the ceiling above. His thoughts went back to the diary as he floated into oblivion, dizzy and gone.

As he rode the train home from Grand Central Station, across the bridge where George "Snuffy" Stirnwess of the New York Yankees went to his death in 1958, through the Bronx, High Bridge, the old Pullman Car on the Hudson River Valley Line pulling Buzzie toward home in Croton, he thought about maybe "reordering my priorities" and maybe "making some long term plans."

14

A Family Picnic

Phil Rizzuto and Stolen Wallets

MY UNCLE WAS always an enigma to me. Although not the quietest man I have ever known, he always appeared pre-occupied, even when he was smiling, which seemed to be most all of the time. He was born in 1915 in Canton, Ohio, the youngest of my mother's four older brothers, and, according to my mother, he spent most of his time, beginning as soon as he could walk, getting into and out of trouble, being equally adept at both, at first. He was given his walking papers from the family dairy farm in 1931 at the age of sixteen by my grandfather who discovered that his son's way of shortening his turn at milking time was to make sure that water was withheld from the cows so that they would "dry off." He would then fill the milk containers with one part milk and two parts water and be done with his chore in lickety-split fashion; then hiding in the grain silo, smoking Camels until he felt that enough time had elapsed to account for a proper milking of the herd.

I first met Uncle Didier Mollard when I was ten, in 1952. He had returned from the war in 1945 at the age of thirty he told me, and settled outside of Wichita, Kansas. When he showed up at our family picnic in Irvington, New York, in August of 1952, Mother had not seen him since the day he had left the farm in Canton on the toe of Grandfather's boot in 1931, twenty-one years before, when my mother was but nine-years-old.

I actually took a liking to Didier, or "Uncle Did," as my mother always referred to him. "Did, don't, did not," my father called him. Uncle Did drove up in a new Packard with his Japanese war bride Ayako at his side. He wore dark sunglasses, an aviator jacket with the lining removed (it was near 90 degrees), tan chinos and highly polished brown loafers with argyle socks, pink and black, the chinos an inch or so too short. He greeted everyone with a big smile and took to me and I to him like long lost buddies. Which I guess we were in a way.

"Packards are nice," he said. "But my preference is motorcycles. This is my '49 Harley Indian," he boasted, pointing to the picture he pulled from his jacket. "Check the sidecar."

I spent at least half the picnic with him, playing catch and talking treasures and sports, particularly baseball. I was a big Yankee fan then. Uncle Did was very partial to the White Sox, and told me over and over that day, between and during the dozen hamburgers and hot dogs we ate together, that Chico Carrasquel was a better shortstop than Phil Rizzuto. "No way," I said. "Yes way," said Did. That went on all afternoon. And, "The Scooter can scoot, but his bat is soft as a berry." I wound up laughing.

"He is a future Hall of Famer," I argued.

"If he gets elected in, ever, you can watch me eat my hat."

Over the ensuing forty years, I did not see nor hear from Uncle Didier Mollard, save a single postcard in 1956 when Phil Rizzuto retired, four years after our family picnic, and I occasionally wondered if he were still alive, and if so, where he lived. And over all those years, Rizzuto never came close to being elected to the Baseball Hall of Fame in Cooperstown, New York.

"He is nice," I said, watching Uncle Didier and Ayako disappear down the road in the shiny, black Packard.

My mother and father looked at each other, then at me. "It's been so long," said Mother, "I hardly recognized him."

"He's so full of shit, it's comin' out of his ears," said my father.

"Please watch your language," said my mother, horrified, I thought.

"Sorry. What were you and he talking about?" asked my father.

"Baseball, mostly. The Yankees and White Sox. He once pitched an inning for the Dodgers. Did you know that, Mother?"

"No, I did not, Chuck. I haven't seen him for twenty-one years."

"What else did he tell you?" My father now had the worst scowl on his face.

"Just about his treasure hunting. A little."

"Oh really? He's a treasure hunter too, is he? What has the genius found?" asked my father.

"Lots of gold and sunken ships. I think he is rich," I said with a smile.

"That's why he calls your Grandpa Mollard every Christmas Eve and asks to borrow money, I guess," said my father. My mother looked at Father and now smiled.

"But, what about his brand new Packard?" I asked, sure that that was convincing evidence of Uncle Didier's success and wealth. "He said it cost more than $2,000 without the whitewalls. But, that that was only a few pieces of gold to him."

My mother and father both began to laugh.

"What's so funny? What's so funny?" I asked, ready to cry.

"The car is a rental car. He doesn't own it. He just rented it to try and impress us."

I was slowly being devastated at the thought of my long lost uncle being a hoax, having lied to me all afternoon.

"I don't believe it," I stammered.

"You can always tell by the license plate," said my father.

"And your Aunt Ayako told me they had just picked it up this morning," my mother said. "They had to leave the picnic early to get it back before 6:00 P.M."

"To save an extra $3 charge," said my father. "He's real rich."

"I don't care," I said. "He promised to take me to a Yankees game, maybe ten of them."

My mother and father looked at each other.

"He also promised to send me Christmas and birthday presents every year when he left the farm twenty-one years ago," said Mother.

"Your mother is still waiting," said my father.

"Never even wrote," said Mother.

"Time for bath and bed, Chuck," said Father.

I went to bed that night dreaming of hot dogs and Yankee games with Uncle Didier. And of buried treasure and sunken ships. And I wondered if he had lied to me. About everything. Especially his notebook in which he said he had listed all of the ships and passengers carrying treasures which had disappeared over the last 300 years, from Florida to the North Pole, that he had met and talked with people who knew a lot more than he did. People who gave him information that would make him rich. "Richer," he said. I thought that was more exciting than wondering about Phil Rizzuto and the Hall of Fame.

The next morning at breakfast, my father told me that someone, "Guess who?" he said, had cleaned out Mother's wallet from her purse the day before.

At our family picnic.

15

New Boy in Town

"Give Him a Chance"

IT WOULD BE quite an understatement to say that Levi Thornton was less than enthused to see his nephew standing in the entryway, clothes all tattered, a few stray whiskers sprouting from the boy's fifteen-year-old face. He had had reports that the boy was, at best, disobedient and afflicted with wanderlust, and, at worst, a deceitful troublemaker. But, when the immigration authorities had called, saying that a boy who claimed to be their nephew was being held, with badly forged papers, at the immigration office, Levi Thornton's wife intervened, and convinced Levi to help her brother's son. "A good boy," she said, about the nephew she had never met.

"An urchin, I've heard you say, and your brother writes the same," Levi said to his wife Priscilla.

"Give him a chance. Just one."

Levi gave the boy a chance. The New York investment and insurance man had more than modest amounts of money and influence. He was tight with the mayor and tight with anyone who mattered in New York City in 1862. The boy was out of the lock-up and in the Thornton entryway in a flash. The boy knew it would happen.

Levi and Priscilla Thornton took their nephew in. The fifteen-year-old boy. They housed him, clothed him, fed him and sent him to school, and gave him a train ticket and weekend in Washington, D.C., as a graduation and eighteenth birthday present three years later. And the boy was not at all like what they had heard. He was not a troublemaker. He went to school with a smile. He scored high marks. He took a job in the market, to "help pay back what you have given me." He was a model boarder and model nephew. And when he graduated with honors from high school, they wanted to send him to college. He wouldn't hear of it. "You've already done too much for me," he said. He wanted to help with the family business, "A family I never knew," he said. He wanted to work for Elmont & Thornton, Investments and Insurance. "To do anything. To help pay back what you have done for me."

And Levi Thornton hired the eighteen-year-old boy, his nephew, to work at Elmont and Thornton. Menial tasks, at first. Then more responsibility as the young man proved himself capable and competent. "A real winner," Levi told his partners.

Levi Thornton trusted the young man. And he was the man's biggest supporter in the firm.

But his trust was misplaced, or was it?

The young man it was said, went on to defraud the firm of Elmont and Thornton. Rather, theft on a monumental level.

And at age twenty-five, in 1872, he, Dunkerque Chamonix, in a raging gale, one hundred miles off the coast of Halifax, Nova Scotia, watched, semi-conscious and hallucinating, as the ill-fated S.S. *Claxdow* went down in the North Atlantic Ocean.

16

Missing Cargo

IN THE SUMMER of 1871, the year before the S.S. *Claxdow* went down, nine years after Dunk Chamonix arrived in America, a three-masted schooner, the HMS *Truro*, departed Edinburgh, Scotland, bound for Montreal, Canada by way of the Shetland Islands and the North Sea with stops at St.

John's, Newfoundland and Halifax, Nova Scotia, on the other side of the Atlantic. Among the *Truro*'s cargo were $20 million in newly-minted sterling notes destined for the Royal Bank of Canada, and sent by the Royal Bank of Scotland.

The voyage was longer than the captain had estimated, but otherwise uneventful; the only gale encountered lasting less than four hours. Uneventful until the schooner tied up at the end of its journey in Montreal. Guards from the Royal Bank of Canada greeted the vessel at the wharf and removed the locked strong box, which had been checked by the captain in St. John's and Halifax.

But the *Truro*'s captain was frequently slip-shod and frequently drunk. And when the guards counted to one million dollars they found the rest of the strong box to be filled neatly with green canvas.

$19 million missing.

One of the passengers on that voyage of the *Truro* had disembarked at St. John's.

His name was Jersey Ipdown.

The New York investment and insurance firm of Elmont & Thornton had insured currency in transport more than one hundred times, without ever a claim, not a single loss. This time was different. And the $19 million loss exceeded the firm's capital, pushing the company to the edge of bankruptcy.

17

Pistol Shots in Ford's Theater

FROM THE FIRST week he arrived in New York in 1862, at the age of fifteen, until his hypothermically ravaged brain no longer ceased to function normally in 1872, he read and reread every book by Horatio Alger, Jr., that he could find. *Luck and Pluck, Sink or Swim, Bound to Rise,* etc., etc. Stories, books, of teenage boys, frequently orphans who were born with little or nothing in New York City and, against all odds, rose to become financially successful; employing all of the best attributes of determination, honesty and frugality; encountering and beating adversarial people and forces that would stymie the average of the best and brightest. And, indeed, it was in large measure due to those books, which captured his imagination, that the young and formerly rebellious boy from England, fleeing from boarding school and crossing the Atlantic to live with his aunt and skeptical uncle that Dunkerque Chamonix went from wayward lad to an outstanding achiever in school in New York and became a pride and joy to his relations in that city. And when he graduated high school, and disdained his uncle's offer to pay for a college education, Dunkerque was sincere in his desire to repay his aunt and uncle by working instead for the family firm of Elmont & Thornton, and sincere in his desire to become one of whom Horatio Alger might be proud. From the first day on the job at Elmont & Thornton, he reminded himself, and he said it daily thereafter. Horatio Alger's words. "In short, the way to wealth, if you desire it, is as plain as the way to market. It depends chiefly on two words, industry and frugality." And Dunkerque wanted wealth as much as he wanted to show his aunt and uncle and his parents in England that he was not doomed to be a failure. He put in eighteen-hour days and worked seven days per week.

And he met John D. Rockefeller, Andrew Carnegie and John Pierpont Morgan when they were also young men, and convinced his uncle and the other Elmont & Thornton partners to write insurance policies for them when no other firm would.

Between 1868 and 1871, when Elmont and Thornton experienced the pinnacle of its glory years, the young man from London was a very major contributor. He was only twenty-two in 1869 when he brought in the largest and most profitable insurance contract in the firm's history. And he opened up business, first in Germany and then in South America at the age of twenty-three; Hamburg and Cuxhaven, then Brazil and Venezuela; never suspecting and never once told that a surname of Thornton or Elmont was a prerequisite to full acceptance, to becoming a partner.

He was driven by the Horatio Alger image and his desire not to disappoint. But two things were to shadow Dunkerque Chamonix for the rest of his life. The first was the visit he made to Washington in 1865 at the age of eighteen, the birthday and graduation present from his aunt and uncle. The second was the suspicion that he was directly involved with the disappearance of the $19 million from the HMS *Truro*; disappearance from the vessel that carried the man named Jersey Ipdown, Dunkerque's boyhood friend; the man who vanished during the layover in St. John's, Newfoundland. The proof was scanty, but it ended Dunkerque's short career at Elmont & Thornton. In disgrace.

He had thought often of his trip to Washington. But his thoughts were not of the play, *Our American Cousin*, which he had been given a ticket to watch, the night of April 14.

As he looked out the window, the train swaying from side to side, rolling from Washington back to Philadelphia, he had kept his hand on the overnight bag next to him on the seat. Four times between Washington and

Philadelphia and then two times between Philadelphia and New York he partially opened the bag, slid his hand in and touched the gold watch carefully wrapped in his handkerchief, touched to make sure it was there, that it had not all been a dream.

He looked across the aisle and read the headlines over a man's shoulder. "President Lincoln Assassinated." And then below that, "Murdered at Ford's Theater. Assassin Flees." As the train slowed in its approach to Philadelphia's Union Station, young Dunkerque Chamonix thought again to the events of the night before. It was all unreal.

He saw himself returning toward his seat from the gentlemen's room, two men standing outside the curtains leading to an opera box. He had watched, unseen. And then one of the men running headlong into him, knocking Dunkerque flat onto the marble-tiled floor, the man staring at the boy, the boy staring at him from his back on the floor, the man's mask falling to reveal his face and his gold pocket watch tinkling glass, its face broken, as it landed next to the boy. The man continuing to stare, then reaching down, half in a running position, reaching for the watch as the boy made a move to right himself, his hand landing on top of the watch and its broken glass as the man turned toward the shouts and screams coming from the theater and then bolted down the hall away from the direction of oncoming policemen.

Dunkerque Chamonix had stood up, reached down and thrust the watch in his pocket. He walked slowly down the hall, past the onrushing policemen and out into the night.

The heat was off in his room when he returned to the hotel. He had wished his aunt and uncle had come with him to Washington. "It is your birthday present and Uncle Levi is cloistered this weekend," his aunt had said. So, he was alone in his cold room. He pushed papers under the grate and set a few lumps of coal on top. He pulled a cigarette from his pocket and then a match and lit the paper. He loved to smoke and he couldn't do it in his aunt and uncle's big house in New York. Uncle Levi occasionally smoked a pipe and even a cigarette or two at times, and he had seen his aunt actually smoke a cigar when she played the piano thinking that she was alone, everyone, her husband Levi and nephew Dunkerque out of the house. He thought of that as he watched the paper light the coal, the coal lumps beginning to glow, first on the bottom then all round. He stubbed out his cigarette and flopped on his bed. He pulled the blanket up and lay back with his clothes on, his fingers touching the bulging watch in his pocket.

He thought about the evening again. The shouts and the screams, the sound of the two pistol shots, the scuffle before his very eyes, then the masked man running into Dunkerque, Dunkerque flattened prone on the tiles, broken glass and a pocket watch next to him on the floor, the man looking and running, the watch to go into Dunkerque's pocket as he fled.

He had wondered what the shots meant.

He wondered if he was to be in trouble for "stealing" a watch.

He wondered what the initials on the back of the gold pocket watch meant.

18

Her Name Was Conswella

"IT'S OKAY, Daddy. It's okay not to remember everything."

The old man, bent over his coal stove, looked at her, tears forming in the corners of his eyes. He loved his daughter more than anything in the world. "Thank you my little one. I love you, Hansie."

And then he was gone. At the age of ninety-three. September 1940.

Hansie Chamonix Van Ogtrop carefully pulled the old wool blanket over her father and kissed him gently for the final time. She went to the crude oak writing table, opened the center drawer and removed the faded yellowed newspaper clipping with its photo of Abe Lincoln. She studied it, turned it over and read the five words written on the back, "Child of the Island Glen."

She was sixty-eight, and she had looked at the photo and the five words with her father dozens of times since she was a little girl. Since not long after he returned in 1872, the year she was born.

"I will do one final thing for you, Papa," she whispered to the dead man as she took her leave from the cold, granite alcove at the top of London's St. Paul's Cathedral where Dunkerque Chamonix had lived alone with his parrot. Alone with his thoughts and a memory erased by the icy waters of the North Atlantic Ocean at the age of twenty-five, sixty-eight long years before. A memory which thereafter was confined to his first fifteen years, ending in 1862, the year he jumped the fence and stowed away on the ship which was to take him to America.

He did not know who had written the five words on the back of the newspaper photo of Lincoln nor what if anything they meant. Or why he had a photo of Lincoln. All he "knew" was that the words were supposed to lead him to something which he believed was rightfully his. That was all he could remember. Or, was even that an hallucination?

And the tears had flowed often over the sixty-eight

years as he tried to remember. Tried to put forgotten pieces together. Tried to find a clue. He wanted to find it for her. For Hansie. Motherless since childbirth.

"I will. I will, Papa," Hansie said to herself as she wound her way down the long winding steeple staircase to the huge cathedral below. "I will do it for you before I die."

Hansie Chamonix Van Ogtrop didn't fulfill her last promise. She couldn't. The woman died two months later in November of 1940 at the age of sixty-eight.

But Hansie had had a son, Luther Van Ogtrop, born in 1905 and thirty-five-years-old at the time of his mother's and grandfather's deaths, Luther to inherit Guyane, the stubborn parrot.

And Luther Van Ogtrop's wife gave birth to a son, Frederick, in 1935, Frederick Van Ogtrop missing and presumed dead at the age of thirty-two after his Red Cross helicopter went down over Vietnam in 1967.

His daughter was only seven-years-old at the time.

Her name was Conswella.

19

Diary of Confusion

I WANT TO WRITE some things about Dunkerque Chamonix's diary for a moment, as much to remind myself how things got pieced together, as anything else. The whole thing still gets a bit confusing for me at times, to say nothing of poor Hector. Dunkerque began the diary in 1861 when he was fourteen, the year before he jumped the fence with Jersey Ipdown and hit the road from Eton, the boarding school north of London. The diary spanned eleven years, until Dunkerque's firing from Elmont & Thornton in 1872.

We do know from the diary that he spoke of it to Jersey Ipdown, his best friend. And that Jersey mentioned it and who knows what else to one or more members of the Ipdown family circle; knowledge of the diary's existence then to be passed down three generations to Fury Ipdown, born in 1930, who believed the stories and went to New York in 1964 to try to search the record rooms at Elmont & Thornton on the chance that the diary might be there, ninety-two years later; a search which he was denied; the same trip on which he traveled to Swarthmore College to look up Dunkerque Chamonix's great-great-nephew, Elmont Buzzie Thornton IV, my college roommate.

"Got to mean something," Laura said when she came upon the "word" which I had stared at at least one hundred times before; the word "GIPUSOLLILANNTD" in my copy of the diary, when I eventually came to show it to her. Well, it wasn't even exactly "spelled" out in the diary. The fifteen letters ran one to a page, always up on the right hand corner, on fifteen consecutive pages.

But when I replied, "I think you might be right," neither one of us had a clue as to whether the letters should be strung together as they appeared, or even, indeed, what they might pertain to; although the fifteen pages were all written in 1871, the year the $19 million disappeared from the HMS *Truro*. And to make things even more confusing, there were thirteen other pages in the diary covering the year 1865, six years prior, when the diary keeper was only eighteen, which had letters on consecutive top right hand corners of thirteen pages as follows: "AJNODHRNESWON."

"Okay, what does that mean?" I asked Laura in frustration, shoving the piece of paper on which I had strung those letters together in front of her face.

"Beats me," she said.

It had been exactly one month before that a letter from Conswella Van Ogtrop had arrived and with it a sketch drawn for her from memory by Frederick Wenzel, keeper of the old tavern in Cuxhaven, Germany.

It was then that I first felt the heat really begin to turn up. I had before me, the diary copy, a sketch reproducing the top half of the map, and a rendering of the bottom half of the map as concealed in a green leather bound book. But none of it would make any sense at all until I was able to understand what Dunkerque Chamonix meant by the diary entries, "GIPUSOLLLILANNTD." As for "AJNODHRNESWON," that took even more doing.

"Diary of Confusion," I said to Laura.

"You got that right." She smiled, putting her arm around Hector, the little bastard running his hand up and down her leg.

And I had no knowledge then of the fact that a man named Igamuche had found something else in the old boxes of Elmont & Thorton records. Or, to be sure, that what he found might be enough. The slip of paper on which Dunkerque Chamonix had written a series of twelve numbers at some uncertain time between 1861 and 1872.

15 letters. 13 letters. 12 numbers.

"Rather bizarre," I just said to Hector.

"What bizarre?"

Forget it.

20

Thick Leather Covers

WELL BEFORE I began to discuss anything about the Buzzie "mystery" or, certainly, showed her my copy of the diary, and before everything began to hit the fan at once last year, I turned to see Laura standing next to me.

"Want to see something interesting?"

"Sure," I said.

Laura swung her hand from behind her back and thrust it toward me, the hand holding a book, a book I had never seen before. It sits beside me now as I write.

It is a small book, in terms of size, about 6 1/2 inches long, 4 1/2 inches wide, 1 inch thick, including the thick leather covers. The book binding and cover are green. There is no title on the cover. The only printing is on the binding piece. Raised gold letters.

The words on the binding read *Child of the Island Glen*, the book's title. Then, "Kellog," the author. Then "Pleasant Cove Series." Then "Lee and Shepard," the publisher.

The fly leaf has a penned inscription: "To Maitstill Church. From Aunt Dorcas. Nov. 27th, 1878."

The fly leaf is followed by a lithograph, nicely done; of a ship, in the process of being launched, at night. It is a sailing ship; double-masted; an old-time square rigger. The caption reads, "The Midnight Launch." There are many, many people; and two bonfires lighting up the night in the litho.

The next page reads, "Entered, according to Act of Congress, in the year 1872; By Lee and Shepard; In the Office of the Librarian of Congress, at Washington. Electrotyped at the Boston Stereotype Foundry, 19 Spring Lane." Seven years after the death of Abraham Lincoln.

I must tell you. It was the strangest thing I had ever seen. Bound with all the other pages, but this page unnumbered and precisely in the middle of the book. A page with but one word, "Bay," written twice, on both sides of an irregular "V." I sat there, dumbfounded. Then, I looked at Laura as she bolted out of her chair, saying, "Candle work, candle work, Chuckie; you figure it out; candles, soap and Christmas."

I moved to the couch, got up, and threw a log in the wood-burning stove. Then, I watched as she dipped candles; and then as she turned to me, and said, "Let's talk about a man named Chamonix." I froze.

Then I thought back about some things Buzzie had told me. Then I wondered how Laura Reo knew about everything. Then, I thought that maybe she knew nothing about the things. But, how did she know the name, Chamonix? I had never mentioned his name to her.

I decided then that I would not ask her. Ask her anything. Anything at all. Nothing about the old man or anything else. And my mind came to set not on what she knew, but rather on my objective.

I took the kerosene lamp after she went to bed and stole into her "secret room."

21

Her Name Was Laura

SARA KELLOG was only thirty-six years old when she died in her bed at home in Boston during the Great Blizzard of 1888, sixteen years after the birth of her daughter Rachel and sixteen years after the sidewheel steamer S.S. *Claxdow* sunk in the North Atlantic. But she kept her promise to the dashing, adventurous, young man from London and New York whom she met just once, in 1872 on the ill-fated voyage from Hamburg to Halifax.

The Reverend Elijah Kellog had married Sara in 1871, when Sara was only nineteen, the year before their daughter Rachel was born. It was a loving, caring relationship cut short by Sara's untimely death. Elijah Kellog was a minister and a writer. And it was between the covers of his first book that Elijah helped his wife keep the promise she had made to the young man in 1872.

Daughter Rachel lived to be eighty-one. She married a man from Boston by the name of Abbot Manchester. Rachel and Abbot had one son, Charles Manchester, who was born in 1890 and died in 1962 at the age of seventy-two, nine years after his mother's death.

Charles Manchester and his wife had one daughter, Helen, who was born in 1920. Helen married, had a daughter of her own at the age of twenty-five, and died an early death from polio at the age of thirty-five in 1955.

Helen's husband's name was George. George Reo.

Their daughter, born in 1945, they named Laura.

Laura Reo's great-grandfather was thus the Reverend Elijah Kellog, minister and writer. Her great-grandmother was thus Sara Kellog.

And the title of Laura Reo's great-grandfather's first book was *Child of the Island Glen*.

And there you have it. All neatly penned in her own handwriting, in her little spiral notebook, in her "secret room." But, there was more. Things. None of them to have any real meaning to me at the time. I didn't know enough then. Now, I sit here and shake my head and say, "Of course, of course," to myself. Look and not see. Listen and not hear. That's me, Charlie Wingate!

I took and nonchalantly accepted her explanation of why she had not told me of her "lineage," and only questioned her about the other "things" I had found, snooping, out of curiosity, barely listening to her answers. I then plunged ahead with her in my task of deciphering the diary puzzles, by then feeling an urgent desire to help Conswella and, it turned out, her soon to be "new friend."

22

Nagasaki to New York

When General Douglas MacArthur arrived in Tokyo on the island of Honshu on September 8, 1945, six days after Japan's formal surrender aboard the U.S. Battleship *Missouri* in Tokyo Bay, a fourteen-year-old boy lay in his bed in a hospital in Sasebo, fifty miles northwest of his home in

Nagasaki on the island of Kyushu, 25 percent of his body covered with burns, his face spared, but his eyes blinking involuntarily and his vertigo rendering him unable to sit up save for short periods. He gazed out of the hospital window to the Sea of Japan to the north as the nurses rolled him over and changed his bandages, tears welling up in his eyes and he wishing he would die. The nurses tried to comfort him by telling him how fortunate he was to have survived, "You are a lucky boy, Aki," that he was more fortunate than the 35,000 people who died in Nagasaki and the 90,000 who died in Hiroshima. But the boy was not sure. His family gone and he a bedridden shell.

After the nurses went out, he glanced at the newspaper next to his bed, a newspaper printed by the American forces and brought ashore by the thousands for the conquered to read. There, on the first page, was an article and a picture describing the effectiveness of the atomic bombs, the picture showing an airplane on a runway with its crew standing next to it. The caption read, "The B-29, 'Bock's Car' and its heroic crew," followed by the crew members' functions and ranks, but with no names. He noticed that all twelve of the men carried somber expressions except for the bombardier, who was smiling.

The boy tore out the article and picture with its caption and placed it in the pocket of his robe at the head of his hospital bed.

And he began a ritual that day which would continue for the rest of his life. He had long-stemmed yellow roses placed on five graves.

Two years later in June of 1947, a year to the day before

the Tokyo International War Crimes Trial began, the boy, now nearing his seventeenth birthday, walked out of the hospital in Sasebo on the island of Kyushu, burns scarred but healed, vertigo less frequent, but not gone, eyes involuntarily blinking, thick glasses on his eyes and closely cropped, bristling black hair on the top of his head, a paper bag with scorched sandals under his arm and tied up with string, and periodic black-outs which would stay with him as a constant reminder.

He lived in Osaka for three years, working in an accounting department of Mitsubishi, as a clerk by day and, in the last year of his stay in Osaka, attending accounting classes at night. In July of 1950, he was transferred to the financial department of Mitsubishi's new Tokyo business machines division and four years after that, 1954, at the age of twenty-three, he received his degree in finance and accounting from Tokyo University, near the top of his class, all A's and B's save for a solitary D in investments.

He would work for Mitsubishi for nineteen years more, until the year after he met Fury Ipdown in 1972, and at age forty-two he did the unthinkable, unthinkable in Japan. Aki quit his job; and then traveled to England and then to the United States, by that time the man an accomplished financial analyst and computer programmer. In London for two years, he was introduced to "Mandy" Mandalay Mandarin by Fury Ipdown. And when he landed at New York's JFK Airport on March 10, 1975, he had in his pockets and suitcase, dozens, hundreds of newspaper articles saved over the years, including the one he had stuffed in the pocket of his robe in the Sasebo hospital thirty years before.

And on his feet were the scorched sandals he had removed from his father's feet on August 9, 1945.

Today was not a good day for me. Things are going well here at the farm, lambs now all healthy and fattening up, other animals and fowl pretty much fine, greenhouse seedlings coming along — except for the damn rats in the barn again, but I was rather depressed. Actually, quite depressed.

I traced my blues to my writing, strangely enough. Reflecting on Laura as I wrote, I became very sad. I still am. And I feel the same way, though to lesser degrees, and for different reasons, about Uncle Didier and Luther Van Ogtrop. But maybe I am just feeling sorry for myself.

I drove Hector to the Goneville Dairy Barn up on the Waterboro Road after we finished castrating Chaucer, our polled Hereford steer. Thought it would be a treat for him and might pick me up. Hector was quite frankly, a pain in the ass. Sullen and snappy. Rare for him. He claimed nothing was wrong, spoke only in Spanish and slammed his hook into the top of the picnic table. I'll be glad when he is in school. Maybe not. He is real good company for me 90 percent of the time. 75 percent. But no Edison. And no Einstein. For sure.

23

Olympic Regimen

SHE COULD HAVE been training for the Olympics as she gradually regained the trimness of her youth. The regimen continued on and off for four years; four days per week, an hour a day at first. And then, the interlude, when it all seemed hopeless, a waste of time. And then the discovery. And then the regimen resuming in earnest. Seven days of every week. Three hours each day. Shooting. Lifting. Running. Swimming. Climbing. Boxing. "Boxing?" she said to herself. "I hate boxing." And shooting lessons. And then shooting, practice shooting every day. Hours. Digging. Practice with a shovel. Dig. Dig. "How fast can I dig?"

The terrain. She studied the geodetic maps. Put on snowshoes in the black of night and tromped across fields covered with frozen snow. On the snowshoes, she imagined what it would be like. She imagined the old oak tree would be gone, and the marked spot hard to find. She began to think that she was a woman gone mad. "Mad as a hatter," she said to herself. "Mad as a hatter."

(I've got to take a break here.)

Before I return to the Olympic training regimen story, let me digress a bit.

When I first started to write all of this stuff down, what has happened, at least what I know of so far, I was at Finnsheep Farm, my farm, in Maine; as I said at the outset. Well, I am not now. I did what I earlier indicated I was thinking of doing. Three feet of snow and 20° below zero temperatures sent me to the airport and south. To the island of St. Martin, the same island where I came to encounter Billy Waddie outside the Sandy Ground Church of God, last year, and where Boogie to Go, *my old 36′ clipper ketch, is still in a slip at Simpson's Bay Marina. I had not been here since last October. Lots of cockroaches.*

I just returned from the town of Philipsburg about an hour ago to purchase a beach chair and cooler for the very uncomfortable cockpit in the boat. Too hot to write below decks, and *cockpit cushions are not comfortable to sit on while writing. Now, I'm very comfortable; sitting here, in my new chair, cooler at my side; boat rocking gently; me in tee shirt and shorts. This is the life. And the best part is that I pay less than $10 per day for the slip! 80 degrees warm. Is this it or what?*

St. Martin on the water for $10 per day. Can you believe it? Of course, that does not include insurance and maintenance on the boat. But so what? And I cancelled the insurance. And I don't do much maintenance, as the facts that the engine won't start and the fresh water pump won't work attest. But, so what?

Okay. Where were we? Oh, yes.

No. Wait.

Got to tell you something I thought was funny at the time. When I came out of the store with the beach chair, I saw this male dog, an island stray. This place is amuck with them. I had seen the same dog chasing a reluctant female dog down the street just yesterday. Her teats were all distended, obviously nursing some newborn pups, and thoughts of more were probably too much for her to take. Today, it was a new female dog, about one-third the size of the male; and she was just getting ready to take her medicine; happily, apparently, as I exited the store. I swear to Godo, the male was smiling as he pounded away. And, get this. When he finished, he dismounted, looked away from his new mate and YAWNED. So much for love. Well, that has nothing to do with anything. I just thought it funny at the time. Still do. And yes, I did stand there and watch. So, I'm a dog voyeur. So what.

Okay. Back to the Olympic-like training regimen.

But, not before I tell you another little story. This place is a gas. All you have to do is observe. Most people, in my experience, can't or won't do that. They look, but they don't see. Not much of anything. And I wish I had a buck for every numbnut in the world. Christ, I'd own the world. This is minor, but representative.

In the slip next to mine is a Peterson 44; a ketch, nicely maintained; a fast and solidly built boat. That combination is rare. The owners, a couple in their early fifties, are from Tulsa, Oklahoma. She is a peach. He is a flamer. Nice when he greets you. Big smile and Howdy Do. A pony tail. Hear him yell at his wife and order her around when they go below decks, out of sight. What? Is everybody deaf? It turns out that this arrogant blow piece worked thirty years for Southwestern Bell Telephone, an upper level manager with lips I'm sure that kissed every set of rosy cheeks above him. And pissing all over anyone below him who didn't smooch his rosy. His name is Jack. His boat's name is Storm Ruler. *Now, spare me.*

"Storm Ruler Jack" was just standing on the dock as I began to write again about the oft-interrupted "Olympic Regimen." He was talking to Mervin, the marina dockboy man. I suddenly remembered that Mervin had a part for my self-steering device in his pocket. I hollered, not too loudly, "Mervin, you got that part?" Well, Jack the dork, ex-corporate blow piece with pin-striped suit, now turned ocean conqueror with ponytail, looked at me as if I had pulled his pants down. I had interrupted his private conversation. He closed his eyes, turned his head to me, and said, "I'm speaking with Mervin, now." He then moved his wife-abusing body between my line of sight and Mervin. Poor Mervin. He knew the guy was a fart gone wild, but he also knew that Jack the dork paid big bills at the marina. (Unlike me, and my low maintenance sailing vessel.)

I was mildly, only mildly, pissed. I have seen hundreds of Jack the dork types. I mostly laugh now. But a vodka martini spoke up. I said, "Mervin, Jackie boy's boat is sinking!" Then, I went below and closed the hatch on my boat, Boogie to Go. *Jackie dork ran around* Storm Ruler *for ten minutes, checking the water line, and looking for leaks. Finally, I poked my head into the cockpit, looked across to Jackie, crossed my eyes, and yelled, at the top of my lungs, "Just an in house, big corporation joke. No offense."*

Jackie Jerkhouse looked at me as if I had just come out of Wingnut Hospital, tugged on his ponytail as if he were straightening his blue and red necktie, and said, "I see no humor in what you just did."

"Good Humor. Want one?" I asked, slipping below and closing my hatch.

Am I crazy or what? Don't think so. But if you roomed with Buzzie Thornton for four years you would have a quite different and, sometimes, strange view of things, too.

So.

She built herself into a lean, disciplined physical 10. The lifting, running, snowshoeing, swimming, climbing, boxing, shooting and digging. She wanted to be as ready as she and her body could be. And her mind. She studied maps of the terrain. Over and over. She could now virtually duplicate, draw the topographical and geodetic maps from memory.

She became very tough, physically and emotionally.

But I don't like writing about her now. For she was not what she seemed. Give her the highest marks possible for deceit. A master liar. She had everybody fooled. Even herself. For, murdering the woman, if she succeeded, would not have marked the end of the long road. Rather, a beginning. I can see that now. Very, very clearly.

Boy. The gestation period on that little account was like giving birth to an elephant.

24

A Parrot and Two Crooks

I AM GOING TO tell the story of Guyane. But, before I write of him, I must write of something that places me in the certifiable category, like Buzzie; certifiably crazy. I wrote of the new beach or lawn chair I purchased to make the cockpit on *Boogie to Go* more comfortable; more comfortable to write. Well, it, the chair, did not solve all the problems. It did not solve the problem of the sun frying me while I sat in the cockpit, trying to write. Or the ten passing squalls every day. In and out. Below and topsides. Ducking the sun. Then the showers. Getting in the sun. Out of the sun. My comfort problem is now solved. I ordered a very large awning today, to cover the cockpit. Lets the wind in, but not the sun or rain. If I want sun, I will go to the beach. And I decided to do something else. Showers (body) are a problem here. *Boogie to Go*'s water pump doesn't work. And I don't want to waste my time fixing the thing for the tenth time. So, no showers unless I want to pay five bucks at the marina. Problem solved. Fresh water hose hook-up to the dock, with nozzle, and hose led along deck and then into the head opening port. Better yet. The cockpit on *Boogie* is big and deep. Too big for an off-shore sailboat. Fills with water, dangerously so, in a bad storm with breaking waves over the stern. But, a great bathtub in safe harbor. So that's what is happening now. I plug the drains with corks and fill the cockpit with water. My own hot/cold tub. I filled it this morning, let the sun hit it, and now its like heaven. I love it. As I sit here and write.

And now let me tell you about Guyane. All of which I learned from my copy of Dunkerque Chamonix's diary; courtesy of my buddy, Buzzie, and something his once bloated ex-wife didn't steal.

Guyane was born a free bird. A free parrot. He was less than a year old by Dunkerque's estimation when the man traveled to South America on a boat-insuring mission for Elmont & Thornton, Dunkerque's fourth year with the investment and insurance firm in 1869.

The parrot was teaching himself to cut corners, live on the cheap, hang around restaurants in Buenos Aires, picking up crumbs, rather than scrounge out an existence in the jungle. He met the wrong, or right, man. He landed on the table of Dunkerque Chamonix. Picking up some crumbs, the parrot was seized by the man, who grasped him gently, thrust him in his baggy, jacket pocket, snapped it closed and went back to drinking his gin, giving no thought as to why he had subdued the flying friend, the green and yellow yearling parrot.

But, as Dunkerque Chamonix rose from his table, wiped his mouth, pushed his chair back and said adieu to his client, he fingered his pocket to make sure the little bird was there. Which it was.

And the man named the bird Guyane.

And Guyane would come to love, trust, be a best friend, and outlive his master. He would see and remember, everything.

Boy, I was just thinking about how things happened at a rapid clip down here last year. Made Herman Wouk's *Don't Stop the Carnival* seem like sand box stuff. When I was here early last year, the governor of the island, Dutch side, was still Billy Waddie, the native Antillian, my "buddy" from Sandy Ground Church of God fame. He ran the place like it was a private business — his own. And his "friend" on the island, namely Tony Spedarrone, from New Jersey originally. "Fat Tony'"weighed a good 300 pounds, neatly stacked and stashed on his 5'8" frame, always had a Cuban cigar in his teeth, spent the days being gunned around by his driver in one of his two

"Cigarette" powerboats, and he spent the nights prowling his glitzy casino, hotel, night club, the Maho Reef. A few months later, both rich and powerful gentlemen were leading new lifestyles. Ex-Governor Billy Waddie spending his days and nights off-island, in Antigua, in jail. Now, politicians here have long been involved in graft, skimming, kickbacks and you name it. But, it seems old Billy went a bit too far on the proposed airport project, appropriating the $1 million construction deposit directly for his own use. This would have ordinarily gone by the boards except for the fact that the higher-ups in Holland decided that the local St. Martin bullshit had gone too far for too long. Hence, Billy was sent inside for what I heard then was likely to be a good long stint. I also heard that Billy was very upset that the authorities at the Hague denied his request for a two-day furlough to be home with his family for his wife's birthday. The Dutch didn't buy that one. And they didn't even know about the cocaine shipments at the time.

As for "Fast Fat Tony" Spedarrone, he came to reside a couple of islands down the Lesser Antilles chain. Guadeloupe, to be exact. Doing the same things by day and night that his old buddy Billy was doing up to the northwest. It seems Tony was engaged in more than the casino, hotel, nightclub business at Maho Reef. The biggest gun and drug running operation in the Caribbean, my sources told me. Unfortunately, neither one of the two men stayed locked up for long. And, those two crooks, whom I had pretty much viewed from afar, came to confront me face to face last October. And I'm not referring to the little incident in front of the Sandy Ground Church of God.

Praise the Lord.

I passed Tony's sole remaining Cigarette at anchor yesterday. It has not been out for a long while and is clearly, visibly now owned by the local pelicans and other birds, barnacles and sea grass. He won't be riding in it again. Unless he rises from the dead.

Who needs to make up stories when you're sitting on a stage like this?

And oh, yes. When I was last here, none of the merchants would take 50 or 100 dollar U.S. bills. The place was rife with counterfeits. Today, merchants are rubbing (for smearing) the faces of Alexander Hamilton and Andrew Jackson on the tens and twenties. Some even rub Abe Lincoln on the fivers. It's down to that. Quarters will be next!

I feel like a boxer who has taken one too many punches. A little giddy right now. No reason for it, to be sure. Hector's flying in tomorrow to work on the varnish. I've missed him. Sorry I called him a little bastard. My "irrational other" was talking.

25

Pigeons, Chimps and Rabbits

Final Dismissal

Of all the crazy stunts and capers Buzzie pulled over the years, the carrot caper was one of his most bizarre.

Buzzie's final dismissal from the family firm came after three previous final dismissals from which he recovered long enough, regained his sanity enough to talk his way back into his monthly paycheck, a gift from his father's benevolence to be sure. The dismissal, the final, final one in 1980, came directly from his father's mouth and in front of all of the firm's senior partners, in the executive dining room of Elmont & Thornton, the 200-year-old firm at 10 Hanover Street, a stone's throw from the New York Stock Exchange, where thirty-eight-year-old Buzzie had set loose a burlap bag full of thirty live pigeons and a burlap bag containing three one-year-old chimpanzees the week before, "to really show them what chaos can be like," he had said to me after the fact. Reminded me of John Irving's book, *Setting Free The Bears*, at the time (which reminds me of something also. Something I did last night. I may, may not tell of that later).

Buzzie's final dismissal. Back to that. Pretty stupid, and not really funny. As the partners of Elmont Thornton entered their executive dining room for lunch, their stomachs collectively growled, knowing it was Wednesday. Rack of lamb and wild rice day. But, it was not to be on *that* Wednesday. Buzzie had fired the cook at 9:00 A.M., cooked up the rice and dumped the 10 pounds of it, together with 10 racks of lamb out of the kitchen window at 10 Hanover Street. The pre-prepared desert, Bavarian chocolate layer cake, followed shortly thereafter. When the partners sat down at their tables, their hors d'oeuvres were already in front of them. There was no smoked salmon. No toast points. Just a bowl full of freshly sliced carrots for everyone. And a glass of freshly squeezed carrot juice. The partners looked at each other, and then at the new cook/waiter, Buzzie Thornton, the

Elmont & Thornton legacy, the legacy gone sour, mad. The Swarthmore grad. Buzzie was dressed in a head to foot rabbit suit, complete with three-foot ears, a waiter's towel deftly draped over his forearm. "The main course, Father first," quipped Buzzie, as he placed a steaming platter of steamed carrots with fresh dill on top in front of his father's place at the table.

Mr. Elmont Thornton III, Mr. Buzzie, was a conservative, reserved man. Not one prone to excess, or profanity. But the final straw, or carrot, had landed. He rose from and kicked back his chair. He glowered at his only son, knocked the three steaming platters of carrots balanced on Buzzie's arm to the floor, and said, only a little to Buzzie's dismay, "You are a God-damned fool, Elmont." He then stormed out the door, knocking over and upsetting every glass of carrot juice, fresh carrot hors d'oeuvres and main course of steamed carrots that he passed.

Buzzie then held court as everyone rose to leave, following his father's last words, "Meet me at Luchow's, everyone. My son has gone mad."

Buzzie, with smiling eyes downcast, a finger in the air, the waiter's towel draped over his forearm, hollered, "Carrots for all of you. All of you. It is time to learn to see in the night. I know it works. Look at me. I can see in the night. You fools can't see in daylight. And you missed the boat. Literally. Remember the S.S. *Claxdow*." Then, he smiled, poured a full pitcher of carrot juice over his grandfather's head, an eighty-seven-year-old head, ran behind the kitchen door, grabbed a burlap bag, opened it, and set free nine Belgian Lop-Ear rabbits. The rabbits ran like stink, jumped and jumped; the carrot juice, fresh carrots and steamed carrots were like a Rabbit Nirvana.

"Carrot Cuisine," said Buzzie, looking at no one, climbing out of his Rabbit suit, and disappearing for the last time from the esteemed firm of Elmont & Thornton.

Why am I telling of Buzzie and the great carrot and rabbit caper? I'm not sure, except that it may provide a real picture of Buzzie. I think. Maybe. Because, I am not sure about Buzzie. Crazy, ugly Buzzie. Even to this day. Maybe.

One last thing. Last night. The great parrot caper. Setting free the parrots. Strangely, not Buzzie. It was I. Old Charles "Chuckie" Wingate. (I think, as I said earlier, I spent too many years around the crazy man.) But let me tell you about my bolt shearers and the parrots to windward. The parrots, lately, of the "Turtle Pier Bar and Restaurant."

But before I do or don't do that I want to mention that the day after Buzzie's caper, he sent a telegram to his father at Elmont & Thornton. A telegram to his father and his grandfather allegedly from the Chairman of the Board of Trustees of Princeton University informing the two men that their degrees had been revoked by the board in an unprecedented but unanimous action for "conduct over the years, business and personal, grossly unbefitting the high standards of Princeton graduates."

He was good at sending telegrams.

How he lasted almost sixteen years at Elmont & Thornton is a major mystery to me. I think if I were his father, I would have killed him.

Part II

26

"Tombe Mort"

"HE COULDN'T have cared much for me," she said. "Unsinn, my child. Nonsense."

"Why did he go?" she asked.

"He was an adventurer of indomitable spirit," the man said, looking directly into her eyes. She looked away, uncrossed her arms and looked at her palms, each in turn, which had been holding her elbows. "An independent man. Person. Just like you. Full of order, you are. Full of order. Just like you."

She looked back at him, she had just turned twelve, smoothed her skirt and stood up.

"You think so, Grandpa, do you really?" she said slowly, unsmiling and without emotion. She wondered to herself whether she should think that to be good or bad, whether she wanted to be like her father, the father who left her alone at the age of seven. The father who chose to risk his life and his role as a father to volunteer for a dangerous peace mission aboard an International Red Cross helicopter in Vietnam; a mission which did not involve her father or his country's business, and certainly not Frederick Van Ogtrop's daughter's welfare. He did it for his own reasons, she thought to herself now, while her grandfather watched her in thought and fiddled with his pipe. Luther Von Ogtrop never really could tell what his twelve-year-old granddaughter was thinking. Just as he was never able to tell what his son was thinking from the time Frederick Van Ogtrop was born in 1935 to the time he left on the Red Cross mission in 1967 at the age of thirty-two, a mission from which he had not returned.

"Really," Luther said. "And Conswella, you've got the Chamonix genes mixed in you real gütig," he said, then looking over to the cage, smiling.

"Real Gütig. Gütig. No tell. Yes. Tell. Now." The parrot, Guyane, by all of Luther Van Ogtrop's figuring, and based on his mother Hansie's words, was nearing or had passed his 100th birthday. Luther's mother had died thirty-two years before in 1940. Luther was sixty-seven now, in the year 1972.

"Tell me about the Chamonix mix," the young girl said, now bright-eyed and quite fidgety, messing with her hair, adjusting the shoulders of her chemise, checking her hair in the mirror, eyes following her own hand as it moved the top of her chemise to the desired position on her shoulder. "Tell me," she said again, sitting down and now half smiling, looking into her grandfather's eyes. "Tell me all you know about my great-great-grandfather, Dunkerque Chamonix."

"No tell," came a squawk from the cage.

"Shut up," said Conswella.

Guyane shut up. For a moment. And then, "Yes tell. Yes tell."

Luther Van Ogtrop then began to tell his granddaughter all he knew about Dunkerque Chamonix.

And he was excited to do that.

Because his granddaughter listened. And she cared. Something that his son, though he loved him, never did.

And Luther Van Ogtrop thought that maybe his granddaughter might pick up the gauntlet and delve into the mystery his mother had told him. His mother, Hansie Chamonix Van Ogtrop. Born 1872. Died 1940. The same year and only two months after *her* father, Dunkerque Chamonix, died.

"Do you remember the game you and your Daddy used to play?" asked Luther Van Ogtrop. His granddaughter looked at him and nodded her head. "Tombe Mort," she said.

"Yes," said Luther, "one of you would yell 'Tombe

Mort' and the other would fall down 'dead.'" Luther chuckled. Conswella did not and her half smile disappeared. *But she did and would remember.*

Conswella Van Ogtrop was born in 1960. Guyane was born in 1869. Ninety years apart. The life expectancy for women when Conswella was born was seventy-four years. The life expectancy for parrots in captivity when Guyane was born was sixty years. Still the same average life expectancies today for women and for parrots in captivity. Some women live to be one hundred or more. Though most don't. Some parrots live as long as sea turtles. Up to and more than one hundred years. Most don't. Guyane did. Guyane did. He lived longer than that. Guyane lived 132 years. Unusual? Extremely. Unheard of? No.

And, Guyane knew a lot of things. But, he told few things that he heard. "No tell. No tell."

The aged parrot and Luther died in 1988 in Radstadt, Austria, in the Austrian Alps. Most year-old parrots in the wild eventually die from eagle conflicts, parasites or disease in the jungle by age forty. Few die of old age. Most parrots in captivity do die of old age. Guyane did not die of disease or old age. The by then blind bird was deliberately killed.

27

An Uninvited Guest

"YOU WANT TO shoot 'em?" he said as I walked into the room, "shoot 'em up?" I set my book bag on my desk, looked at the prematurely balding thirty-four-year-old dude with the red bandanna around his half-cocked head with squirrel-like cheeks and one eye that was rolled back as if searching the heavens. "Come on," he said, looking down at his hand, aside his waist, a needle in his palm, the needle and syringe half drawn from his pocket," Come on," he said again, "let's all shoot 'em up." I looked at his needle-marked arm as he rose, stood and glared at me, then Buzzie. I turned away and began pulling overdue library books from my book bag, setting them one at a time, slowly on the back of my desk. The dude with the red bandanna and messed up eye punched the "on" button on our stereo player, looked at Buzzie, pointed at me, burped and said with an English accent, "whose the arse-hole?"

Buzzie said nothing.

"Is this one of your crazy friends?" I said to Buzzie. I knew my roommate had a penchant for sniffing glue.

Buzzie said nothing.

"Ye bet yer arse we are friends, old friends," said the dude with the eye and bandanna as he limped across the room mopping his brow.

I sat at my desk, opened a book and began to read. The English dude turned up the stereo and hollered at the top of his lungs, "Let's all shoot 'em up, even the arsehole."

"We are sort of old friends, in a way," said crazy Buzzie.

"Get the jerk out of here," I said. I wanted to punch him.

"Wait, Chuck," said Buzzie.

"Now," I said, "You and I share this room, half and half, my half is being encroached on by this junkie."

The uninvited guest lunged at me, his arm raised, the needle and syringe grasped in his hand, the thumb on the plunger as the arm came down, the needle just grazing my shoulder as I kicked him in the groin, the needle and syringe flying through the air, bouncing off the cement block wall, my arms now around his neck.

"Get the hell out of here," I screamed, looking at the man's eye. "Do you hear me? Do you hear me?"

"Okay, laddie," he said burping again, "not to worry. And I see your not an arsehole. But, ye better heed what I tell ye."

"What's that?" I said, my arms now wanting to crush his neck.

"Let me up, and I tell you what I told yer friend, here, yer friend, Buzzit."

"Buzzie," I said, looking at Buzzie.

"There is times to live and there is times to die. And me know that Mr. Buzzie knows what I say. You must ask him when I'm gone."

He left.

"There is times to live and there is times to die," I said to myself.

"What the hell was all that about?" I said to Buzzie, wanting to settle into my desk and books, having trouble doing so.

"Easy Chuck," said Buzzie the Elmont Thornton IV. "He is a descendant of a man named Jersey Ipdown."

"Who gives a road apple?" I said.

"I do," said crazy Buzzie. "His great-great-grandfather, a hundred years ago, was a friend, the best friend I think, of an ancestor of mine, a man by the name of Dunkerque Chamonix. Dunkerque was my great-great-uncle on my mother's side. Sort of. Priscella Thornton was his aunt."

"Wonderful," I said.

"Chuck," said Buzzie, "it is not that simple. There is a mystery, you know; Dunkerque Chamonix supposedly left a diary. And a map to a fortune. I am related to that long dead man. And you know something? The man who just left thinks he knows where that diary is. I mean to study it. There are things to discover."

I looked at Buzzie and knew that this crazy roommate of four years, this crazy roommate of mine was dead serious. About another caper.

"What is that fool's name?" I asked.

"He is no fool," said Buzzie.

"His name is Fury Ipdown."

That was 1964, Buzzie's and my last year at Swarthmore. We graduated the next month. It was great rooming with Buzzie, for four years, crazy though he was.

28

"The Great Fabricator"

HIS CAR WAS not owned. The Packard, a new black 1952 convertible model, was rented, as my father had said. And he never pitched an inning for the Brooklyn Dodgers, striking out "Willie Mays on three pitches, not including the foul tip," in the "bottom of the ninth, with the bases loaded at Ebbets

Field on September 7, Labor Day, before a packed house in 1949." And he never took me to a Yankee game, let alone the ten Yankee games he talked about.

It was not long after our Wingate family picnic in 1952 in Irvington, New York, that I discovered that Uncle Didier Mollard had lied to me. I remember receiving the postcard from him when Phil Rizzuto retired. I remember asking my mother from time to time if she had heard from her brother. "Nope. But Grandpa said he called on Christmas Eve again, looking for a loan." Same answer every time I asked, very infrequently as the years passed. "He's rich," I remember saying to my father in 1952. "He's so full of shit, it's comin' out of his ears," I remember my father saying, much to my mother's horror.

I found out that Uncle Didier didn't strike out Willie Mays on the three pitches in 1949 on Labor Day, September 7, when I went to the library and discovered that Willie Mays didn't break in to the Major Leagues until 1951, and Labor Day in 1949 was not on September 7. I was able to chuckle about it by then. As much so when I went to the library and looked up the name Didier Mollard in the *Baseball Encyclopedia*, which lists every person who so much as appeared in a game since 1876. "Unc Did" was not listed. "Did not. Uncle Didier Didn't, Uncle Did Not," as my father would have said.

And I did (not did not) get some good laughable gossip from my mother over the years, about her brother, all of which came from the yearly Christmas Eve calls he made to his father, Grandpa Mollard, always asking for a loan. Neither Mother nor I ever hearing from him directly, for sure.

Things that Mother heard about Uncle Didier included enough to "make a movie," according to my father. My uncle at various times reportedly communicated to Grandpa Mollard that he, among other things, had been a migrant worker in the California wine vineyards after leaving home at sixteen in 1931; had saved a family of eight from a burning house near the vineyards. That he panned for gold in Alaska during the following year "making enough money to live comfortably for (the rest of his) life. ("Quite a feat," my father remarked.) That he dove for treasure off the coast of Florida and flew crop dusters in Kansas during the late thirties and then fought in World War II. ("I never heard about that one," said my father.) And that he had compiled a "soon to be published" book after the war about shipwrecks and missing treasures.

The last bit of "news" Mother heard came from one of her other brothers, Ted, in 1984, thirty-two years after our family picnic, long after Grandpa Mollard had passed away and after two decades of silence. Two decades during which we initially made up our own "news" and stories about Uncle Didier for a while before his name disappeared from our Christmas Eve chats and he was indeed all but forgotten.

I was forty-two at the time and remember Mother and Dad laughing hysterically, aided by a cocktail or two, after talking with Ted on the phone and wishing him a Merry Christmas.

"What's so funny?" I asked.

Mother and Father looked at each other and then at

me. My father said, "Chuck, I'll bet you can't guess what your Uncle Didier is up to these days."

"You're right," I said. "But let me guess. How old is he now?"

"He'd be or, rather, is sixty-nine," said Mother.

"Okay," I said. "Let me guess. He's back pitching for the Dodgers?" We all laughed together. "Rewriting the *Encyclopedia Britannica*?" More unified laughter.

"Close," said Father. "According to Ted, Uncle Did Not is designing a 'super fast' ocean going vessel with 'a friend' for a top secret project he, quote, 'is not at liberty to discuss.'"

"What are his qualifications?" I asked, somewhat tongue in cheek.

"Same as for everything else," said my father.

And then, as if rehearsed, my mother and father leaned forward and whispered, "None."

There were to be no more Christmas Eve phone calls from Harley riding, Camel smoking Uncle Didier to Ted or anyone else.

In June of 1985, Mother's eldest brother called to say that, according to a telegram he had received, the "Great Fabricator" had apparently drowned when he and his fishing partner, also presumed dead, went into the rapids and over the falls and were separated from their pink and orange outrigger canoe on New Mexico's Pecos River. Neither body was recovered. Didier would have been seventy at the time.

"May he rest in peace," said my mother.

"Amen," said my father.

29

Jubilee Chosen

When I now picture a pretty green-eyed trim nineteen-year-old woman sitting across the desk from Buzzie Thornton in November of 1964, I do not ask myself the questions: What did she know? How did she know it? When did she know it? And, whereas "obsession" would be the last word to describe Conswella Van Ogtrop's curious and casual interest in her great-great-grandfather as she ghosted down the Elbe toward Cuxhaven aboard *Weitra*, her 40-foot, old wood Bristol Channel pilot cutter in 1993 at the age of thirty-three, obsession with the name Dunkerque Chamonix had already gripped Buzzie Thornton's nineteen-year-old interviewee twenty-nine years before; when Conswella Van Ogtrop was but four-years old, three years before her father's ill-fated Red Cross mission. What was a curiosity to Conswella at the age of thirty-three had become an obsession for the other woman by the time she turned nineteen in 1964.

"I didn't know for sure whether you were hiring," she said to Elmont Buzzie Thornton IV, a twinkle in her eye.

"I'm not sure we are," said Buzzie, smiling, deciding that she would be a delightful addition to Elmont & Thornton, a nice contrast to the sixty-year-old, ugly battle-axe secretaries who had held down the fort since Columbus.

"I'm an excellent typist and am studying library science at NYU at night," she said.

"Miss Chosen," Buzzie began.

"You can call me Jubilee."

"All right, Jubilee Chosen," he said, "let me show you around the offices. Have you ever been in an investment library?"

"Many times," she lied. "As a matter of fact, my concentration at NYU will be in investment and business library science," she lied again.

"Excellent," said the Buzzer, trying to hid his extra long nose with his right hand, wondering if he should use his left hand to cover at least one of his prodigious ears, thinking then that the right hand over the nose did both jobs at once, hid the nose and distracted her eyes from his ears. "Boy, is she a knockout or what?" he said to himself as he began to escort Jubilee Chosen through the offices of Elmont & Thornton, dowdy old secretaries at their desks peering over their glasses and the firm's partners and associates, all in three-piece suits and wing-tipped shoes, taking a moment to eyeball Jubilee and Buzzie as they passed.

"My guess is that you are about twenty-two, Mr. Thornton," Jubilee said as they finished the tour, returning to Buzzie's office, then lingering over cups of coffee, Buzzie distracted from time to time by a fly that had occupied his office for most of a week, driving him nearly crazy as it buzzed and buzzed, landed and took off.

He looked around for the fly swatter and said, "Exactly twenty-two, Jubilee. Call me Buzzie."

"All right," she said, her green eyes and long lashes causing him to knock over her coffee.

"Are you always alright?" he asked.

She looked at him strangely, he was smiling. "Always," she said. They both laughed.

"What do you know about the fine old firm of Elmont & Thornton?" Buzzie asked, pushing his chair back and placing his feet on his desk, picking up a pencil and beginning to tap it on the edge of the desk; Buzzie the crazy; Buzzie the up and coming Elmont & Thornton rising star, he thought to himself.

"Really nothing, Buzzie," she said.

"Good. You will fit right in."

Buzzie hired the pretty young woman right on the spot and enjoyed the barbs of the old dowdies and questioning looks from his associates and criticism from his grandfather and father for hiring such a young and inexperienced woman, and after only one interview and no reference checks, by-passing the personnel manager and all Elmont & Thornton protocol.

Jubilee Chosen had first heard of Elmont and Thornton when she was eight-years old, in 1953. She knew that it was where a man named Dunkerque Chamonix had worked back in 1872 before he sailed on the S.S. *Claxdow* bound from Hamburg to Halifax. And when Jubilee left Buzzie Thornton's office, job offer in hand, she smiled to herself. "This may be easier than I thought," she said to no one as she boarded the subway headed uptown.

She rode the subway and looked at her shoes and dress and scoffed. She reached into her bag and pulled out a book. She began to turn the pages of the small book. With a green leather cover. Written in 1872 by Rev. Elijah Kellog.

30

General Robert Creighton and A Bombardier

Russia	20,000,000
Poland	6,000,000
Germany	5,000,000
China	2,500,000
Japan	2,000,000
Yugoslavia	1,600,000
Romania	700,000

France	600,000
Hungary	400,000
Great Britain	400,000
Czechoslovakia	350,000
Austria	310,000
Italy	300,000
USA	300,000
Netherlands	200,000
Greece	100,000
Finland	90,000

He looked at the computer screen and felt dizzy again. He blinked his eyes and thought, and then remembered back; to June 6, 1945, when the Japanese Supreme Council's resolution came across his parents' radio as they sat in their small home in Nagasaki, eating dinner. Both of his brothers dead in Burma, killed during the Japanese assault on the city of Mandalay three years before, in April 1942; and he a fourteen-year-old boy sitting in his uniform on June 6, 1945, two months into his membership in Japan's 28 million strong civilian militia, part of "Ketsu-Go," the Supreme Command's plan for the defense of Japan, the defeat of U.S. beach landings which everyone knew were coming.

"We will fight to the end, uphold our kokutai [national essence]. We must and we will." And then the radio station had signed off for the night. He had looked at his mother as she began to cry, touching his militia uniform. His father took her hand from the uniform and stood up, gave her a stern look, scuffled away in his sandals and knelt below the portrait of Emperor Hirohito. Then those of his mother and father and his grandparents and great-grandparents. "Family, country, love and honor." He looked to his Japanese-born wife, then to the pictures on the opposite wall of her father and American-born mother, Noriaki and Ada Nishikata, and he spat. "American," he said, ripping the portrait of Ada Booth Nishikata from the wall.

Two months later on August 9, 1945, a plutonium bomb, an atomic bomb, nicknamed "Fat Boy" by the Americans, left the bomb bay of the B-29 *Bock's Car* and exploded over the City of Nagasaki, killing 30,000 people, severely injuring 6,000; killing Aki's mother, father and sister, and burning more than 25 percent of the skin from his own body; the fourteen-year-old boy to pull the smoking sandals from his father's feet as the legs stuck out from under the burning rubble; Aki to save the sandals as if a treasure.

He snapped his mind away from 1945, looked down at his feet with the old sandals, the burn and scorch marks still unchanged, and then his eyes went back to the computer screen with its list of the number of dead, by country, the number killed in World War II. He focused on Japan's 2,000,000 and the United States' 300,000.

Photographs and newspaper clippings slipped through his hands. He watched in turn the images he passed from hand to hand as he leaned over the table, his hunched back and neck supporting his bent down head with its close-cropped, bristling, black hair; then, setting the pictures down, running his fingers over the scars on his legs, arms and neck, he scuffled his little sandaled feet back and forth on the floor under the table.

He looked at an old photograph of himself and his two brothers, Naotake and Fumimaro, at a school outing in 1936 when he was five, and he unfolded a newspaper article and picture detailing the successful Japanese assault on Mandalay; the picture of U.S. General Robert Creighton, who commanded Chinese troops in their unsuccessful defense of Mandalay, the troops who, under Creighton's command, killed Naotake and Fumimaro.

He looked at a photo of himself, his sister, his mother and his father; Aki in his civilian militia uniform, the photo taken in 1945 under the flowering pink cherry trees by the pond in the park in Kokura City when he was fourteen and one month before *Bock's Car* dropped the plutonium bomb on Nagasaki. He unfolded a newspaper clipping and picture detailing the horror in Nagasaki on August 9, 1945; the picture of the crew of the B-29 *Bock's Car* standing proudly next to their plane. He looked at the faces in the picture and then at the caption below. There was only one name he cared about, that of the bombardier. The airman first class. The man who was smiling. The only one. He would find his name. No matter how long it might take.

And General Creighton was long dead. As was his son, killed in Korea at the age of forty in 1953. But there had been one grandchild. A granddaughter living in London.

Finding and killing her had been easy.

The bombardier, however, seemed to have simply vanished into thin air.

31

Caught Snooping

THE FIRST TIME was on a Friday afternoon in 1968, three years after their marriage. She had been away from her desk for almost three hours. He found her on the top floor where all of the records of the 200-year-old firm were kept, everything; everything saved, nothing thrown out. Old and not so old all mixed together. Insurance policies dating back to 1780, saved in case some crazy descendant came across some crazy loophole. Ledgers, cash books, stock transaction slips. Eight rooms heaped from floor to ceiling. Eight rooms of boxes and files and nary an index to anything.

She was kneeling and sifting through a box in Room #1 when he appeared out of nowhere. "What in heavens are you doing, Jubs?" he asked.

"You scared me," she said straightening up.

He looked at her, waiting for an explanation. "What are you looking for?"

She flashed her green eyes and fluttered her long lashes. "Just trying to sort things out," she said.

"This room is not part of your job. You know that. I suggest you get out of here before father or grandfather finds you up here. This room is off limits. All the rooms up here are off limits. How did you get in?"

"The door was unlocked," she lied.

It was only a month later that he found her up there again and became very suspicious.

"If I must tell you, Buzzie, I am trying to find out information about a man named Dunkerque Chamonix." She had been caught snooping with her pants down, hand in the cookie jar, what to say? Her normal quick-on-her-feet lying had failed her this time. While she waited for a response from the Buzzer, now standing with his hands on his hips, his normally relaxed good humor less and less evident the more he had gotten to know Jubilee, she thought that if she came clean and told him all, what little she knew, that he might actually help in her search.

And then she thought that her best approach was to continue to use him without telling him anything.

"How do you know of Dunkerque Chamonix?" asked Buzzie Thornton, looking down at her and the piles of records and documents strewn about her feet.

"I read about him at the library," she said, lying now well in gear.

"Oh?" asked the Buzzer, looking at her curiously.

"What did you learn about him at the library that causes you to come snooping here where you know you're not supposed to be?"

"I was just trying to help you. Surprise you. I've heard he was your great-great-uncle and that he worked here back in the 1860s," she said, withholding the rest she knew. "I wanted to do a biography of him for you, for your birthday."

"I don't think a biography of Dunkerque Chamonix is something the firm of Elmont & Thornton is interested in seeing in print."

"Okay," she said, rising. "I'll drop it."

"Please do."

Buzzie Thornton stuck his tongue out as his now very plump wife turned and headed for the door. He ushered her out, closed the door and had a new padlock put on the entrance to the floor that afternoon, a padlock to which he had the only key. And while Jubilee was temporarily locked out of any further search for information in the old files of Elmont & Thornton, Buzzie was not; and *his* curiosity now, caused *him* to begin snooping once more through the old files when he had time between what little work he did and dreaming up inventions and capers. And he began to think with renewed and heightened interest back to his encounter with Fury Ipdown at Swarthmore in the spring of 1964, four years before.

It was on October 11, 1973, a Saturday morning, when Buzzie, alone in the building, took time out for a break from a project he was working on on the roof of 10 Hanover Street and began to rummage through the piles of boxes on the top floor as he had done on numerous occasions before.

And it was in the back of the bottom drawer of a dusty old file cabinet crammed to overflowing in Room #3 that he found it. The diary begun in 1861 by a fourteen-year-old boy; the diary with entries covering eleven years.

Buzzie's find. Twenty-one years ago.

I didn't have either half of the map early in 1993, the top half or the bottom half. But I did have the copy of the diary given to me by Buzzie for safe-keeping, in the event that anything should happen to him; given to me two days after he was fired from Elmont & Thornton in 1980 as the two of us sat in a corner of a dive in New York's Soho district eating Thai food and drinking "Wobble-Walkers," as Buzzie called them, the night before he left for his Conestoga wagon excursion, and the first time I had seen him in years; but still each other's best friend I believe now; though neither of us would ever have owned up to it to the other. And that was the last time I saw Buzzie. Crazy, paranoid Buzzie. Telling me he thought his "brainless" and by then fat ex-wife, whom I had never met, might try to kill him. And that if she succeeded, he wanted me to carry on with his search to unravel the one hundred-year-old mystery, the mystery of Dunkerque Chamonix, Buzzie's great-great-uncle or "Unc Dunk" he would say.

Now, I had not the slightest interest then in the so-called mystery, viewing it as just another weird tangent to which Buzzie was channeling his energies. But I took the diary copy and assured him that it was safe with me, and that no one wanted to kill him, but that if someone did and succeeded, that I would carry on his "research." Buzzie had clapped his hands, patted me on the shoulder and smiled. "Best dork I ever met," he said. "Best and worst roommate, too." I laughed.

"I'll make a deal with you," I said, pulling an old photo from my wallet. "I'll get my brains focused on your mystery if, in your travels, you do something for me. Keep an eye out for this man." I handed him the photo taken at our family picnic in 1952, twenty-eight years before. "Last known address, Wichita, Kansas," I said. Buzzie rolled his eyes.

I thought of that final meeting with my old friend as I sat down by the wood stove at my Finnsheep Farm in Dayton, Maine, in May of last year, 1993, and began to look through the copy of the old diary again; Dunkerque Chamonix's first entry made at fourteen. As I scanned the diary, I smiled to myself. He reminded me of Buzzie. That wayward gene seemed to have found its way down through Dunkerque Chamonix's aunt, Buzzie's several times great-grandmother, right down to Buzzie himself. I thought of Buzzie scaling the fence at Swarthmore College when we were freshmen, to climb into the opening overlooking the open showers in the women's locker room, as I read of Dunkerque's vault over the school fence to freedom in 1862.

I went back to scanning the diary. There were big gaps in terms of time, entries often widely separated by several months in places. Other periods were very detailed and intense, entries sometimes made twice each day for a week or more, some entries very extensive, others short and quite oblique. The last entry was made in 1872, when the writer was twenty-five, the year he was dismissed from Elmont & Thornton. "Fired," I said to myself, "just like his wingnut great-great-nephew Buzzie more than one hundred years later."

I got up from my chair, went out to feed the sheep, all 146 of them, all Finnsheep, the prolific of the prolific, the latest ewe to give birth having dropped sextuplets that morning. She had fooled me. She was big with lambs but not "bagged up," the teats weren't. I thought that she was three weeks away, but I was wrong. Worse yet, after she dropped three lambs on her own, I pulled the last three out and then found that her teats were not just plugged, but that she had mastitis; no colostrum or milk would be coming from her, none at all. I filled six bottles on the rack and placed the lambs' noses at the nipples, got them started, thought of the stupid diary, and told Hector to feed the rest of the flock; hay for all and grain for the lambs, and I went back into the house.

I reread Dunkerque's last entry in the diary, and then sat back and thought. In truth, I wondered why Buzzie had even bothered to give me a copy of the diary. What could I ever make of it? It was interesting, in part, some places, accounts of events and happenings, particularly his entries regarding the *Truro*'s missing "cargo" in 1871 and the Ford's Theater "incident" in 1865, if they could be believed, and the descriptions of times and places; but even at that late date, I had not yet developed the sustained fascination for it that had long ago gripped my old friend, Buzzie.

It was only when I began to discuss things with Laura, living with her, on and off, sometimes at Finnsheep Farm, sometimes at her farmhouse, ten miles away, sometimes for a week or two, other times for just dinner and a few hours, sometimes not seeing her for weeks at a time, that things began to gel. My little, spectacled, retiring blue-eyed librarian with her interest in candles and soaps, seeking, asking my help when she had embarked on her first entrepreneurial venture into Right & Ready Reo Candles and Soap, Inc.; I suggesting the "Inc.," she dipping the candles.

"What's new with the moldy diary?" she asked, peeling onions, bouncing to Bob Marley and the Wailers, in the summer of last year.

"I think you are right," I said, looking at the entries in the diary.

"I am always right," she said, putting down her peeler, turning to me and tugging on her apron. "About what, now, though?"

Right and Ready Reo, I thought to myself. "Gipusollilanntd," I said.

"Got to mean something," said Laura.

"I'm sure it does, maybe," I said, and "Let's think for a moment. Do you think it is possible that Buzzie's ex-wife is still snooping around all of this?"

"We don't even know whether she is still alive, do we?" asked Laura.

"Why wouldn't she be?" I asked.

"I just have a feeling," said Laura, smiling at me. "I just have a feeling."

"Interesting," I said. "Very interesting."

32

Hanover Street Roller Coaster

THE INSURANCE and investment firm of Elmont & Thornton had prospered at 10 Hanover Street in New York for ninety-one years, from its founding in 1780, until the disappearance of $19 million in sterling notes from the HMS *Truro* in 1871. That loss, insured by Elmont & Thornton for the Royal Bank of Scotland, the first loss of insured currency sustained by the firm in its ninety-one-year-history technically bankrupted Elmont & Thornton, the loss far exceeding its capital base, the firm avoiding bankruptcy only through a series of loans arranged by the partners, utilizing all of the contacts and goodwill that the firm's name could muster among the financial circles in New York that had been cultivated for decades and, for the first time, a little help from fading Boss Tweed. But the loans were terribly onerous and Elmont & Thornton never fully recovered the status and financial strength it had enjoyed before the *Truro* loss, and indeed, became a roller coaster for the firm's partners. They took to riskier insurance because it generated higher premiums and riskier investments because the potential returns were higher. As were the potential losses.

Elmont & Thornton remained in family control and limped into the 20th century, barely surviving the depression of 1896; had a mild resurgence in the 1900 to 1915 period when it invested in A & P, which grew from 200 stores in 1900 to 400 by 1912. But Elmont & Thornton sold its investment in A & P in 1915 to repay loans and offset insurance and investment losses in other areas. It was unfortunate, because A & P would go from the 400 stores in 1912 to more than 11,000 over the next ten years, making untold fortunes for the investors who stayed in.

The firm invested in the Ford Motor Company in 1908, the year production of the Model T began. But, again they sold out too early and put the money into cars produced by the axle manufacturer Harry Stutz and backed the Pierce Arrow, Locomobile and the Stevens-Duryea, all losing propositions. But Elmont & Thornton continued to limp along, successfully avoiding any large insurance losses between 1916 and 1930. And they survived the Great Depression due to a series of individually small but collectively large investments in risky propositions in the 1920s — filling stations, roadside diners and automatic traffic lights — all of which paid off handsomely.

The 1940s and 1950s were successful decades for Elmont & Thornton; insurance boomed and the firm moved away from the riskier private investments to publicly traded securities on the New York Stock Exchange.

When Elmont Thornton IV joined the firm in 1964, its capital base was sound enough but the partners were aging and unwilling to go beyond family ownership, and Buzzie was the last male Elmont or Thornton on the family tree. Somehow, the partners sensed that the end of Elmont & Thornton as a privately-owned entity was inevitable, and when heir Buzzie went to Swarthmore, then joined the firm, married Jubilee Chosen, had no children, proved himself as bright a prospect for investment and insurance as a one-watt light bulb, it became just a matter of time.

The year that Buzzie pulled his last caper at Elmont & Thornton, the great carrot and rabbit stunt, 1980, was the same year he left the firm for good, his father and eighty-eight-year-old grandfather both to pass away the following year. In 1982, the firm suffered catastrophic insurance losses from its imprudently created title insurance business, the same year that it lost millions on its largest investment holding and old nemesis, the Royal Bank of Scotland, when it elected to play the currency game and switched its holdings from dollars to pound sterling, and proceeded to watch as the pound plunged in value relative to the dollar. Elmont & Thornton was bankrupt, this time with no strings to pull.

On the morning of September 10, 1982, two years after Buzzie's departure, the remaining partners of Elmont & Thornton gathered in the now spartan offices and signed the papers selling the firm to a diminutive, short and near bald, burping, limping man with one bad eye, a man whom none of them liked. They signed and sold to avoid the embarrassment of a publicly bankrupt Elmont & Thornton. The sellers received nothing from the sale save removal of their names guaranteeing the firm's debt. No small matter. The selling price was $1 plus assumption of the debt, the debt assumed by the buyer, the diminutive, balding man with the bad eye and limp.

The diminutive man had visited the offices of Elmont & Thornton eighteen years before in 1964, but no one remembered that visit, a visit that had ended with the man being literally thrown out the front door, refusing to go on his own, until he got "the information I came for."

His purchase in 1982 gave him the firm's name, Elmont & Thornton, and debts well in excess of assets.

But, the assets included two things not even recorded on the books.

Two hundred years worth of records crammed into eight rooms on the top floor.

And perpetual rights to the all but forgotten $19 million missing from the HMS *Truro* and insured by Elmont & Thornton 111 years before.

I read about the sale of Elmont & Thornton, a one-liner in the *Wall Street Journal*, the following day. "In a move designed to avoid filing for bankruptcy, the 202-year-old insurance and investment firm of Elmont & Thornton was sold yesterday to an Englishman by the name of Fury Ipdown."

But the Chamonix diary was now gone from the records room. Found and removed only 9 years before, 101 years after the last entry in 1872.

Silence. It was somewhat disturbing. For the fourth time in less than the three days I have been back at the farm (why I left St. Martin and the sun, I'll never admit), the phone rang last night and the caller hung up without saying a word; several seconds of silence the first time, almost thirty the last time, after I picked up and said "Hello" or "Finnsheep Farm."

Same silence I got from Hector when I came in from the barn this morning and surprised him on the phone. He hung up immediately.

I think it's the hormones at work. Adelade at the store says Hector has started hanging around in the parking lot again after dinner with the loose young tart from up the Buzzell Road. One of Jim Morrey's eight kids, that one the worst. An abortion at thirteen? Give me a break.

Either Hector shapes up or he is headed back to Santo Domingo or Dominica. He can forget about school here this fall. I hope it does not come to that. I plan on talking to him again tonight. He has been far too casual about his chores here the last three days, and he is not expending enough effort on his reading and writing. I don't need this garbage. I feel like a God damn baby sitter.

33

GIPUSOLLILANNTD

LAURA AND I were at it again. "Trying to make sense out of nonsense," she said, making a Buzzie-like expression.

In truth, the map itself, I mean even the whole map, the two parts together would have been near useless to anyone without some knowledge of why it was drawn, when and by whom. "It was dog do," as Buzzie would have said.

So, there was an oak tree, maybe, probably long gone now, I thought then; near the shore of a bay to the west, and a marked spot 76 meters from the tree on a north by northwest heading, 330°. Where? What Bay? In what part of the world? I thought that one could dig 76 meters from every oak tree on every shore of every bay in the world for the next thousand years and still come up empty. And to make matters worse, if that were possible, the marked spot, the spot marked with an "X" appeared to be under water!

"Gipusollilanntd," I said again. "Let's try breaking it into two or three words. What do you think?"

"Something to do with Gypsies?" wondered Laura, aloud.

"Sometimes I think *you* are a Gypsy," I said, smiling.

"A Gypsy candlemaker I am. Nomadic and naughty."

And the bottom half of the map, the portion given to Laura's great-great-grandmother, Sara Kellog, by Dunkerque Chamonix in 1872 as the S.S. *Claxdow* was sinking, seemed to be of little help at first; the sketch, reproduced in the Rev. Elijah Kellog's, Sara's husband's first book, *Child of the Island Glen*, only possibly reproduced accurately; the original of that half of the map having long disappeared.

All that sketch seemed to indicate, and it was impossible to be sure even of this, was that the oak tree was situated somewhere on a peninsula jutting to the south, southwest with a bay on each side, one to the west and one to the east. Again, probably thousands and thousands of such peninsulas in the world. Unless the draw-

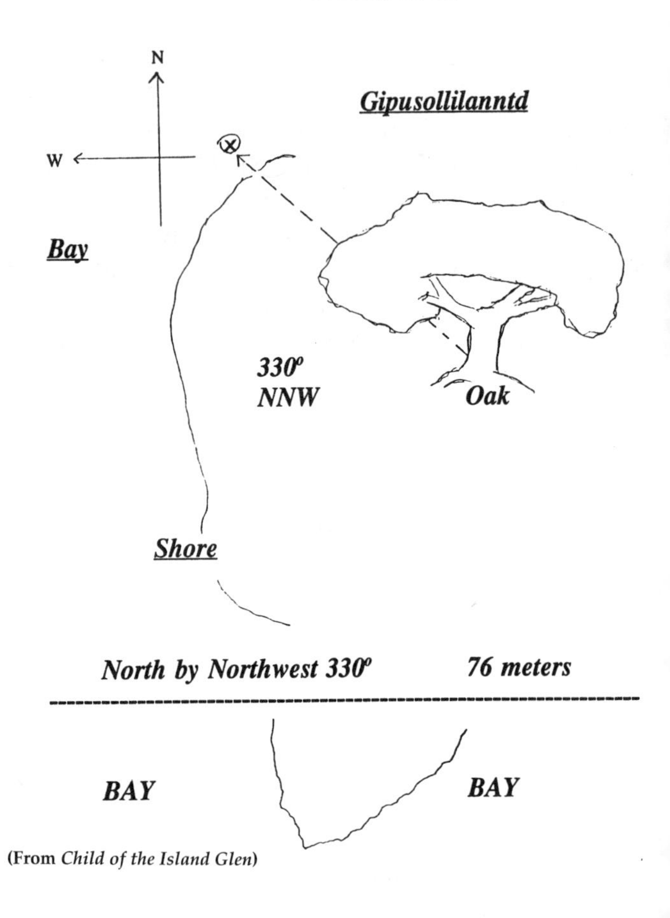

(From *Child of the Island Glen*)

ing was truly accurate in its detail, in terms of coves, inlets, etc., and had been drawn in its entirety in a consistent and accurate scale. A lot to ask by a possibly untrained map renderer in 1871. Unless he or she had traced that peninsula from an atlas or another accurate map or had walked the peninsula him or herself. That set my mind to wondering.

Up until last year, I was reluctant to air any of my thoughts, few though they were, with anyone, even Laura. But I must take my dirty cap off to her. She tolerated my mood swings, highs and lows, as I took to my task in earnest for the first time last summer. Buzzie's legacy to me. It suddenly became somewhat of an obsession with me and I came to see how Buzzie got so wrapped up in it. And I guess it was with him in mind that I was initially so secretive about the whole thing, as he had been. I thought of his crazy capers, stunts and his ugly face, and I missed him. A lot.

And long before I admitted to the existence of, and, much later, let her actually read the diary from cover to cover, eventually giving her free access, Laura tried to help in any little way she could, and she didn't pry, not at all, taking only information that I gave her and little queries that I made aloud for her to hear; sometimes working for hours trying to come up with a thought or a clue that might help me unravel the mystery, piece bits and pieces together.

When the letter and the replicated drawing with the oak tree came from Conswella, with word that she was departing Cuxhaven to continue her journey, solo, in her sailboat to retrace the 121-year-old route of the *Claxdow*, I was incredulous at first. I didn't really know what kind of woman she was. But it was then that I resolved to double my efforts and solve the mysterious "map," a faithful replica of the top half sketched last year for Conswella by Frederick Wenzel, the original drawn by Jersey Ipdown in 1871 and then hidden in the old tavern in Cuxhaven the night before Dunkerque sailed on the ill-fated S.S. *Claxdow*.

I don't think I would have gotten anywhere even then without Laura's help, without her thoughts and, indeed, without her *Child of the Island Glen*.

"Let's assume that the drawing is accurate," I said, "in terms of two bays, west and east, inlets, coves, etc., and that the scale is at least consistent."

"All right," she said, tapping her pen against the back of her hand, "then what?" smiling, taking off her glasses and setting them on the table, then looking down at her pointed shoes, red flats, and running two fingers across her plucked eyebrow.

"Good question. How about getting the world atlas and focusing on the area in the North Atlantic where the HMS *Truro* traversed? Canada, Labrador, Newfoundland, Nova Scotia, etc. The area to which our friend Conswella is headed," I said. "We know the money was gone when the *Truro* arrived at Montreal."

"Chuck," said Laura, putting her pen down. "Just because the cargo supposedly disappeared somewhere between St. John's, Newfoundland, where the captain said he last checked it, and Montreal, doesn't even mean it was necessarily hidden in that part of the world. And worse yet, just because the captain of the *Truro* recorded that he had checked the cargo in St. John's and it was intact doesn't mean that he did and that it was. Am I right?"

"You're right," I said, kissing her on the cheek. "But, the only passenger to disembark during the whole trip, Jersey Ipdown, did so at St. John's. And you know something Laura," I said. "We have to start somewhere."

"How about a martini?" she asked.

"Get the atlas," I said.

Laura brought the atlas and a martini and we began the slow (but I now found interesting) process of comparing the shape of the bay-sided peninsula reproduced on the page of *Child of the Island Glen* with every piece of coastline from Eastern Canada to Scotland. I thought Scotland. Laura thought Newfoundland.

And it was about 6 P.M., 1800 hours GMT on the evening of September 10 last year with Hector grinning, his hook secured in an overhead beam in my farmhouse kitchen as he dangled and swung back and forth, testing my eroding patience when Conswella Van Ogtrop raised me on her short wave radio; she aboard her old Bristol Channel pilot cutter, *Weitra*, 50 miles east of St. John's, Newfoundland, Laura and I sitting next to my short wave radio at the kitchen table at Finnsheep Farm in Maine, a map of Newfoundland spread before us. I had waited days, excitedly, for Conswella's call.

"*Weitra, Weitra*," I said, trying and failing to conceal my joy at hearing her voice, and anticipating her reaction to what Laura and I had discovered, what I was about to tell her. "Good copy, good copy," I said, "How do you copy me? Over."

We listened to a crackling sound, I switched from lower side-band to upper side-band, Laura watching me adjust the knobs. We waited and waited. And then, "Roger that. Good copy here. Over."

"Conswella," I said into the transmitter, Laura lifting her head from the map in front of us, her eyes scanning the kitchen and then fixing on mine as I began to speak for the first time to Conswella rather than the sailing vessel *Weitra*. "I have great news." I caught Laura's blue eyes with mine, as I began to speak through the transmitter to a woman for whom, incredulously, I had subconsciously begun to turn myself inside and out, day and night; never, ever having met her. I caught myself. "I have great news *Weitra*," I said. "I have a match. Over." Laura pushed her chair back, stood up and began to chop onions for the pasta, wielding the cleaver like a woman gone mad.

"A match with the drawing in the book. With Newfoundland. Over." I waited.

"Roger that. Roger that," came the voice from *Weitra*. I was more than a little surprised that she showed no excitement. No emotion. Then I remembered all I knew, not very much, about Conswella Van Ogtrop and realized that she was cooler than an iced-down quail. Three thousand miles alone in a sailboat across the North Sea, through the Shetland and Orkney Islands of Scotland, then the raging North Atlantic. "Christ," I thought.

"Newfoundland. South coast," I said. "Over."

"Roger that. Confirms my thinking," she said. I looked up to see Laura's reaction. Laura had left the room. "Exact coordinates?" crackled Conswella.

"Peninsula with St. Mary's Bay to the West and Trepassey Bay to the east," I said.

"Specifics on Gipusollilanntd?" she asked. "And exact coordinates?"

"I don't know yet about that. Hope to have more detail tomorrow," I said, but not very convincingly. "Over."

"Roger that," she said. "Nothing I don't already know. Over."

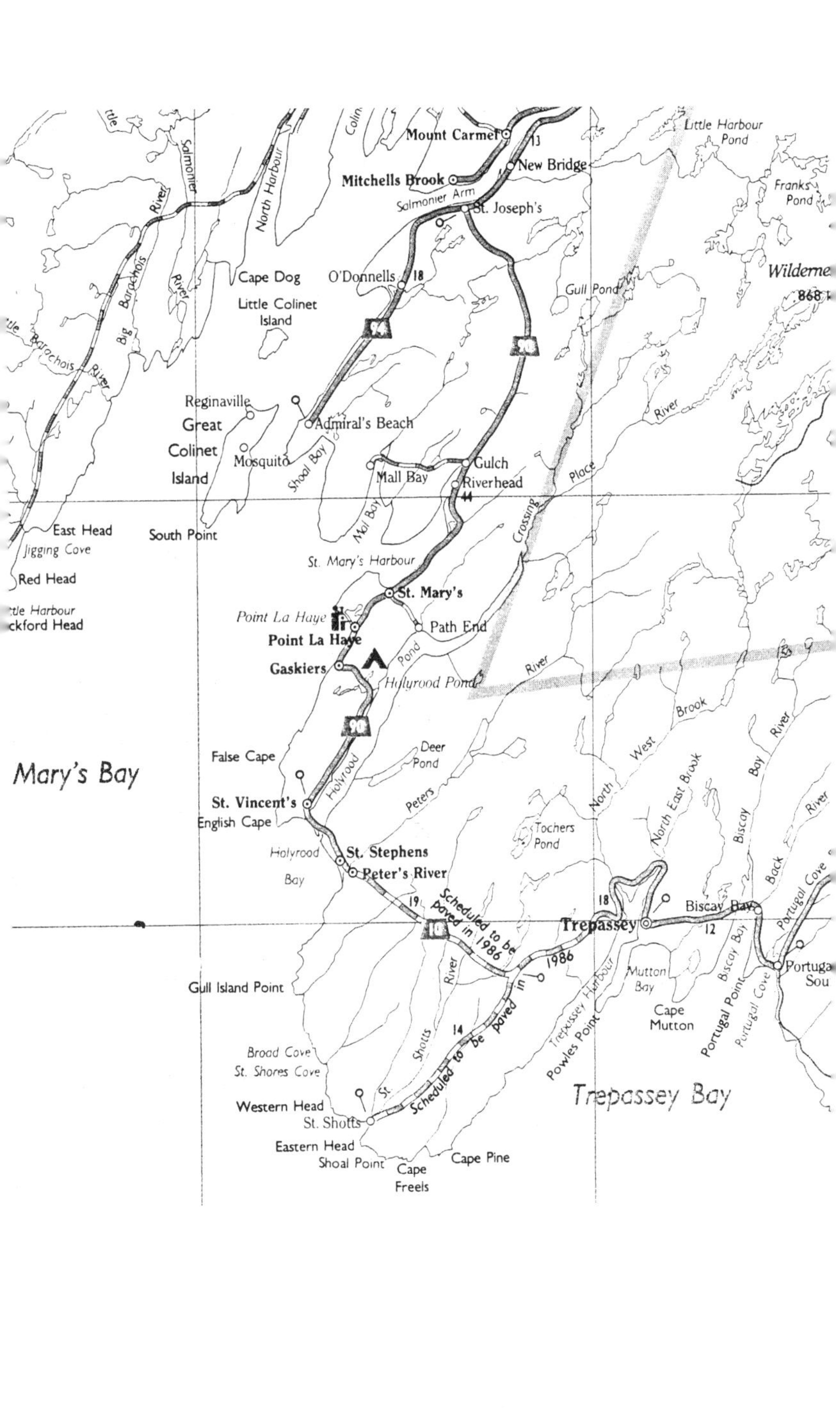

Mount Carmel
Mitchells Brook
New Bridge
Salmonier Arm
St. Joseph's
Little Harbour Pond
Franks Pond
Salmonier
North Harbour
River
Big Barachois River
Cape Dog
Little Colinet Island
O'Donnells
Gull Pond
Reginaville
Great Colinet Island
Mosquito
Admiral's Beach
Shoal Bay
Mall Bay
Gulch
Riverhead
Place
Crossing
East Head
Jigging Cove
Red Head
South Point
Mal Bay
St. Mary's Harbour
St. Mary's
Point La Haye
Path End
Gaskiers
Holyrood Pond
Pond
River
Brook
False Cape
Deer Pond
Mary's Bay
Holyrood
St. Vincent's
English Cape
Peters
North West
North East Brook
Biscay Bay River
Tochers Pond
Holyrood Bay
St. Stephens
Peter's River
Back
Scheduled to be paved in 1986
Trepassey
Biscay Bay
Portugal Cove
Gull Island Point
Mutton Bay
Trepassey Harbour
Cape Mutton
Portugal Point
Powles Point
Broad Cove
St. Shores Cove
Shotts
Western Head
St. Shotts
Trepassey Bay
Eastern Head
Shoal Point
Cape Freels
Cape Pine

"Roger that," I said.

Conswella Van Ogtrop did not sign off. She merely hung up her transmitter, set her wind vane and climbed into her bunk, probably disgusted with the hapless fool she had been talking to.

I did not know for sure then that Conswella Van Ogtrop and *Weitra*, her Bristol Channel pilot cutter, were being followed; followed by a vessel which tried to lie far enough back to be just beyond the horizon from the pilot cutter ahead.

When I told Laura that I had a suspicion that Conswella was being followed, it was as if she were struck by lightning. She dropped her fork and stared at me. "Jesus Christ," she said, "What in hell is going on?"

"Any thoughts?" I asked.

"Fuck you, Chuck," she said.

I looked at her, my mouth agape. "What did you say?" There was no response.

Later that evening, I broke the "Gipusollilanntd" code. Dunkerque's fifteen letters.

Laura smiled. Hector laughed.

The following morning, I received a telephone call from a man I did not know, a man who issued a warning.

That same day, September 11, 1993, Laura disappeared.

34

Dizzy and Sick

Incomprehensible Computer Programs

"DIMINUTIVE?" she asked.

"Yes," he said. She didn't laugh. Her younger male friend had only been working at the company for less than a month and he did not yet share her reverence or fear.

"Short," he said. She looked away, brushing the hair from her eyes as a man with hair implants dotting his head and one eye rolled back opened the door from his office, burped and limped out past the two of them, glancing at his secretary and then the boyfriend sitting next to her desk. He turned the top half of his body only slightly, raising his chin, puffing out squirrel-like cheeks, and pointed to the young man.

"You are fired," he said. "Do you, did you work here?"

The young man sprang from the chair, "Yes, sir. Yes, sir."

"Well, me boy," said the limping short man. "Now you don't." He walked down the hallway, away from his office, mopping his brow and trailing his leg, the shoe dragging a line through the thick carpet, a white line, between separated pile carpet fibers, scribed by his shoe tip. The cleaning lady watched him disappear down the hall and turned on her vacuum cleaner, following the trail of the foot, erasing the marks of his shoe.

He entered the conference room and shut the door. Four people in suits and ties no longer spoke. He took his seat. The table had chairs to the left and chairs to the right and one at the other end, down from him. Two empty chairs, to the left and to the right sat next to him. A man on the right side of the table, about half way down fumbled with a pad and dropped his pen on the floor. He pushed back his chair, bent down and retrieved the pen. Everyone looked at him. Except the man at the head of the table.

The man who had found his pen rose from his seat and walked to the door. He turned to look back and then made his leave. The table was silent. The men at the table looked at the door and then to the man at the head of the table.

"There is nothing here for that," he said. He looked up and down the table, flicked a speck from his collar, pulled a wadded, soiled handkerchief from his rear pant pocket, blew his nose, returned the balled wad to his pocket, his cheeks again puffed like a squirrel's, and then he sat down.

"Let's go, Igamuche," he said, his head tilted down, eyes fixed on the papers in front of him. "I said, let's go."

"Yes, sir. Yes, sir," said the man to his left with close cropped black hair and thick glasses. "I will begin if I may."

The head of the table man with the gimpy leg and wadded-up handkerchief and squirrel-like cheeks stared at him, the old needle tracks on his arm concealed beneath his shirt and suit coat.

The man with the thick glasses to his left dimmed the lights, turned on the overhead projector and began to report. "As of the close of business at the end of last month, we had, as you can see, $1.25 billion in assets distributed as indicated. Cash and Equivalents, $575 million, mostly in 30-day notes, bills, etc.; Notes Receivable, $200 million, principally the two casinos and the Royal Bank of Scotland, due in 60-120 days."

"Useless casinos," said the man at the head of the table.

"I'm sorry, sir?" asked the man with the glasses, eyes blinking rapidly.

"Useless casinos, I said. The casino notes were originally due a year ago. Where has all the God damned cash gone?"

"Yes, sir," said the man with the thick glasses, pausing, and then hearing nothing more, he continued. "That's $775 million in Cash, Equivalents, and Notes Receivable. The remaining $480 million as follows: $450 million in listed securities, New York, London and Tokyo Stock Exchanges, the small amount on the Munich Exchange. $30 million balance in private, venture capital investments of which . . ."

"Where is the breakdown of that $30 million?" the gimpy-legged, squirrel-cheeked man asked.

"I am now to summarize that, sir. We did not have time to develop that slide," said the man with the glasses and close-cropped black hair.

"Let's go. And I want some fast answers on the God damned casinos. Somebody's gettin' rich, and it sure as Hell ain't us. Not me, anyway." He glared across the table.

"All right, yes."

"This is like a bunch of pigs in shit." He took out his handkerchief, rubbed his forehead and blew his nose again, glared again at the man with the glasses and burped.

"The electronics company in Singapore, Tengco, $10 million; the export company in Panama, $12 million; the salvage company out of Grand Cayman, *Glory Be*, $7 million; and the cinema in the Caribbean, $600,000; the balance of $400,000 in sundry accounts receivable, mostly from the salvage company people, $50,000 of it from the cinema." He paused and looked away from the wall to the man at the head of the table who had burped again, louder.

"What are you stopping for?" asked the burping, gimpy-legged man, now alternately cleaning his nails with a pocket knife and gingerly touching the hair on his head.

"Yes, sir."

"Yes, sir, what?"

"No, sir." His eyes began to blink uncontrollably. He began to feel dizzy and sick to his stomach.

"Get on with it unless you would like to get on with it somewhere else, you fool."

"Yes, sir." The glasses man slowly reviewed the results for the month of the $450 million in listed securities, the payment schedules for interest and principal of the $200 million notes receivable in place with the two casinos and the Royal Bank of Scotland, and then the $30 million in venture capital investments: Singapore, ($10 million); Panama, ($12 million); the salvage company, *Glory Be*, ($7 million) and the cinema, ($600,000).

"Do you know how long we have had the $7 million invested in the salvage company?" asked the gimpy-legged man. "Salvage companies, casinos and cinemas. Jesus Christ. How long?"

"Yes, sir," the other man said, flipping through his stack of print-outs.

"How long?"

"Quite a while, sir."

"How long? This is 1993."

"Several years, sir."

"And can you tell me what our return has been?"

"Yes, sir. None, sir." His eyes were scanning the room.

"None. Yes. Nothing. The same amount as the good

you've been since we restructured this company, together. That was eleven God-damned years ago. You peaked in '82."

"Correct, sir." He folded his hands and knew what was coming.

"Damn right I'm correct, and can you tell me whose idea it was to pour two, then another two, then another two, then another one million into that wasted venture?"

"Yes, sir. Who?"

"Who, God-damn, who? I'll tell you who. You. You. You God-damned idiot."

Igamuche was silent. He ran his left hand over the scars on his neck and felt his pulse racing, anger ready to explode.

"Yes, sir," he said.

The gimpy-legged man at the head of the table was tight as a cork, his face red, veins in his neck bulging, eyes riveted on the glasses man whose face was stretched tight. "Seven million in the salvage company, another $600,000 in the cinema, plus the additional $50,000 in accounts receivable from the cinema. May I ask what our current prospects are in those two black holes at the moment, when you think we will begin to get a return, our money out, if ever? And what about the casinos? That's where the real money is. Was. The others are piddle in comparison. You seem to think that we've endless supplies of cash."

"Yes, sir. No, sir."

"Yes, sir, what? God damn it."

"Yes, sir. Well, sir. If I may. It seems a bit unfair that . . ."

"Unfair? Unfair? What's unfair? That we have gotten

our money here into worthless bags of shit? Unfair? You idiot. You should have stayed in Nippon. I'm fed up with your incomprehensible computer programs and losing our asses because of your wretched investment judgment. You should have stuck with accounting. Stayed a shiny-assed bookkeeper." He was banging his fist on the table and shouting, neck veins bulging.

"No, sir. I mean, yes, sir. No, sir. Only that it seems a bit unfair for me to be taking blame here." The three other men stared, motionless and mute, at the walls and ceiling.

"I see," said the gimpy-legged man. "I see. I see that you will be working elsewhere. Beginning now you no longer work here. Leave the papers in front of you. Leave the building. Now. We'll settle things later. In private. Am I clear?"

"Yes, sir." And then he was gone.

Igamuche was gone.

But, he had unfinished business. And he was glad that he had not lost his composure. Yet.

"Am I right?" bellowed the gimpy-legged man mopping his brow at the head of the table. "Am I right?" The three other men left in the room nodded their heads in agreement.

The three men left. With their suits and ties. Their pads and pens. What they had come with. They left with what they came into the room with. They left the room without their self-respect because they had not brought it with them into the room. They had lost it long ago. Each of them, the day they had decided to join the firm, work for this tyrant Englishman.

The short, gimpy-legged man with squirrel cheeks and a wadded-up ball handkerchief in his back pocket sat in the room alone. He ran his fingers through his hair and touched the new hair plugs on the front of his head; they were very sore, and he wondered if his eyes were still black and blue from the last hair transplant session he had early that morning.

He sat alone.

He pulled up the sleeve of his suit coat, loosened his necktie, unbuttoned the cuff of his shirt sleeve, rolled it back, pushed it back as far as he could against the sleeve of his suit coat and then took the suit coat off, standing up. Sitting down, he pushed the shirt sleeve all the way up to his shoulder and he looked at the old marks running like a lost dot marker up his arm.

"Never again," he thought to himself.

He got up from his chair, looked at his arm and stumbled, the chair falling in back of him. He walked around the room. He thought back. He limped to the side board, placed his hand on it, leaned over and began to cry, looking to the door, closed.

A nasty, mean, vindictive, short-tempered son-of-a-bitch. That's how his acquaintances used to describe him. What did his friends say? He didn't seem to have any, at least no one seemed to know of any. A heavy drug user at an early age. An intermittent, depressed user later on. But there was another side to the man I had stood face-to-face with and threw out of the room I shared with Buzzie Thornton at Swarthmore College in 1964, the man I would not see or hear from again for almost thirty years.

Fury Ipdown lived and breathed what he had learned about his great-great-grandfather, Jersey Ipdown, the young boy who had gone over the fence with his Eton schoolmate in London in 1862, Dunkerque Chamonix; the latter to die sad and broken, alone with his parrot, Guyane, in St. Paul's Cathedral; in his steeple alcove, cold and damp; in 1940 at the age of ninety-three. Outliving, chronologically, his friend Jersey by sixty-eight years. It is strange how some people learn a bit of history and then lock into it, onto it, become obsessed with it as if the present were the past, the past the present, nothing other to matter but to live through dreams, facts, fantasies and bodies long turned to dust. That was Fury Ipdown.

Break here. I thought I was perfect. But, now I know I'm not. Sitting here, writing, in the bathroom, my feet up on the tub, I just noticed that the little toe on my right foot is smaller, relative to the adjoining toe, compared to the little toe on my left foot. I don't know of any other imperfections that I have. Except maybe for the short score on sanity or rational behavior. No, not true. But I must confirm that by checking with my "rational other." Did I write of him? I think I did. I will definitely check him out. Tomorrow. Or next week. Oh, my gosh, I ask myself. Like Mrs. Lincoln. "Aside from the incident in the opera box, Mrs. Lincoln, did you and Abe enjoy the play?" On, no, my rational other wants to say. But, I won't give him a chance to talk to me until I want to. He is the one who told me last year that I couldn't possibly be in love with Judy, after knowing her for only one week [but I was], Laura and Conswella at the same time. It was probably unfortunate for me that Red Stripes cost only 50 cents in St. Martin.

One little observation for wealthy absentee boat owners. Across the dock in St. Martin's Simpsons Bay is a 60- or 70-foot motor yacht named Othello, *from Miami. The owner was aboard for a week last April. He comes for only about one week out of every two months. And he has a live-aboard worker whose job is to keep the boat clean and the varnish in Bristol condition. During that April week, things were very quiet on the boat. The worker, Basil, about twenty-two or twenty-three, and from Holland, was busy as a bee every day, sanding and varnishing, arms and hands moving faster than a hummingbird's wings. The varnish work is a never-ending process on the boat, literally. By the time you finish sanding and varnishing from bow to stern, it is time to head to the bow again. Boat looked good.*

The owner left with his bags for the airport at 8:00 A.M. after eight days. I watched Basil sitting on deck of Othello, *eyes following the American Airlines plane overhead as it rumbled from St. Martin toward San Juan with* Othello*'s owner aboard. Ten minutes after the plane passed overhead, Basil collected up his sandpaper and brushes, capped the varnish can and went below. Five minutes after that the Neville Brothers were blasting from the stereo in the main salon. Five minutes after that, Basil was on deck with his guitar, strumming away.*

By noon, Basil had been joined by three young ladies and a case of Heineken. The Neville Brothers still playing. Louder.

Oh, my. Hector, get back to work. I don't want him reading that and getting any ideas.

35

Sound Truck in Philipsburg

UH, OH. Look out.

As I previously mentioned, up until two years ago, and at least since I began coming to Sint Maarten in 1980, the native Antillians pretty much ran the island their own way. At least that was true for Dutch Sint Maarten which

I know a lot more about than French Saint Martin, the other half of the island, the whole of which I loosely refer to as St. Martin.

Dutch Sint Maarten, comprising sixteen square miles, the southern half of the island, is part of the Netherlands Antilles, the five island group, all territories of Holland. The island of St. Martin was settled by the Dutch and French in the 1630s and divided between Holland and France in 1648.

In 1992, in the face of the growing drug-smuggling, money-laundering, government and political corruption and the like, Holland's laissez-faire attitude toward its possession suddenly changed, and the Dutch "Supervision Program" was put in place. The native Antillian government no longer could assume it could do whatever it wanted. The 1993 jailings of Billy Waddie and Tony Spedarrone, which I referred to earlier, were a reflection of the tightened screws. I did a fair amount of business on the island in the 1980s, and can tell you from experience that whatever the Dutch laws said, the local government did whatever it pleased. Not so true today, although corruption is still alive and well down there, even with Spedarrone and Waddie now pushing daisies.

To my point. A lot of resentment built against Holland, by the Antillians. And one night early last year marked a first there for me.

I was driving from Simpson's Bay to Philipsburg to visit a favorite watering hole of mine after dinner. Just outside Philipsburg on the main drag, was a sound truck and a crowd of people. And the message blared, "What have the Dutch done for us? Nothing. They come here three hundred years ago. They promise to help us with all their money. All they do is take our property. It now time to take our island back."

"Uh, oh. Look out," I said to myself. And I didn't suspect then how right my gut might be.

During that same month last year, approximately a week later, and nine miles away on the island of Anguilla, people rose from their seats and began to head for the exit doors, no more than ten or twelve people in total. Almost all of the patrons had seen the old film more than once before. He waited until the last person had disappeared through the exits before opening the door to his booth, descending the ladder to the cinema floor below, pushing the rewind lever on the projector as he began to descend.

He looked up at the screen from time to time as he pushed his broom down the aisle and across the rows; empty paper cups, candy wrappers, popcorn and a solitary condom piling up ahead of his broom; a hood with cut-outs for eyes, nose and mouth over his faceless head. Gregory Peck, David Niven, and Anthony Quinn flashed by backwards on the screen with Gia Scala and the big guns of Navarone, 1961 vintage.

All eight lights in the small theater were on as he emptied the trash, stowed away *Guns of Navarone*, placed Peter Sellers and *The Mouse That Roared* on the projector for the following day, locked the booth, returned to the floor below, counted the meager evening's receipts and placed the few bills and coins into his green cloth zippered bag. He stopped in the single toilet lavatory without a sink, swabbed the toilet and put out a fresh roll of toilet paper, glancing and grimacing only momentarily as he passed the mirror. He closed the single panel door, crossed the ten-by-ten lobby to the light panel where he shut off the switches and turned to see three men in front of him, standing between him and the entrance door.

"Last day of the month, paste face," said the first man.

One of the other men reached for the small green bag under the cinema operator's arm, pressed between upper arm and side. The cinema operator flinched and stepped back. "Bitte," he said. "Bitte. Da ist nicht Geld jetzt. Ich nicht Könne. Aussehen zu mir. Aussehen zu mein kleider." There is no money now. I cannot. I can't (even afford to) eat. Look at me. Look at my clothes.

The first man laughed, took a gun from his belt and shot twice across the lobby toward the screen at the far end of the short aisle.

"Your choice, paste face. You're already a month behind."

The second man spied a folding chair near him, picked it up and hurled it toward the small counter with its hot dog warmer on top. The chair crashed through the glass front of the counter, covering its contents of Mounds Bars, M&M's and peanut bags with splinters of glass.

The third man lunged for the small green cloth bag, caught its end and ripped it from the cinema operator's grasp. He opened it, looked at the meager contents, spat and handed it to the first man.

"Two weeks to pay up what you owe plus another five hundred on account."

"Es ist nicht möglich. Es ist unmöglich." It is not possible. It is impossible, said the cinema operator.

"Take your choice, my friend. Pay up or this place gets burned to the ground," and then, "Let's go."

They were gone as quickly as they had appeared.

The cinema operator stood there, running his hands over the sides of his face. Tears began to well up before they gave way to anger.

"Nicht mehr. Nicht mehr." No more. No more, he said aloud.

He locked the front door and went into the tiny maintenance room with its sink, mops, pails, tools and a folding cot next to a hot plate on a wood crate. He took off his shoes, lay down on the cot and leafed through his ledger book.

He set the book down, reached above his head for the dangling string and pulled it; the solitary light bulb going out for the night. A downpour suddenly drenched the entire island easing the oppressive heat. He thought of his daughter and he felt his face.

"Schmutzig Bastards." Dirty bastards, he said, before falling off to sleep and dreaming once again of Me Yong.

36

Hand-Scrolled Sword

Reunion at the St. Moritz

THIRTY YEARS had passed since their most famous missions and thirty-five years since the first prototypes were ordered in 1940. The B-29 American Superfortress undertook its first combat in the Pacific Theater in the early summer of 1944. More than 3,000 of the advanced bombers were in the hands of the U.S. Air Force one year later. An extraordinary feat.

He briefly had toyed with the idea of clearing the entire ballroom with hidden explosives when the time came, but never really seriously planned or considered such a monumental act, an act which would surely result in a nationwide manhunt and probably his capture. When he left his taxicab and walked into the lobby of the St. Moritz Hotel on Central Park South in New York on August 6, 1975, his plan was a more modest one.

The *Enola Gay* and *Bock's Car* had each carried a crew of twelve men in the early August of 1945 when the first atomic bombs were unleashed on Hiroshima and then Nagasaki. Nine of *Bock's Car's* crew were still alive thirty years later, and seven of them were listed as returning for the "Superfortress Reunion" at the St. Moritz along with six of *Enola Gay*'s crew, eleven members of Boeing's 1944 engineering staff and thirty assorted other former employees of the five companies which produced the mammoth bomber.

And among the attendees listed on the reunion program was the bombardier aboard *Bock's Car* on August 9, 1945, the Airman First Class. The man who had pushed the red button, sending the atomic bomb hurtling down from the sky and 30,000 people to their deaths in the city of Nagasaki. A smile on his face in a newspaper photo to follow.

Aki checked into his room, unpacked his clothes, sat down at the little desk and opened his briefcase. He reviewed his plan, carefully penned on a single sheet of legal paper, and lifted the stainless steel handle from its compartment. The blade was honed to razor-edged sharpness and he clicked it into the handle, holding the assembled sword with its hand-scrolling out in front of him. He rose from his desk, walked to the bed, paused, and then plunged the sword into the pillows.

The hotel operator answered his call and informed him that the hotel guest had not yet arrived. Arrival was not guaranteed said the operator. That meant the guest planned to arrive before 6:00 P.M. Aki looked at his watch. It was 5:45 P.M.

"Thank you," he said, hanging up the phone.

The taxicab pulled to a stop in front of the St. Moritz. The passenger reached for his wallet, paid the driver and opened the back door. One leg out, he stopped. His mind began to race. Thirty years flashed through his mind, back to August 9, 1945.

The former Airman First Class, bombardier aboard *Bock's Car,* pulled his right leg back into the taxi, paused and said aloud, "No."

"What's that?" asked the driver.

"Back to the airport."

"We just came from there, Bud."

"Back to the airport."

The sixty-year-old man slammed the door shut.

The taxi driver shrugged and hit the meter, the cab heading across town back to LaGuardia.

Was it a desire to block out the memory of a thirty-year-old mission or an inkling of lurking disaster in wait? A little of both I was to learn eighteen years later when I sat with the man, forty-one years after first meeting him.

37

Visitor to the Alcove

THE OLD MAN watched as the motorcycle with its sidecar disappeared in the direction of the motorway. He placed his bony hands and fingers on the shutter knobs and took one last look. Then he slammed the window covers closed and sat down at the crude desk in the corner of his damp steeple alcove. He fumbled with the matches, the wind whistling through the granite, blowing out match after match. The kerosene lamp was finally lit with a piece of straw inserted in, and then carried up from the coal stove two stories below; the old man cupping his hand around the faint glow as he climbed the winding stone steps, back to the small alcove at the top of the steeple in St. Paul's Cathedral.

Dunkerque Chamonix huddled over his desk and notebook, the oil lamp flickering, a full moon casting a glow across his pen and paper. "No," he said to himself, "I will not [let things] end this way. There is still much to be done. I must not take my leave." He turned his wrinkled face, just a half turn, and said "You know, you know."

"I know. I know. You know, I know. No, no, no, no. Squawk." Guyane then fell silent and looked at the man eyeing him, the parrot's head cocked to the side.

Dunkerque Chamonix ceased to glare at his parrot, turning his head back to his notebook, beginning to write. "Tell no one," he suddenly said, swinging his head back in the direction of the old wood cage, "but me. Tell me."

"No tell. No tell. Squawk." Guyane the parrot poked his beak and head under his wing, sleep on his mind. And then "Cover, cover." Dunkerque laid his pen down, took the mildewed cloth cage cover from the foot of his bunk, and placed it over Guyane's cage.

"Thank you," came the words from under the cover.

"No tell?" asked Dunkerque.

"No tell," squawked Guyane.

But the old man knew that his best and claw-footed

remembered to anyone and no one. But he would not tell his master, Dunkerque, who had sworn him to secrecy, of things which Dunkerque's long vacant memory had no recollection.

His eyes dropped as he turned the yellowed pages of his old notebook. He watched his bony fingers run down the new entries he had written, beginning two months before, in June 1940, at age ninety-three, when he began to remember, or was it imagining? He did not try to check the flow of tears that clouded his monocle and ran down from the corners of his eyes, through his beard and the few drops which wet the pages in front of him. He turned his head to the parrot's cage. He thought about taking the cover off, opening the cage and bringing Guyane to his hand, to his face, to hold him and love him, stroke his beak and back. Dunkerque Chamonix squinted at his notebook and once again turned over the old newspaper clipping and photograph from 1865 and read the five words written on the back.

He looked toward the closed shutters, he looked down at his feet, he thought back to the day in 1862 when he jumped the fence with his school friend, Jersey Ipdown, and they ran across the clover meadow and hid in the woods as the headmaster ran after them, shouting, cursing, swinging his switch; Jersey to head north to the Cotswalds, Dunkerque to make his way to the London docks and ball himself up in a mail bag in the ship bound for America. But, he had been able to remember only isolated images beyond that, and he sniffed his crinkled nose and remembered the smell of the mail bag and the hold in the ship, and he could now smell it again.

But as he watched the motorcycle with its sidecar race away from St. Paul's Cathedral, he wanted to run down the old, cold steps, run down to the entrance of the cathedral, to touch, grab the man, the young man who had visited him frequently over the last two months. The man who talked with the old bony man and kissed the parrot. The young man who wanted to know everything. But until today, that man had talked with an old man who could not remember anything of what he wanted to know.

Until today. When Dunkerque Chamonix remembered. The watch and its broken glass. It cutting his fingers. Seventy-five years before. At Ford's Theater.

And today he remembered what he was bound for when he boarded the S.S. *Claxdow* in 1872, sixty-eight years ago. $19 million and the watch. But where?

His natural death in September of 1940, one month later, went largely unnoticed.

But his twenty-five-year-old visitor with his motorcycle and sidecar and interest in lost treasures had learned enough to begin a fifty-three-year odyssey of his own.

38

The Hunter

SHE SAT IN the tree and waited. She had been there for four hours. Sitting and waiting. Cold, tired and hungry. She poured coffee from her thermos. It was cold. She brought her binoculars to her eyes. Nothing but the wind-driven snow and the wavering pines.

And then she saw him. The massive head. The suspicious, large brown eyes. The bulging neck, muscular chest and long legs. She was downwind, but the eyes seemed trained on her. Trained on the tree limb on which she was perched.

She had waited a long time to meet up with him. And now, there he was, magnified into something close enough to touch. She raised her hand to reach out and touch him, realized her stupidity, and let the hand swing back to her side.

He stood still, like a monument. The eyes were still staring at her and the limb on which she sat as she slipped the shaft of the arrow with its razor sharp, stainless steel broadhead hunting point over the arrow rest and set the nock around the bow string, carefully sighted, and then slowly drew the string back, the eccentric cam wheel letting forth with a slow, low squeak. "Damn," she said under her breath.

He was gone in a flash. A flash of breath-taking speed. And then there was only the wind-driven snow again and the wavering pines.

She descended and broke the snow.

From the hill she looked north across the Gulf of St. Lawrence to the hills of Labrador and Newfoundland; east to Cape Breton Island and the open expanse of the Atlantic Ocean beyond; and south across the North Umberland Strait to Nova Scotia. She buttoned the collar of her old blue pea jacket and began walking; the icy wind clinging to her nostrils and bringing tears to her eyes. It was rare to have snow here, the moderating influence of the Gulf Stream making the island a rare summer paradise at this high latitude. But there was snow now, and she was proud of herself for remembering to bring her snowshoes. They were serving her well.

As she walked toward her truck, the sky clear, bright and now exploding with stars, she reached up and touched the upper limb of her compound bow slung over her shoulder; and then with the other hand, reached back and ran her fingertips across the smooth steel of the broadhead hunting points on the tips of the arrows in her quiver. She smiled to herself. She could put arrow after arrow into a four-inch circle from thirty-five yards. Without so much as a sound, save the "whoosh" of the arrow against the wind. And the sound of the bow string, a "snap," as her firm and steady fingers slowly opened, and the string eased down and off the ends of her index and forefinger.

She would be ready when the real time came. She had no doubt of that, or that the time would come.

39

"Cat's Ass" and Desert Loon

FOUR BELGIAN draft horses, giants, hooves the size of five-gallon pails pulled the wagon ever so slowly, the wagon inching forward and rocking from side to side on its old scissor-type springs as it went; a long wooden flatbed trailer, forty feet, drawn along, attached to the back of the Conestoga wagon; the draft horses seemingly pulling without effort, feed bags in place on the two aft horses; the wagon driver sitting high on his wide wood seat, an inner tube surrounding his bottom cheeks atop a second, larger inner tube beneath; a Sony Walkman blaring forth Bob Marley and the Wailers' "Jamming"; a Sony Watchman, battery-powered, set next to the seat, the screen's image reflected in a two-foot by two-foot convex mirror astride a stainless steel telescopic pole attached to the wagon's sideboard; the television image in the mirror, now Oprah Winfrey talking to a transvestite in prison to the left, no more than eighteen inches from where the wagon driver sat; his eyes moving to the transvestite on the large, screen mirror, then to his horse team pulling his old Conestoga wagon and flatbed trailer. "Desert Loon," read the letters painted in fluorescent orange on the canvas-hooped covering of the wagon. "Desert Loon - Boy at Work."

He shut off Oprah and Bob Marley, loosely tied the reins around the spring under his seat and crawled into the covered wagon. He took a big thick steak, marinating for two days in Italian dressing, from his battery driven ice box and threw it on the charcoal grill with its wind protector in the recessed hole to the right of the driver's seat in the front of the wagon. The steak and its fat and dripping dressing sucked up the coals' heat; yellow and red fire and the steak went aflame, blackening. "Cat's ass," he said to himself, and then aloud, "cat's ass." He took a tin cup of water and doused the flames of the steak, the coals sizzling, not dying. He looked to his team of horses, lit the kerosene carriage lamp hung from the top of the front of the covered wagon's first iron hoop, looked up to the Polestar, the North Star, and with his thumb and index finger, the index finger pointing toward the North Star and his thumb pointing toward the horizon, he estimated the number of degrees between his index finger tip and his thumb tip and thus his current position in degrees of latitude. "Thirty-three degrees north latitude," he said to himself, "give or take a few degrees, two hundred miles or so," smiling.

He looked for Pleiades in the heavens, to the north, and found it. "Cat's ass," he said.

He thought about standing again on his head in the covered wagon, Desert Loon, and looking toward the southern horizon for the Southern Cross in the beautiful, clear, crisp, star-filled night. But, he did not. He knew the only way that he would see the Southern Cross again was to get down to 25 degrees north latitude. This time he would see her from the ocean.

Ocean Loon, the stainless steel, 44-foot sailboat projectile with twin screws and three bladed propellers sat on the 40-foot flat bed trailer behind Desert Loon, as if a whale looking for water.

"Cat's ass," he said as he chewed his thick steak, sucked on a St. Pauli Girl and looked first at his team of Belgians, then back to the sleek, stainless steel whale on the flatbed. "I will polish you, tonight," he said to no one but Ursa Major, as he looked up. "Tonight. Cat's ass."

Desert Loon rolled along at a pace that would embarrass a rejected snail. For thirteen years. Traveling the untraveled, living in his home, his old covered wagon, the old Conestoga, buying the old lady on wheels from the long-departed cowpoke who was more interested in the stock market than the open plains of America. He bought it for nothing, close to that, and the crusty cowpoke had simply said, "Done," when he was offered $200. And then the new team, the four Belgian giants with five-gallon bucket feet; and he had a home, a workshop, to amble along ostensibly without a care in the world; the horses pulling Desert Loon and *Ocean Loon*; the old wagon, the man's home and workshop, a workshop filled with ideas, inventions and tools, tools, tools and more tools.

He had ridden the plains of Kansas, Oklahoma, Nebraska and the Dakotas, looped down into Texas and New Mexico, and then retraced the entire route; graveled slowly east toward Georgia, sometimes stopping for a day, a week or months; always the mystery of Dunkerque Chamonix not far from his mind. His welding torch now out every day, welding the stainless steel of *Ocean Loon* with pieces of stainless that he bartered for at every junkyard from Boise to Wichita and now Erie, Pennsylvania. He made his living with his wits. He traded wagon wheels and he bought and sold old odds and ends and junk like a medicine man; he bartered, bought, and sold anything his crazy mind could think of. He survived. "No problem," he thought.

He printed short card decks on a press outside of Wheeling, West Virginia and sold them to card sharks in Roanoke and Washington, D.C., and he made $1,200 off that caper.

Before he settled into his sleeping bag, he thought of his plan to get *Ocean Loon* into the ocean for a test, and he looked over his shoulder at the mass and mountain of mess he had produced over the years. The "no-stick shoe sole department" at the far end of the covered wagon. "Didn't work for that," he thought to himself, eyelids heavy, "but a good water-proofer." He thought of his other projects, and thought of his great rabbit, carrot caper. He smiled at that.

"Virgin Mary, Mother of God," he cried out. "Mary of God." The lead draft horse ate from her feed bucket, eyes downcast. She did not look at him.

"Virgin Mary, look at me." She did not look at him. She chewed and chomped, stomping her hooves, snorting and farting.

"Mountain Mary," he called out. Mountain Mary took her eyes and mouth from the feed bucket and looked at him. She ceased to chew, stomp and chomp.

He laughed aloud.

Then he poured himself black coffee from the blue metal pot on the grill and got very solemn as he thought of what he knew about the mystery of Dunkerque Chamonix. The "black sheep from London."

And then he watched as the older man who had been sleeping in the rear of the wagon made his way forward to join him for coffee. "I guess I don't need this picture anymore," he said, looking to the older man and smiling. The old man listened and oiled a hand gun as his companion of eight years, since 1985, began to tell more stories about his days at Swarthmore with the old man's nephew.

"Do you trust Fury Ipdown?" asked the seventy-eight-year-old man.

"I don't know, but he believes that a man whom he just fired has stumbled upon the exact coordinates. Numbers. Not letters."

"Well, why wait? Let's go."

Elmont Thornton IV looked at him. "You might want to stay dead. *The name of the man is Aki Igamuche*."

40

Hamburg to Cuxhaven

ON THE EVENING of August 1, 1993, a solitary figure dismounted an old bicycle, lashed it securely on deck and began the 120 kilometer, 72-mile journey down the Elbe from Hamburg to Cuxhaven where the river empties into the North Sea. The journey would take approximately twelve hours.

Hopefully, no more than a day would be spent in Cuxhaven. And then the real test would begin. Northwest, 550 miles across the North Sea to the passage between the Orkney Islands and Shetland Islands of Scotland. And then, assuming that passage could be made successfully, would come the 3,500-mile journey across the Atlantic Ocean; west southwest, Iceland and then Greenland to the north, and then southwest past Newfoundland to Nova Scotia on a heading for Halifax. Once in Halifax, her search might begin. But there could be no thinking about that now; at an average of four knots per hour or one hundred miles per day, Nova Scotia was more than a month's sailing away, thirty-five days at best. And that assumed a kindly North Sea, by no means certain, and indeed unlikely. But there was no choice to be made in her mind.

As the forty-foot wooden cutter slipped past Wedel, dodging giant ships headed to sea, the skipper of *Weitra* stood at the helm and wondered if any sane solo sailor would make a trip across the North Sea at this time of year. Probably not. And then wondering if she were the first woman solo sailor to attempt it. Probably so. The preferred route at any time of year would be to run down the North Sea, southwest to the English Channel and then into the Atlantic.

She then thought of Cuxhaven at the mouth of the Elbe, twelve hours away, and wondered. If all went well there, once she cast off and was headed northwest toward the Orkney and Shetland Islands, there would be little chance of anyone interfering with her until she got to Halifax. If she got to Halifax. If she got to Halifax before the North Sea or North Atlantic got her and *Weitra*. But no time to think of that either. She locked the wheel, scanned the river ahead and astern, went below and made coffee.

There was no way for her to know whether her stop in Cuxhaven would unearth anything. She suspected not. But that wasn't the real purpose of the voyage. She wondered whether Halifax or even Nova Scotia itself was the correct conclusion as to where to begin a search. But that really didn't matter either. It was the voyage itself. Retracing a very old one. That was why she was going. The stories told to her by her grandfather, Luther Van Ogtrop, and the tidbits she gleaned from Guyane the parrot were interesting. But that was all. Her interest in her great-great-grandfather, Dunkerque Chamonix, as she glided down the Elbe was a curiosity, and nothing more.

That would begin to change that very night.

She had no way of knowing that in a matter of weeks someone would be watching her, waiting to kill her.

Someone whom she did not know. Waiting to kill her with razor sharp stainless steel.

41

Pool of Blood

Numbers from a Window

HE WAS NO genius but he knew the man would come. Aki Igamuche had worked for Elmont & Thornton and Fury Ipdown for eleven years when he discovered that a man named Dunkerque Chamonix had left more than a missing diary among the firm's boxes and boxes of records more than a hundred years before. By the time of his discovery, Igamuche knew that his days as an employee were numbered, and he decided to keep the information to himself, at least away from his employer. It might come in useful he thought to himself. And well it might.

On the night of August 10, 1993, exactly one month to the day after Igamuche was dismissed from his job, he slept lightly in his bed as a figure with an infra-red light searched the room next door to the bedroom.

Igamuche heard a sound and turned his ear to the wall. Soft footsteps coming.

A body slid along the hallway wall, slowly, almost silently, carefully, back hunched and pressed against the peeling wallpaper. The old halting figure reached the doorway, stopped and listened. The slow, rhythmic tick-tock, tick-tock of the grandfather clock was the sole sound to ears. The moonlight cast a quiet dim glow from the window inside the room, the door half open.

And then one could hear it. A low, long, deep rumbling in the distance. The man looked down at his watch and eased himself carefully into the room. The rumbling noise slowly rose. He began to move across the carpet. The noise was now filling the night. The house began to shake. He thrust open the bedroom door and emptied his hand gun into the mound on the bed covered with blankets. The headlight of the on-coming train illuminated the side of the house. He stepped to the window beside the bed, and hurled the paper-filled suitcase as the train began inching to a stop, the station one hundred yards away.

He turned toward the door and began to walk quietly toward the living room, the only noise now again the rhythmic "tick-tock." The razor sharp wire was around and half through his neck before he was able to move a muscle.

The train and its noise began again and disappeared in the night. The man lay on the floor in a pool of blood. Igamuche stepped over him, exited the room and slipped out the house front door, climbed into his car and coasted down the hill before engaging the starter and heading off rapidly in the direction of the train.

Two men sat in the train's club car, sipping martinis as the train sped toward New York. One craned his long neck to look at his watch; the other, with one eye rolled back, looked at the numbers he had taken from the pile of papers in the suitcase and written on the pad in front of him. He smiled. He had guessed it. So simple. He looked at the numbers in his book. 532813465122.

He had a match.

53° 28.13′. West.

46° 51.22′. North.

As he roared on in his old Plymouth, Igamuche wiped the blood from his hands and thoughts began to pour through his brain in disjointed fashion. Even in the dark, the man who had tried to kill him while he slept, Igamuche watching from the closet, did not limp and he was not built like Fury Ipdown. His thoughts raced back to August 1945 in Nagasaki, to August 1975 at the St. Moritz Hotel in New York, and to the glimpse he had caught of a man years ago, Igamuche searching for him with a crazed heart and dizzy emotion. A man whose face smiled out in the photo as he stood by the B-29 *Bock's Car* in 1945.

"No," Igamuche hollered aloud. Then, "Yes. Yes." Then, "Yes," again.

Igamuche's old Plymouth could not catch up with the train. He knew that. He slowed, turned off the road and pointed his vehicle in the direction of Stamford Harbor and the salvage trawler, *Glory Be*.

Fury Ipdown sat in the club car of the train and studied the twelve numbers with the man sitting next to him. Fury Ipdown, one eye rolled back, cheeks puffed like a squirrel's, burped and then smiled. The man next to him crossed his eyes and took the sombrero from his head.

He had no idea that his former traveling companion and fishing friend lay on a floor in a pool of blood.

As he wound his way through the traffic on the outskirts of Stamford, Igamuche thought that time was running out. The twelve numbers, from Dunkerque Chamonix's old files, his ticket to fortune, were no longer a secret. And he thought of the incriminating print-outs in the suitcase. Then of his American-born grandmother and the old pocket watch. Then, the child.

But was it possible, finally, and by sheer luck that he had avenged his parents' and sister's deaths after all these years? He wondered. The woman had been so easy. Years before. General Creighton's only surviving heir. A granddaughter.

Mandy Mandalay Mandarin.

"Family, country, love and honor," he said to himself as his little foot and scorched sandal pressed down on the gas pedal, and his vision began to blur, his head suddenly dizzy. Again.

42

Geronimo and the Vanishing Prairie Dogs

"SI, SENORITA," the man said, trying to put his hand on the knee of the woman interviewing him, a hand which she repeatedly brushed away, a hand that kept coming back, to the knee and then the thigh, each time getting knocked away, the woman with the microphone sitting bolt upright with each touch, her eyes flashing, her voice picking up speed and volume. "Si, Senorita," he said again.

They were "live" on "CBS This Morning" she said to him, and Paula Zahn was not enjoying her assignment. The man is preposterous, she said to herself, then saying, "Back to you, Harry."

I had been simultaneously stoking the woodstove and brewing coffee, having been up since 4:30 to feed the sheep and cattle (pigs, goats, chickens, turkeys and also Hector's solitary goose), and flicked on the tube only casually, as I seldom watched the thing except for college football, when Boston College was playing.

I had watched Paula Zahn as she approached an open campsite, it was definitely not "live," even though Paula Zahn said it was. She was, "Somewhere in the Southwest," she said. A man sat by the campfire, drinking coffee, a long, very long handlebar mustache, obviously waxed, turned up at the ends, the ends not far from his ears. He had a sombrero on his head and though the sun was only beginning to show its orange glow to the east, he had sunglasses on, taped to his prodigious ears with what appeared to be silver duct tape, a ukulele on his knee, a ratty looking mongrel dog next to him, a cat sitting on his shoulder. Black pants, black shirt with a bolo tie around his neck.

"Why do they call you Geronimo?" she had asked.

"My name, my name," he said, smiling broadly; his head defined by his ears and nose, and perched on a long neck.

"CBS This Morning" had a crew on site to discuss and show the habitat of the vanishing prairie dog. Paula Zahn had spotted the old Conestoga wagon and campfire in the distance and sped there in the Land Rover with camera men filming away, hanging off the sides of the vehicle.

I didn't catch much of it and wasn't really paying much attention. I flicked off the television and sat down with my coffee. And I thought of Buzzie Thornton for some reason.

It had been nine years, since 1983 and the telegram from the "Santa Fe County Sheriff's Office" and Buzzie's expressed wish, "granted," the telegram read, for cremation with no service and no mourners, his ashes to be thrown into the air at midnight toward the southern horizon in the direction of the Southern Cross. Buzzie "dead in a bull fight." I wondered whatever happened to his ex-wife, Jubilee, whom he had divorced three years before in 1980, the same year he walked out of Elmont & Thornton for the last time and headed west for his vacation, never to return. I thought of his marriage to a woman whom I had never met in the entire fifteen years that they were man and wife, from 1965, the year after he graduated from Swarthmore, right up until 1980. And then I thought again of the copy of the diary he had given me the night before he left, the night we sat and ate and drank at the dive in Soho - Thai food and "Wobble Walkers." I chuckled to myself.

I thought about the old parrot, Guyane, dead at the bottom of his cage, and the old man Luther high in the Alps. And then I wondered, for some strange reason, what had ever become of the balding, burping young drug addict with the limp, red bandanna and needle pocked arm who had appeared out of the blue just before Buzzie and I graduated from Swarthmore together. The young man who sat in our room and spoke of an old mystery. I wondered what became of Fury Ipdown and his cockney, British accent and lousy disposition.

I remember that morning well, watching Paula Zahn, and it was eleven months later, on August 1, 1993, that I received a telegram. A telegram, unsigned, addressed to me. Eleven words.

"I found him, but he is gone," it said. "Should have told you."

It had been paid for with cash and sent from a Western Union office in Erie, Pennsylvania.

And it was signed, "Ocean Loon."

And I remember the Paula Zahn telecast with Harry Smith on September 1, 1992, because of how it ended. As the film crew began to leave, milling about, "Geronimo" shouted, "Somebody cleaned out my wallet. Three hundred bucks." His elderly traveling companion pointed to Paula Zahn and said, "She did it. I saw her."

August 1, 1993, was also the day I got truly suspicious, and imposed upon an old police officer friend of mine to do a little sleuthing for me. One week later he called to give me his report. There was no record at the mortuary in Santa Fe of cremating one Elmont Thornton in 1983. Nor any bullfight in Santa Fe that year. And, indeed, no record in the Santa Fe Sheriff's office of the death of anyone by the same name in 1983. Or any other year.

"You sneaky bastard," I said to myself.

Well, Hector seems to have cleaned up his act a bit. He is back at his books, doing the chores like there is no tomorrow, and smiling. And talking. As much English, as broken as it is, as Spanish. And the anonymous, silent phone caller has not called again. Let's hope that Hector has said a final goodbye to the Morrey tart. Looks like it. Adelade says he just walks right past the girl now. Good.

Today is January 18, 1994, and it feels like spring here at the farm. Fifty degrees and sunny. Just like St Martin. Hardly. What am I doing? Why did I come back?

Now I'm concerned again. It can't be the Morrey tart who was calling and hanging up. Her family's home, shack, doesn't even have an indoor flush, let alone a telephone. Oh, boy. Who cares. I'm paranoid. Who wouldn't be after the past year.

43

"You Win"

"SOMEONE IS here," announced Laura, the month before her disappearance.

The dogs went into their glorious barking show at about 9:00 P.M. on the evening of August 6, 1993, five days after the eleven-word telegram from "Ocean Loon" in Erie. They seem to hear any vehicle the moment it turns into my driveway at Finnsheep Farm, the entrance concealed from and more than a quarter mile from the farmhouse and barn. I was sitting at my desk charting a course from Portland, Maine, across the Atlantic Ocean to the Azores, half asleep, listening to a Phoebe Snow tape and "Don't Let Me Down," when the barking commenced. Like usual.

What was unusual was that when the machine appeared in front of the house and an old man gingerly stepped towards the front door, bending down to pat the two behemoths, the dogs stopped barking and commenced to wag their tails. Wonderful watchdogs, I thought to myself. I watched through the window as the frail figure wearing aviator glasses and a too short pair of worn, tan chinos together with old, but polished brown loafers stood up straight and continued to walk carefully toward the door; turning his head from side to side, looking all around as he went; the two dogs walking right next to him, continuing to wag their tails. A sixth sense.

I'm embarrassed to admit that it is not uncommon for me to ignore a knock at the door if I do not recognize the knocker, as I surely did not then. But the dogs' wagging tails roused my curiosity.

There was a smile on his face as I opened the door. He held his hat in front of him at his waist with two hands.

"Can I help you?"

"You win."

"Excuse me?"

Again, "You win," followed by an even bigger smile.

I watched, incredulous, as the old man raised his hat to his mouth and began chewing on its brim.

A half hour visit and then he was off. "In the direction of New York."

44

A Secret Room

LAURA REO'S old Maine farmhouse had a big country kitchen with hand-hewed beams overhead, an antique soapstone sink, and an Atlantic wood stove. The kitchen's number one use came to be for "Right and Ready Reo Soaps and Candles, Inc.," tallow and lye and fumes. And, off the big kitchen was Laura's librarian's library, a 20 x 20 foot room, originally three rooms when the farmhouse was built in 1770. Laura's library had floor to ceiling bookcases on three walls packed with an eclectic collection of 1,000 books. The fourth wall had a huge fieldstone fireplace in the center of the wall. And to the right of the fireplace was a large wall hanging from the Far East, about three by four feet; the wall hanging an old woven rug with an embroidered face in the middle; the face in the middle surrounded by embroidered long-stemmed yellow roses; hundreds of them. The rug, "a gift from a friend." And behind the wall hanging was a section of wide board pine, running from ceiling to floor. The middle pine board with a removable knot hole. The knot hole to be removed by Laura Reo at night so she could stick her finger through and open the door with its concealed hinges. Behind the door was a room - dank, dark and dirty - concealing the secrets and another face of Laura Reo, Dayton town librarian, erstwhile soap and candlemaker, and great-great-granddaughter of Sara and the Reverend Elijah Kellog.

Things. Secret things. Stupid me. Dumb Charles Wingate. Ears of clay. Eyes of cotton.

45

Haar Auf Der Hund

A Surprise in Cuxhaven

THE ELBE FLOWS in a northwest direction from Hamburg, winding its way 120 kilometers, 72 miles past Wedel, Gluckstadt and Brunsbuttel before emptying into the often ferocious North Sea; the city of Cuxhaven overlooking the mouth of the river and the sea; the city holding a secret of which Conswella

Van Ogtrop could not fully have had an inkling as she brought her old wooden cutter alongside the city float, twelve hours after she had cast off the docklines in Hamburg, to dodge ferries and container ships the entire seventy-two miles from Hamburg to Cuxhaven last year on the night of August 1, 1993.

And, as I earlier related, obsessed was surely not the word to describe thirty-three-year-old Conswella Van Ogtrop's interest in a century-old mystery involving her great-great-grandfather, Dunkerque Chamonix, when she departed Hamburg aboard *Weitra* bound for the North Sea via the Elbe and Cuxhaven. The taciturn, unsmiling woman's only obsession, if she had one at all now, was with sailboats and sailing; particularly solo sailing. And even that was more of a fascination than an obsession; her other fascination — with men — having ended abruptly, and finally, she said, twelve years before. But, the passing curiosity which best described her interest in Dunkerque Chamonix at the outset of her voyage was hours away now from becoming a mental fire.

At the age of fifteen in 1975, she had solo sailed from Hamburg, down the Elbe, to Heligoland in the North Sea, and back. At the age of twenty, and wondering to herself if she were pregnant, she was a solo, uninvited and unofficial participant in the Royal Ocean Racing Club's regatta from Burnham-on-Crouch to Heligoland, the latter once a curious little island with two towns or one town on two levels, an island with no cars and cobble streets, the island turned into a virtual bomb crater during World War II.

When she bought *Weitra*, her old Bristol Channel pilot cutter, Conswella Van Ogtrop already knew that she wanted to solo sail the heavily built vessel from Hamburg to America. It was certainly not a boat which one would ordinarily pick to single-hand, and it was not a racing boat by any means. Rather plodding, in fact. And its rig was gaff, a gaff as long as the boom. Beside the mainsail, the boat carried a jib-headed topsail, and a genoa and yankee-jib topsail for light winds. Built in 1903, *Weitra* was 40 feet on deck, 37 at the water line, had a beam of 13 feet and a keel which extended 7 feet into the water. All in all, not a simple boat for a single-hander, except that it was a fine blue-water vessel with a deep self-bailing cockpit, wide decks and high bulwarks, and built as solidly as any constructed before or after. Conswella's grandfather, Luther Van Ogtrop, would have told her she was foolish to attempt a solo passage of such a great distance and with such a complicated array of rigging and sails if he were still alive. But, it would only have doubled the woman's resolve and increased her stubborn, unsmiling determination.

When Conswella arrived in Cuxhaven, all she knew of Dunkerque Chamonix were the handed-down stories she had heard from her grandfather, Luther; the stories about Dunkerque's travel to America as a young man; a cache of $20 million from the Royal Bank of Scotland, a cache which Dunkerque was responsible for and the firm in which he was employed had insured in total; a cache of which $19 million disappeared en route from Edinburgh to Montreal aboard the HMS *Truro*; a Jersey Ipdown, boyhood friend of Dunkerque's disappearing from the HMS

Truro at its stop in St. John's, Newfoundland, and dying by his own hand one year later. That was what Conswella Van Ogtrop had been told. All hearsay. Stories. No order.

There were other bits and pieces of stray information. None of which made any sense to anyone, but which did provoke curiosity on her part from time to time. Particularly what Grandpa Luther had said about stories of Dunkerque Chamonix being a frequent visitor with his boyhood friend to taverns in Cuxhaven on the occasions Dunkerque was in Germany on business for Elmont and Thornton; in the days and months and years before Dunkerque boarded the S.S. *Claxdow* for his ill-fated passage from Hamburg bound for Halifax in 1872, a similar passage taken by the HMS *Truro* the year prior to that, and the same route Conswella was embarking on in 1993, one hundred and twenty-one years later.

And though the purposeful, serious woman was not given to larks and nonsense, she thought of her talks, alone, with Dunkerque's ancient parrot, Guyane, when she was just a girl; when the normally fun-free girl got Guyane to talk after the bird's years of saying, "No tell. No tell," to its beloved first owner, and then to Grandpa Luther over the years; the girl getting her few laughs when her repeated volleys of, "Yes tell. Yes tell," got Guyane to talk and her to laugh; Grandpa Luther long given up on the apparently two-worded bird loyal to his long dead master. It was Conswella's little secret, for years, and she remembered the few things, none of which made sense; curious things that Guyane the parrot had told her in private years ago, remembering as she rowed ashore in Cuxhaven from *Weitra* and tied her dinghy to the city dock. "Map. Hair of the Dog. Sara Kellog. Boston. Child of the Island Glen. Oak Tree." She shook her head at herself. "Very sane," Conswella Van Ogtrop thought, "very sane," as she began to walk up from the dock. "I am here because of stories, old stories. Here in this city because of old stories from an old man. And because of long ago words from a parrot." She almost laughed at herself. But, she did not. She walked on. "I must be nuts, dumkoff."

If there is one word which best describes what Conswella Van Ogtrop was not, it might be dumkoff. Then, why did she stop in Cuxhaven? She rarely, if ever, did anything for curiosity's sake; maybe a side-long glance every now and then, rarely that; but, stop after barely commencing her passage, anchor the boat, row ashore and begin to walk the streets of Cuxhaven at night? If you were to ask her, she would not be able to explain. But, later, she was to tell me.

"There was some vague order in the old stories from Grandpa Luther, and there was something vaguely ordered about what the old parrot finally, reluctantly told me when I was a girl. No order that I can express. But, here was a parrot who had sat on the shoulder of a man every day for seventy years until my great-great-grandfather Dunkerque Chamonix died in 1940 at the age of ninety-three. Guyane was him. Guyane became him. In a way. Guyane knew everything that Chamonix could not remember. The parrot. I guess that is what, subconsciously, I thought. Maybe. A parrot? Yes. And, I knew that my father, Frederick Van Ogtrop, spent his last night in Cuxhaven, the night before he drove to Hamburg, boarded his flight for Bangkok, to fly the peace missions for the

Red Cross over Vietnam. An indomitable spirit. Just like me, Grandpa Luther used to tell me. Maybe I felt I wanted to get closer to my father, by stopping where he spent his last night in Europe. I don't know. There were other things. A few. I can't explain it. Any of it. For one who is ordered and believes it only when it is there, it was even more strange. But, I did smell order. A possibility. And for some reason I followed the scent. Uncharacteristic of me, but I did it."

She walked. She walked through the dimly lit streets of the old city at the mouth of the Elbe, gateway to the North Sea, a dirty, decadent gateway crawling with bums and hookers at night. She looked over her shoulder as she climbed the Buchenstrasse road, looked out to the North Sea and the ominous clouds in the direction of the island of Heligoland and thought of her first solo sail from Hamburg, down the Elbe to that island at the age of fifteen; and the look then on her Grandpa Luther's face as she had cast off the docklines. And then she thought of him again, now dead, killed by noxious fumes, having lived alone in the Austrian Alps, smoking his pipe, stoking the fire in his old fireplace, and tending his beloved goats. Then she thought of her great-great-grandfather, Dunkerque Chamonix, then her father, again, and then herself. "Are we all alike?" she asked herself. "All alike?"

Conswella Van Ogtrop stopped in front of an old sandstone building on a cobbled street high above the Elbe and the North Sea, "Cuxhaven Wirsthaus," the sign said. She stood for a moment and then opened the heavy wood door with its hinges of iron. She walked past the tables filled with eaters and drinkers. She got, even in her dirty boat clothes, untold looks and cat calls. She gave two drunken German men the finger. They laughed. She didn't. She sat down at the bar, ordered a hamburger and finished two small glasses of Austrian wine. Then a stein of beer. She hadn't had a glass of wine or a stein of beer since her twenty-first birthday. "Order," she said to herself, "order." She was getting tipsy and she knew it, and the dockworker cat-callers rocking to the Om, Pa Bavarian music knew it. She was beautiful. A drunken German dock worker from across the Elbe rose from his table, walked toward her at the bar, and sat down next to her. "Du ist Schön." You are beautiful, he said.

She nodded her head, and tried to glare at him, her eyes beginning to glaze, "I've got to get back to *Weitra*," she said.

"Ya," the man said. "Ich bringen." I will take (you).

"No, you won't," she said, smacking his hand off her neck, "unless you can tell me."

He looked at her, his eyes heavy and his head bobbing. "Ich erzählen." I will tell (you), he said. "Ja. Erzählen was?" Yes. Tell (you) what?

"Map. Hair of the Dog. Sara Kellog, Boston. Child of the Island Glen. Oak tree." She slurred Guyane's words as she brought forth the utterances of a parrot. "A parrot told me that," she said.

The drunken German dock worker looked at her, lit up a cigarette, nodded and bobbed his head up and down, finished his beer and said, "Ja. Haar auf der Hund. Landkarte. Die versteckt Schatz. Folgen mich." Yes. Hair of the Dog. Map. His hidden treasure. Follow me."

Conswella Van Ogtrop sat straight up. "Hair of the dog, map, I just said to you. His hidden treasure?" she asked.

She did not want to follow him. She followed him. They walked and walked, she was tipsy. He was drunk. He took her hand and pointed it to the sign next to the door. The sign read, "Haar Auf Der Hund."

"Mein name ist Frederick Wenzel," the barkeep said, his massive forearms and hands clasped. Conswella sat next to her new drunken friend and ordered another beer. Her new friend was happy and smiled, "Ich bringen ihr Heim." I (will) take her home, he said to himself, then to the barkeep when she went to the W.C. She stumbled back to the bar, cursing herself for drinking, wondering why she was there. She paid her money and thanked the barkeep. She rose from her seat to leave, the German drunk grabbed her arm. "Ich bringen sie Heim." I take you home, he said.

She brushed his arm away and said, "Nein, Dankershern," and then, looking at Frederick Wenzel, "Hair of the Dog?"

"Ya," Frederick Wenzel said, "hier es ist."

"Sara Kellog?"

"Nein."

"Boston?"

"Nein."

"Kind auf die Insel enges Tal?" Child of the Island Glen?

"Nein."

"Landkarte? Eiche Baum?" Map? Oak tree?

There was a long pause and a sidelong glance, followed by a smile and a touch of his massive hand to her arm resting on the bar. Then Frederick Wenzel leaned over the bar toward Conswella Van Ogtrop. He looked into her eyes. "Landkarte. Eich Baum." Map. Oak tree. He swung his head left to right, then right to left. He scratched his head and thought back to 1945, forty-eight years before when he had fallen through the floor of his burned out tavern, Hair of the Dog, burned out by the drunken Dutch. He thought of the old, water-soaked map piece he had found when he reached down to grab his twisted ankle, the map which he had framed and placed on a hook on the wall behind the bar of his re-built Hair of the Dog.

"Wer ist Sie?" Who are you? he asked.

"My name is Conswella Van Ogtrop," she said, chin sticking out, subconsciously thinking that she might be important, no one ever having queried her quite that way before, about her name." Conswella Van Ogtrop," she said again, and then to herself, "Men."

"Osterreich?" he asked.

"Ya," she said.

"Van Ogtrop. Ich Kennen ein Ogtrop. Frederick. Mein Freund." Van Ogtrop, I knew an Ogtrop. Frederick. My friend.

"My father?"

"Wahrscheinlich nicht." Probably not.

"International Red Cross," she said. "Here in Cuxhaven the night before he left for Hamburg and then Bangkok. To his death in Vietnam. 1967."

"Ya. Ya," said Frederick Wenzel. "Was him."

"Oak tree. Map," she said again.

Frederick Wenzel patted Conswella Van Ogtrop's hand, said to her, leaning again over the bar, "Ich denke wir kennen ein ander, da ist etwas. Ich kennen das. Ich brauche sie sehen etwas." I think we know each other, there is something. I know that. I want to have you see something.

He turned with a smile on his face, and said, raising his stein to Conswella and her new German dock worker "friend," now hanging on to the bar, amidst collapsing in a drunken stupor, "Blicken." Look, pointing his raised arm to the wall.

But, the half map, buried under the floor by Dunkerque Chamonix and Jersey Ipdown 120 years before, the same sodden map found and framed, hung on the wall of Hair of the Dog by Frederick Wenzel in 1947, 46 years ago, was gone. Gone from the spot it had hung only hours before.

"Can you describe the map to me?" she asked Frederick Wenzel, "Draw it? Sketch it?"

"Ganz richtig." Exactly, he said.

And Frederick Wenzel surely had no thought then that Frederick would meet Frederick. That Frederick Wenzel would meet Frederick Van Ogtrop. Again. After twenty-six years. In a common mission. Thousands of miles from Cuxhaven.

You know about "OFF - Deep Woods," to repel mosquitos? Let me tell you something. That garbage, which you spray on your body to repel mosquitos is deadly, to everything. I sprayed around Boogie to Go's *cabin one night earlier this month; in the corners and a little on my head and arms.*

You know something, the stuff peeled the paint and varnish off everywhere I sprayed. Bubbled, like a paint remover.

No matter. I think I made some headway with Judy on that brief trip back to St. Martin.

Hector just said I should forget her. "What do you know about women?" I asked. He showed his gleaming white teeth. "Never mind, I don't want to know." The kid is still only eleven. I think.

46

Bows and Arrows

"I HAVE A GREAT deal of difficulty believing that," I said, staring at her. She was not looking at me, but carefully examining the drying candlewicks, which required no examination at all. It was the morning of September 11, 1993. I had spoken to Conswella and then broken the GIPUSOLLILANNTD code the night before. I had just hung up the phone on the "Fat Tony" warning call; Fat Tony's mouthpiece threatening to sink my boat if I didn't call off Conswella.

"That is your choice," she said, finally, turning to look at me and rising from the table.

"I love you, Laura."

"I love you, too. But, I think none of it is any of your business."

I was flabbergasted.

The pot began to boil. Laura grabbed the long-handled wooden spoon from the counter and began to stir the melted fat tallow.

"But it is my business," I said stunned, but putting my hand on her shoulder.

The wooden spoon went motionless. "And how is that?" she asked, smoothing the front of her apron, looking out the window toward the meadow. "Please enlighten me."

"A promise I made to Buzzie, you know that. I've told you that a dozen times," I said as she brushed my hand from her shoulder.

She strode across the room, talking and fumbling with things; aimlessly picking up and putting down things; books, glasses, etc. "Forget Elmont Thornton. Forget Conswella Van Ogtrop. Forget the whole mess. You are asking for trouble, Mr. Wingate. Big trouble. Go to St. Martin. Check your boat. Do you get the idea?"

She walked out the door and headed toward the barn.

I did not get the idea. I had suspected before, but was not at all sure. Not even then. Laura Reo knew more than I ever wildly imagined, and what she knew was not going to be volunteered to me or, probably, to anyone else. Independent Laura, with her own agenda.

I thought back to my discovery. The "things" in Laura's "secret" room that I had found. Not only the carefully penned documentation of her lineage, but also a collection not normally associated with quiet librarian candle dippers. Big game hunting bows and arrows with razor sharp, stainless steel hunting tips.

Together with a map of Newfoundland.

And in the little lavatory off Laura's secret room I had poked around.

Tweezers for her eyebrows. Brown hair dye. Blue contact lenses. And her wire-rimmed spectacles with clear, non-prescription lenses.

And then I caught myself. We were not married, for sure. There were things about *myself* that I had never told Laura. Like my butterfly collection in *my* secret room at *my* farmhouse. And she had told me not long after we had met that she had a "secret room, for my [her] eyes only," laughing as she said it. Butterfly collections or bows and arrows. What's the big deal, I thought, beginning to feel very guilty that I had snooped, invaded her private space. So, she plucks her eyebrows and dyes her hair and changes the color of her eyes. Big deal again.

As I left that room last year and closed the door behind me, I thought back to the first butterfly in my collection, the first one I had caught, a Monarch; the first of more than five hundred that were now mounted in oak framed cases in my little basement room at Finnsheep Farm. I was nine, in fourth grade, in 1951, when I got the butterfly net for my birthday and ran along the stream behind

Gehrig School at lunch hour, chasing the yellow and black Monarch. Hibbie Flondo and Butch Darken were shooting carp from the bank of the stream with spear guns, the two of them covered with mud, as I flew past, my net high in the air, the butterfly clearly within my grasp, new birthday sneakers on my propelling feet. Hibbie stuck out his spear gun and tripped me, the two of them then to push me into the stream, hollering "Fairy, fairy. Fairy and his butterfly net," as I gurgled and waded back to the bank.

So, is it any secret why I have never shown my butterfly collection to anyone? And I wondered as I looked at Laura's tapestry with its embroidered yellow, long-stemmed roses, the tapestry hung over the "secret" door to her "secret" room next to the old fieldstone fireplace, whether she had taken archery lessons in grade school; while her classmates watched her as they pushed each other around on the soccer field and then beat her up. But I resolved to check the color of her roots. Her hair roots.

"Laura," I said, some days later, "do you dye your hair?"

She looked at me quizzically, paused, and said, smiling, "I can't believe it took you this long to figure it out."

"Didn't you like being a blond?" I asked.

"Chuck," she said, "if I were trying to deceive you, I certainly wouldn't leave the door to my little room unlocked. Would I?"

"I wasn't suggesting that you were trying to deceive me," I said.

She looked at me and laughed.

"I wasn't suggesting that at all, Laura," I said again.

And I wasn't.

But, I should have. Obviously now.

"Would you like to see my butterfly collection?" I asked.

"Yes, indeed," she said.

Call me jelly brains.

47

An Unlikely Connection

Spider and Wasp

HIS BACK ITCHED and he was beginning to feel dizzy again. She ran her hands through his bristly close cropped black hair and then began to scratch his back. "Another two or three months and we can just disappear, poof," she said.

"We don't have two or three months," he said. "The

man is not stupid."

"Surely you are smart enough to keep it from him a while longer, or hide the whole mess in your computer somewhere." She kissed him on his arm, careful to avoid the disgusting scars.

"No longer. I am finished stealing money for you and your two ugly friends."

"You seem to have no trouble accepting your share," she said, rising to her feet.

He sat up and looked around, then at her. "No longer. There is far too much money missing already. It has become impossible to conceal any longer."

"Two more months. Columbia to Dominica. Eight trips. There will be more than enough to replace what you, we, have borrowed."

"No more. It is over."

"Don't do anything stupid," she said, walking across the room, then turning to look at him, "you will be the one, the only one, who will be in trouble."

"We are both equally at risk here," he said, sensing for the first time that she might be willing to see him bear the full force of any consequences. Swing alone.

"I don't think so. It's your employer's money. I don't work for him. And neither do Tony or Billy. It's an American company. Do you really think the government in St. Martin would care if we were taking money from the casinos; or the Cayman government care that we funneled cash out of the salvage company? And you are the one who made it all possible, with your computer tricks. I'm just an innocent on-looker. Don't you want to find the child?

That hit him like a thud of thunder. His eye began to twitch uncontrollably.

"Besides," she said, pulling up her skirt, "your chances of recovering the HMS *Truro* money are nil without me. Tony, Billy and me."

He thought once more about the old, gold watch, and whether he could believe those diary entries. He believed.

He wondered if he should kill her. Then he thought of the child. Without her, he would never find the child.

He moved numbers around with uncanny speed, and he could make numbers "sing" according to his boss from 1982-1993, Fury Ipdown. Fury, far from accomplished himself when it came to numbers and finance, was impressed with the forty-one-year-old Mitsubishi financial analyst computer programmer the first time he met him in 1972. And when Fury Ipdown purchased Elmont & Thornton in 1982, he was almost buried under the firm's debts. It was in large measure due to Aki Igamuche's brilliance and creativity in the financial structuring realm that Fury Ipdown's purchase was made to turn the corner and survive in the following year, Igamuche having been hired full-time two weeks before Fury Ipdown's purchase, nine years after the Japanese man had left Mitsubishi for London and then New York.

Igamuche was a computer nut in addition to a financial genius. But he was not an investment genius. To the contrary. Convincing Fury Ipdown to back the two casinos and float the cinema represented an unwarranted endorsement of Igamuche's investment talents. His investment experience was non-existent. Investment judgment worse than poor. But, tapping into casino capital and cash flow with his computer acumen was easy, and something that his boss, Fury Ipdown, had had no knowledge of.

The greedy Jubilee Chosen did have knowledge. So did Fat Tony and Billy Waddie. And Jubilee Chosen used the somewhat woman dumb Japanese man. Igamuche with his financial wizardry, working for little more than "bags of peanuts," he said; working for the tough, limping man with the hair plugs who promised Igamuche "a piece of the action," equity of the restored Elmont & Thornton, initially restored thanks to Igamuche's efforts; "a piece of the action" that Fury Ipdown never delivered on; a fact that Igamuche could not ignore; a fact that, with Jubilee Chosen's constant urgings, in part led Igamuche to do many of the things he did at Elmont & Thornton before he was summarily fired by Fury Ipdown.

Igamuche knew the salvage company, *Glory Be*, the two casinos and the debt-ridden cinema on Anguilla far more intimately than Fury Ipdown. And what's more, he had long ago fallen in love with Buzzie Thornton's ex-wife, the woman who showed up and applied for a job, which she never got, at the offices of Elmont & Thornton in 1982, the day after it was purchased by Fury Ipdown, eighteen years after she had first gone to work for that firm in 1964, hired by her future husband, giraffe-necked Elmont Thornton IV.

When Jubilee Chosen initially found that she would have no luck gaining influence over the man who purchased Elmont & Thornton's record rooms and rights to a long-lost fortune of $19 million, she turned her attention to the financial wizard; the man who "worked for bags of peanuts," the wiry man of 5'3" who knew more about the workings of the casinos than his boss. Jubilee Chosen had a bit of trouble at first gaining control over Igamuche, but she was a cunning seductress and she knew that there was money to be made by manipulating the Japanese man. And, indeed, it could truthfully be said that the greedy woman, rather than Igamuche, or certainly Fury Ipdown for sure, plotted the strategy that led to Elmont & Thornton's investments in the two St. Martin casinos, the Cayman salvage company, *Glory Be*, and the little cinema on Anguilla.

Jubilee Chosen's strategy was simple. And Igamuche was her loving tool. An unlikely connection of apples and oranges, spider and wasp. Access was her initial goal, access to the records of Elmont & Thornton, records which she was convinced contained more information about the location of the missing millions than just the diary, which she knew her ex-husband had found, and more information than she had in *Child of the Island Glen*.

The greedy Jubilee first became hooked on gambling during her honeymoon on St. Martin in 1965 when she met Fat Tony Spedarrone at his Maho Reef Casino, won $5,000 and spent the night in the fat man's bed while her husband of two days, big-eared Buzzie Thornton, was snoring through his big nose. Casinos meant money and Jubilee thought she could never have enough of that. The salvage company, *Glory Be*? That was her best chance of getting a private search launched for the missing millions.

Igamuche had cringed when Fury Ipdown asked him why the firm of Elmont & Thornton had sunk $7 million into *Glory Be*, and why there had been no results. No profit. But Igamuche knew that if he didn't continue to push, support the *Glory Be* investment, an investment which he had argued strongly for, that Jubilee would blow the whistle on his financial skull-druggery and then leave him. Alone. Alone without even his bag of peanuts salary.

And he needed more time. More time to make his find. He had no doubt now about the missing $19 million. It would be found by him. It was only a matter of time. To be found because Igamuche himself had spent countless hours searching the old records of Elmont & Thornton. And found because Igamuche had discovered the set of twelve numbers written years ago, more than one hundred years, by Dunkerque Chamonix. Numbers which Igamuche's lover convinced him meant something very important. Numbers which Igamuche spit into his computer. Twelve numbers which the computer whiz's software said were longitude and latitude coordinates.

Coordinates which Jubilee and Igamuche decided marked the location of $19 million. And Igamuche wanted more from that location than just the money.

When I initially learned that Jubilee Chosen was still very much alive, I wondered if she had finally murdered her ex-husband. That he did not die in a bull fight or, later, drown with his fishing partner by "accident" in New Mexico's Pecos River.

It was only later that I came to know for sure that Buzzie Thornton had not been cremated in Santa Fe in 1983, thanks to my old, retired police officer friend. Just as I came to know that Santa Fe had no record of the death at all of an Elmont

Thornton IV, in 1983 or any other year. And the findings regarding the two unknown fishermen reported to have drowned when their canoe went over the Pecos River rapids, neither body recovered, but two fishing licenses with pictures subsequently found in a beer cooler floating one quarter mile from the overturned canoe. The picture on one license bearing a startling resemblance to Buzzie Thornton, despite the handlebar mustache and the name, "Felix Geronimo." The picture on the other license a dead ringer not for one "Horst Gutsfeld," but rather my long lost uncle, Didier Mollard.

And for some reason, I thought of little seven-year-old Hanna, Judy's child, Judy the waitress at the "Turtle Pier and Bar Restaurant" on Simpson's Bay in St. Martin. Maybe it was just because, I thought, that I had promised to look in on them upon my return to St. Martin and help in the child's home schooling.

Part III

48

Tired Eyes Above Oberwölz

White Fly Beak

BUZZIE THORNTON must have really gotten into his sleuthing, snooping and research; big time. It is a wonder he found any time to build log cabin fireplaces on roofs and take Conestoga wagon vacations in Kansas. But, let me get into it. Let *me* tell *you* something.

In 1983, six months before the telegram announcing Buzzie's death arrived, Elmont Buzzie Thornton IV went to see an old man. An old man who lived alone with an inherited, decrepit bird. An old man who lived in a one-room stone house in the Alps of Austria. He was born in 1905. I know because I talked to Buzzie about it. Rather, he talked to me. And I know a bit more, because I dipped into my savings after word of Buzzie's death and I went to see the old man. Eventually. Five years later. To see Dunkerque Chamonix's grandson. Luther Van Ogtrop. Conswella Van Ogtrop's grandfather.

It was a long flight. And I asked myself the whole time whether, rather how, I had caught the Buzzie Thornton sleuthing virus. But I was only temporarily bit then. Crazy, ugly Buzzie and his diary find had me temporarily hooked. You must remember, also, Buzzie, as crazy as he was, had a spot in my heart. I loved the man, fool though he may have seemed. And I was less sure that he was a fool than I was that he might have been a genius. But, I had made a promise to him.

I landed in Munchen on January 25, 1988. I rode the bus east, down and along Autobahn 70, past and through Bad Aibling, Rosenheim, Grabenstatt and Siegsdorf (I had never been to Germany before) and into Salzburg, Austria, where I rented a room for the night. I would have flown directly into Salzburg, if I could. But, the flights were booked, or "rucked up," as Buzzie would have said.

The next morning, I rented a car and pushed on, excited and crazy, I thought to myself. I drove from Salzburg to Oberwölz on good roads and then bad roads.

Then up toward Radstadt.

I climbed higher and higher into the mountains and thought of Julie Andrews in *Sound of Music*.

To be in the Alps was breathtaking. To drive up to the small stone house with its grazing goats outside the door was breathtaking. To meet the man who came to the old hinged door was spooky.

He was frail and very fragile. He didn't look at me as he opened the door and let me in. He went toward the wood stove, picked up a log, turned and faced me.

"I knew you would come, Mr. Wingate. I knew you would come."

I stepped through the doorway and looked around the room. It was quite warm and cozy, and there was a glow from the fireplace and wood stove, a bottle of wine and a glass on the table.

"I knew you would come," he said again, tired eyes fixed on me, unsmiling; the eighty-three-year-old man, his skinny arms and hands and elbows quivering with only a small piece of firewood in his grasp.

"How did you know?" I asked.

"Elmont said you would come."

"Elmont is dead," I said. "Five years."

"Rest you be to do, to do," the old man said.

Then the old man told me his story. He told me about his mother, Hansie Chamonix Van Ogtrop, daughter of Dunkerque Chamonix. And then he told me other things.

He told me about his granddaughter. Luther Van Ogtrop told me about Conswella Van Ogtrop. Her life story. Her father, her solo sailing, her subsequent disdain for men, her focus and determination, indomitable spirit, loneliness, and her long-held dream to solo sail the Atlantic someday.

"I fear she will die," he said.

And he told me of the times he spent with his grandfather, Dunkerque Chamonix, who died when Luther was thirty-five years old, in 1940. And he told me what Dunkerque's parrot, Guyane, had told Conswella when she was a child. "Map. Oak tree. Sara Kellog. Boston. Child of the Island Glen." Things which the parrot never had said to Dunkerque or to Luther. "No tell. No tell."

Luther related that he told no one what little he had learned from his grandfather and mother until long after Dunkerque and Luther's mother, Hansie, died within two months of each other in 1940. Luther's son Frederick was never interested. And the mystery was an old one. But he told me that Frederick's daughter, Conswella, was interested, five years before I would warn her of possible trouble as she approached the coast of St. John's Newfoundland, a vessel shadowing her.

"And did the parrot say anything else?" I asked the old man as he fumbled with his match and long-stemmed pipe. I glanced quickly at the ancient bird in its cage next to the fireplace.

"Only once," said the tired Luther Van Ogtrop. "Only once, one thing to me."

"And?" I asked.

"Nicht sinn" (made no sense), he said.

"Tell me, please," I said.

He looked at me, his shoulders stooped, face drawn, eyes glassy and said, "White Fly Beak."

"White Fly Beak," I repeated softly to myself, and

thought how nice it would be to get home and try to forget all of the nonsense. To just feed sheep and chase more butterflies.

As I watched the stewards and stewardesses jamming up the aisle with food carts, blocking the route to the lavatory, my kidneys bursting, I wondered about the last words from old Luther Van Ogtrop, spoken as I rose from my chair in his stone cabin high in the Austrian Alps. Could Buzzie have foreseen that old Luther would have a visitor after Buzzie's visit? He couldn't have.

"Mr. Thornton, the other one, and now you, Mr. Wingate," Luther had said to me.

"Who?" I asked. I had come to genuinely like the congenial, old man who had introduced me to Gerhard and Gerta, two of his goats, welcomed me into his home, put me up for two days, shared the beautiful spot amidst the meadows of the mountains with me, let me into his life. The grandson of Dunkerque Chamonix. "Tell me. Who?"

"Working on a book about missing money from the HMS *Truro*. 1871," he said.

I stopped in the doorway. I studied my new found, eighty-three-year-old friend. His eyes were quiet and sad as he looked at me. And his eyes were curious, I could tell, to see my reaction. Luther Van Ogtrop's eyes asked me if I knew the other person who had visited him.

I thought, smiled and said, "I can tell you nothing without knowing a name, a physical description."

"I don't remember people well," said Luther Van Ogtrop.

Guyane moved in his cage. The old green and yellow

feathered parrot, long blind and now living in the past began to preen himself and squawk. "No tell. No tell," he bellowed. And then, "White. White Fly. White Fly Beak."

The old man looked at me, only a hint of a raised eyebrow. "If only he would tell a fraction of what he knows." And then he began to smile, closed the heavy wood door, and watched me from the tiny window as I made my way through the field of flowers, to begin my journey home, Gerhard and Greta tugging on my shirt and then my pants. I resolved to add a goat or two more to my menagerie at Finnsheep Farm. After a dozen more butterflies.

The flight home was a long one, with stopovers. But I didn't care. I just thought, ate and had a drink or two. And I thought of words from a song, "You can't always get what you want."

I thought about my friend, back in Maine. Laura Reo. I wondered. And I wondered if Guyane the parrot was full of shit. I wondered if a parrot could lie, make up things. I thought, maybe, yes.

And, for some reason, I kept forgetting that Buzzie Thornton was dead. I wanted to talk to him, desperately.

And, I decided that I would like to find, and talk to the former Mrs. Elmont Buzzie Thornton IV. Mrs. Thornton, nee Jubilee Chosen.

Jubilee Chosen. I wondered. And thought about "White Fly Beak."

In all the years of his marriage to her, I had never heard Buzzie say two good words about his wife. He couldn't stand her. That I knew. I wanted to know more about her.

And that was the day I first began to seriously wonder if she had killed Buzzie.

Six weeks after I visited them in 1988, Luther Van Ogtrop and the parrot Guyane were found dead, five years before the map was to disappear from behind the bar at the Hair of the Dog in Cuxhaven, Germany.

49

Sick at Sea

SEPTEMBER 15, 1993, and things were not going well. The vertigo had returned in full force. His eyesight was worse than it ever had been, eyeglasses now thick as a child's blocks, his right eye blinking so fast and often that he felt as if he were losing total control of his functions. And the ocean's swells made him vomit.

He leaned over the stern and retched. His mouth was dry and like felt as he pulled himself upright.

He thought of Fury Ipdown and the capital invested. And the influence of Jubilee Chosen. The beginning. Then came the skimming of dollars from the investments, Igamuche covering it all with his sophisticated computer programs; Fury Ipdown in the dark. There was no turning back once he began. Jubilee's seductive actions. The coke.

Jubilee, Tony Spedarrone and Billy Waddie saw to that. It went well for a while, and the looming jackpot, $19 million, was on the horizon. He had the twelve numbers which would put him on top of that treasure. And only he alone and the woman he had loved had those numbers. Until the disastrous night. Only a month before. His suitcase of papers thrown from his window, not twenty feet from where he watched in the night, out of sight. Thrown by the man Igamuche thought he had then killed. A man he initially believed to be Fury Ipdown. But it was a man, instead, whose death was more important to Igamuche and his memories. A man who did not die that night. Both the secret twelve numbers and the man to slip from Igamuche's grasp. And it was the second time he had failed to kill that man. As he had killed the woman in London. The woman, sole heir to the long dead man responsible for Igamuche's two brothers deaths in Mandalay in 1942. And his thoughts flashed back once again to the failure of his mission at New York's St. Moritz Hotel in 1975.

Thank God that is now over, he said to himself, looking at the man below.

But he was so entangled with Spedarrone, Waddie and Chosen that he could see no way out. They had coerced him, blackmailed him; the skimming and diverting of more and more of Elmont & Thornton's investment dollars and share of the two casinos' profits. More than $5 million, an almost impossible sum to hide much longer; much of the money diverted to the production of small submarines at $200,000 each to ship illegal drugs from Colombia to the United States and Europe via Dominica. The semi-submersible vessels, each operated by a two-man crew and capable of carrying one ton of cocaine. He recoiled as he thought of watching Jubilee using, convincing him that it could do no harm. She lying there next to him, naked. Fat Tony watching from the doorway. Igamuche wanting to kill him. Jubilee saying, "Think about us Aki." Aki believing her.

Fifteen vessels in number, all built in the Colombian Caribbean ports of Santa Marta and Baranguilla. The vessels 30 feet in length, constructed of fiberglass, fitted with Nissan car engines and capable of traveling at 12 knots with a range of 600 miles. When operating, two-thirds of the submarine was under water, making it virtually impossible to detect by radar. But, when one of the subs was washed up on a beach in the Dominican Republic in July, 1993, the whole operation began to unravel before Igamuche's eyes. Within two weeks, Dominican and Puerto Rican patrol boats had seized seven more. And then the arrest warrants for Tony Spedarrone and Billy Waddie, the two men out on bail from the earlier charges. Igamuche knew his days were numbered. Even if he could continue to conceal the missing funds from the eyes of Fury Ipdown. Which he knew he could not.

He told himself that he had not sought to steal from the firm. That it had started as a short-term loan to his lover's two friends, to fund the cinema on Anguilla. A modest amount. Then came the casinos. Then the salvage company. A slow spiral.

He sat down now and tried to focus on his objectives.

He felt wretched. The dizziness and the sea caused him to vomit again. He struggled with his pen. He wrote to himself. Told himself to get to and recover the $19 million, and what he was sure was buried with it. Then, make good on the funds borrowed or stolen from Elmont & Thornton. Maybe.

And then disappear.

Back to Japan. Under an assumed name, if need be. No doubt that would be needed, at minimum.

He had betrayed his employer in America. Just as he had betrayed Mitsubishi in 1973, when he had resigned to go to London.

As he inched the trawler, *Glory Be*, closer to shore in St. Mary's Bay, he re-checked the twelve numbers, the numbers detailing the coordinates in longitude and latitude, and he tried to block *his child* from his mind.

And he watched as he rowed toward shore, his now dizzy mind elsewhere, asking himself why he needed to have the $19 million. Then stopping and lifting his oars, dropping one, when he spotted the woman and two men now down on the shore, seventy-six meters from the old oak. Jubilee Chosen, Tony Spedarrone and his dimwitted henchman. She had betrayed him. Betrayed his love. He wanted to kill her now.

He felt the treasures slipping from his hands as everything else seemed to have done, wondering if he now cared at all about the money. Thinking of his blood - *his* great-grandfather. And then he watched as the violence erupted against two people initially hidden from his view. In the hole on the beach at low tide. The hole now twenty feet deep.

And, as Aki Igamuche watched an arrow and an axe fire through the air on shore, the man who had slipped from his bed in Room 113 of the Grasslands Hospital in White Plains, New York, almost 1000 miles away, the man whose neck was nearly cut through by Igamuche's razor sharp wire on the night of August 10, Igamuche driving away in his old Plymouth, the man who had slipped from his hospital bed, a score of his own to settle - that man lay dead, stuffed under the starboard settee, a hand-scrolled sword run through his back.

Family, Country, Love and Honor.

50

A Warning Call

I REMEMBER PICKING up the phone in the kitchen at Finnsheep Farm. I listened for a few seconds, covered the talking piece with my hand, turned and looked across the room to Laura, got her attention with my hand, and whispered, "Do you know someone called 'Fat Tony'?"

Laura looked away, shrugged her shoulders, turned back toward me and, eyes and head astonished, said, "Tony who?"

I listened to the voice on the phone tell me without identifying himself that he was calling at the direction of "Fat Tony"; was I Charles Wingate?

"Yes," I said.

"Then you better pay heed to what I say. I say it only once. Comprenez?"

"I don't speak Spanish and I think you've got the wrong number, Pancho," I said, hanging up the phone.

"What was that all about, Chuckie?" asked Laura as I inched my way toward the sports section of the Portland paper. It was just before 10:00 A.M., a Sunday morning, on September 11 of last year. I had been scooping fat from a large pot on the stove containing simmering garbage for my pigs, the separated fat to be saved for Laura to use as tallow. Laura was stirring melted tallow again with the long wooden spoon in an adjacent pot. And we were perplexing over "White Fly Beak." Again. My now five-year-old gift, the parting words from Luther Van Ogtrop in 1988.

"Some crank," I said, studying the box scores.

The phone rang again.

"Don't answer," Laura said before the first ring was done with.

"Why?"

"Probably the crank again."

"Doubtful," I said, picking up the phone, and, "Finnsheep Farm here. Lambs on the hoof, one dollar a pound. Two-twenty-five per pound hanging weight plus slaughtering and wrapping costs. Sheep pelts at thirty dollars."

That's all I got out before the voice said "Better listen shit toes. Better not hang up on me until I'm fini. Fini."

It was the same crackpot again, and my irritation began kicking my mouth into overdrive. "I don't speak French either," I said, and then deciding to play with crackpot, "How is Fat Tony?"

"Lay off the case, Wingate. Fat Tony's gettin' pissed."

"What case? I'm not a lawyer," I said, and then "*who* is Fat Tony?" Now, I was getting curious.

"You'll know when your boat sinks, wise ass."

I thought of my old 36' Cheoy Lee clipper ketch sitting in Simpson's Bay Marina, in a slip. I hadn't stepped aboard her or been to St. Martin in some time, and as I thought of her, I remembered the bag of flour I had left on the galley counter. I could see the cockroaches having a field day again and multiplying by the hundreds. Thousands. I pulled open the kitchen counter drawer in front of me and lifted out a relic from my by-gone corporate days, a Norelco tape recorder, dictaphone with an attachment for recording telephone conversations. I smacked the suction cup at the end of its lead to the side of the phone and started talking.

"Tell me what the problem is," I said. My thoughts went to the old lady, my boat *Boogie to Go*. We had been through thick and thin together, for more than twenty years. She was my best friend, leaks and all. The thought of someone wanting to sink her immediately got my attention and did a mind job on my head. She was worth little in dollars, but untold amounts to me.

"What is the problem?" I repeated into the phone, glancing over at Laura, she now leaning back against the soapstone sink, arms apart, hands gripping the soapstone edge, biting her lip I noticed, and looking down at her feet with the pointed red flats.

"You may not be a lawyer, shit toes," the foul-mouthed voice said, "but you are as dumb as them. I'll tell you once more dog face . . ."

I interrupted my friend on the phone, irritation now in overdrive. "Shit toes," I said. "Not Dog Face. It is Shit Toes Wingate. At your service." As soon as I came out with that moronic utterance, I regretted it, thinking of my old lady, my bucket of wood and bolts, floating; at the moment.

"The woman shows up, she's fish food. It's cold up der. The fish is always hungry." He uttered a baleful laugh into the phone.

I didn't have a clue what in the name of Jesus he was talking about.

"She shows up, your boat sinks."

I looked at Laura and whispered to her, now at my side, clinging to my arm, "They want to sink *Boogie*." Laura knew what *Boogie* meant to me.

"Don't let him," she said. "Do whatever he wants. We can't lose our old lady." Laura had sailed *Boogie* with me in New England waters before I sailed the boat south. I looked at her and smiled. She gripped my arm tighter and kissed me on the cheek.

"What do you want, my friend? I will do what you ask, if I can, if it is reasonable," I said into the phone.

"Put the arm on your loose cannon friend," Fat Tony's caller squawked through the phone.

"Who might that be?" I asked, now as much curious as concerned and irritated.

"The Kraut."

"The who?"

"The Kraut."

"I don't speak German."

"The Kraut."

"The war was over almost fifty years ago," I said.

"The woman from the Alps."

And then I thought of Conswella. And then I thought of my old lady again; my boat, and the island of St. Martin. Then the light bulb went on. I thought of Tony Spedarrone. Maho Reef Hotel and Casino.

"Fat Tony," I said to myself. I remembered Buzzie first mentioning his name many years before in connection with Jubilee's "gambling disease," he had said. And I knew of the trouble he was now in with the authorities. Some of it. Not all of it. That was to come later. My hearing of the mini-subs. The coke runs.

I did not know that the phone call from Fat Tony's friend presaged a killing on the shore of Newfoundland.

And I did not know what to think, just as I had felt the night before when I had nestled in bed with Laura, finding a matchbook and cover only an hour before, beside the wood stove, as I was oiling sheep pelts. A matchbook from The Turtle Pier Bar & Restaurant. I found it next to Laura's half-empty glass of wine just before she went to bed.

"The Turtle Pier Bar & Restaurant," the matchbook read. It was a bit strange. "Simpson's Bay Road, Sint Maarten."

"Strange," Laura said to me before she snuffed her cigarette out and climbed up the stairs to bed. "That matchbook was not put there by me. It's not mine. I would love to go to Sint Maarten. I've never been there."

I wondered if I were losing it big time when I poured out my glass, loaded the dishwasher and then climbed the stairs. Going into the fetal position with Laura's warm form. And I wondered what in hell was going on.

"Laura?"

"What?"

"Do you have the feeling that someone was in the house today?" We had spent the day in New Hampshire checking out Border collies and corn planters.

"No. Why do you have that feeling?"

"The matchbook for one."

"White Fly Beak," she said, laughing. "Something white that flies. And I think beak means point. Beaks come to a point, don't they?"

"Like your head," I said, rolling over, and then, "why do I even waste my time talking to you?"

Laura sat up and turned on the light. "I think it has something to do with Gipusollilanntd," she said.

"What does?"

"White Fly Beak. Sea gulls are white. And they fly. And they have beaks which come to a point."

"Actually they don't," I said, deciding to humor Laura a bit rather than attempt to understand what was going on in her clouded head. "Sea gull beaks actually turn down at the end. No point."

"A mere technicality," she said, switching the light off as she lay back down on the pillow.

"What about that matchbook?" I asked.

"Now, that is a puzzle," she whispered, "I would guess that it belongs to you, the only person I know who has ever frequented the 'Turtle,'" Laura then slipping into a low, muffled snore.

When I had put some things together after the phone call the following morning, I said, "Why in hell would the Caribbean crook, Tony Spedarrone, have someone call me? And threaten to sink *Boogie to Go*?"

"Beats me," said Laura, then she telling me, me flabbergasted, that I was asking for trouble, that I should forget Conswella and Buzzie and "the whole mess."

"Do you think he was referring to Conswella?" I said, almost inaudibly.

"I'd bet on it," said Laura.

"But how would they know anything about Conswella and have any inkling that I might know her?"

"Beats me," she said again. But if I were you, I'd head to Sint Maarten and make sure that *Boogie to Go* is secure. Stay on the boat for a while or pay someone to watch over it. If I hear any news from Conswella, I could let you know."

"I'm going to try and raise her again this evening, on the short wave. See if she knows anything about why Spedarrone would be interested in her activities. This is unbelievably strange," I mumbled.

"What is? The matchbook? You're nuts."

"No, the whole thing," I said, staring at the floor.

"You can say that again. I don't think you should call lovely Conswella again."

"I plan on doing just that," I said.

It was two hours later that I went to the barn to look for Laura, and she was gone. Three hours later, I took off for St. Martin.

Hector read that, with my help, and asked all sorts of questions. I answered every single one. Took two hours.

He got a letter today. From outside the States. Lots of postage. He won't tell me who it was from. But he is smiling. That's okay. A letter from a young, lovely in Santo Domingo or Dominica beats a rendezvous with the young Morrey tart in the Dayton woods. I'll take that trade off. Any day. I asked him if the letter was from the orphanage. He said, "No." And that was that.

Today we worked on one of my old tractors here. Rebuilt the carburetor and water pump. I think the radiator will have to be next. The bottom is about rusted out.

Then we went fishing for rainbow trout in the pond up back. Hector can now cast better than I can. He loops the line around his prosthesis hook and gets the line and lure going in a circle around his head. A bit unorthodox to say the least, but he gets unbelievable distance.

He caught two good-sized fish. I got skunked. As usual.

51

Murder in the Alps

"DO YOU remember me?"

The old man, stooped and frail, withdrew the pipe from his mouth with two bony fingers and squinted through the opening between door and frame, the sun high and warming his face, the figure in front of him glowing in the sun. "Yes," he said, opening the door fully.

"May I come in?"

"Yes," he said again. "The book."

"Yes."

"Have you finished it?" asked the eighty-three-year-old man, gazing off, somewhat quizzically.

"Almost. But I still need more information."

"I have told you all I know," said Luther Van Ogtrop.

"No tell. No tell," squawked Guyane.

They sat for tea which the old man made.

"It is important that no one else know what you have told me, that no one tries to put the pieces together, especially your granddaughter."

That evening when Luther and Guyane were again alone, he rose from his chair by the wood stove, the now blind parrot on his shoulder, and he put the kettle on for tea. When the water came to a boil, he dumped the little packet into the kettle, the packet which his visitor had given him that day, suggesting that it was a special blend.

It took twenty minutes. The closed, one-room stone house, high in Radstadt, high in the Alps of Austria to fill with odorless fumes, and the old man to lie dead on the floor next to the old parrot. Dead at the bottom of his cage.

It was almost three years before I learned of those deaths, termed "natural" at the time; the deaths but six weeks after my visit to Radstadt in January of 1988.

52

Following Sea

THE SUSPICION that I had voiced to Laura on the evening of September 10 was confirmed two days later as I sat at my chart table aboard *Boogie to Go*.

"All is a Roger except for the following sea. Follow the leader." I listened that afternoon of September 12,

1993, and plotted the boat's position, now approaching Mutton Bay, Newfoundland, and knew that Conswella was trying to tell me something, something that she did not want to say over the open air waves. I adjusted the control knobs on my short wave radio, eliminating static and nearby interference.

"Come back," I said.

"All is a Roger except for the following sea. Follow the leader. Wind 15-20 knots out of the southwest."

"Roger. Roger. Roger," I said. With the weather conditions having been what they were for the past week, and the wind now out of the southwest, the vessel on a westerly course, port tack, there would not be a following sea. I had to try and figure out what she meant, later. Now, I had to let her know that she might be in danger.

"Possible strong gale ahead," I said into my transmitter. "Possible strong gale ahead," I said again.

I knew she had a weather FAX aboard *Weitra* and that there was no gale ahead at all. I needed to warn her that there might be trouble waiting for her. But, again, I had to choose my words carefully. Who knew who or what might be listening? I just hoped that her weather FAX was working and was showing a clear weather pattern ahead.

There was a long pause, and then "Roger that. Weather FAX is *clear* on that."

"Good," I thought to myself and wondered again about her words, "except for the following sea. Follow the leader."

"Could be a violent storm," I said, thinking about the call to the farm from Fat Tony's mouthpiece just the morning before, and the words, "The woman shows up.

She's fish food. It's cold up der." And "She shows up, your boat sinks." And "Put the arm on your loose cannon friend." There was no use trying to tell Conswella to give it up. No use at all.

She asked what I was doing back in St. Martin, signed off, and promised to call me the next time, at the same time, the following afternoon; a call which never came.

To say that I was concerned for Conswella Van Ogtrop's safety as I switched off my shortwave radio would not fully convey my feelings. I smelled big trouble. And later that night I heard omens. Two, three things. "Except for the following sea. Follow the leader." Of course, I thought to myself. Following. See? Follow the leader.

I climbed up the companionway, spraying cockroach killer on the way, to sit on deck, drink a Red Stripe and think. A distant crack in the night was followed instantly by a thud. Another crack. Another thud. Boogie to Go *began to take on water. Someone in the mountains across the lagoon had put three holes in the boat's hull, each less than an inch apart. I dove below decks, switched on the bilge pumps, pulled a handful of wooden plugs from the hanging locker and went in search of the holes.*

What a night.

And someone indeed was following Conswella and her sailboat Weitra. *And the shadowing vessel had nothing to do with Fat Tony Spedarrone or any of his thugs, or indeed anyone from the Caribbean. And as I went to my berth and climbed in for the night and began to reflect further on the whole picture, I thought, I've got to get the hell out of here. What in God's name am I doing here? Somebody's taking pot shots at my hull, trying to sink* Boogie to Go *right in the slip. My long distance friend, whom I'd been helping to try to unravel a mystery was possibly in very serious danger on the open ocean 1500 plus miles to the north, off the southern tip of Newfoundland; alone on a 40-foot sailboat, having sailed thousands of miles fraught with danger, across the North Sea, and then the treacherous North Atlantic, alone. And I was sitting on my boat drinking Red Stripes? Something was wrong.*

Yes. Something was wrong. Goddamn Buzzie Thornton had dragged me into shit which was none of my goddamned business. Laura is right, I said to myself, missing her. So what about Conswella's plight? I'd never even met her. Not my crazy problem.

I decided then, "I'm out of here. Tomorrow. First light."

I got up and had a Red Stripe.

I had another Red Stripe and sat in the cockpit, scanning the hills across the lagoon, waiting for another bullet to pierce my hull. Then I had a late dinner at the "Frog" across the road.

Where am I going to head if Boogie to Go *and I pull up stakes tomorrow? I wondered. I didn't know. I knew nothin' right then. "Shit toes." That's a good one. If I find the grunt who called me that I'll probably find the bastard who tried to sink my boat, I thought to myself. Damn guerrillas in the lush green mountains of sixteen-square-mile Dutch-owned Sint Maarten. I wondered if that could happen. A revolution I mean. Real doubtful, I decided.*

Uh, oh, I thought, I'm really out of here tomorrow. I could still tune in my on-board shortwave to listen for Conswella's call at the agreed time. I thought I loved her. Unfortunately, I'd never met her. Actually, I was madly heels over cheeks in bliss with Laura. Where the hell was she, *I asked. Dipping candles.*

Sure. "Right and Ready Reo Soap Making & Candles, Inc." What a cover. She's probably setting her wire-rimmed glasses on the night table, I thought, switching contact lenses, and preparing to give someone the bronco ride of his life. Only kidding. I would've liked to bottle Laura. Clone her. Have a dozen Laura Reos around Finnsheep Farm. No. I would never have gotten anything done. Laura Reo. Kiss me in your dreams. "Good night, Mrs. Kalebash, wherever you are." Thank you, Jimmy Durante.

I said, "Uh, oh," and told myself I'm really out of here tomorrow, for a couple several reasons. Let me try and get this straight.

This did me in. This capped the stone, the iceberg, whatever; it capped me. No question I was "down the road tomorrow."

When I got back from my late dinner at the Frog, I tuned my radio into the local station broadcasting from Antigua. Cheery news. Forget Clinton's budget package and the fruit salad in Sarajevo, Bosnia, Somalia and indeed New York, New Jersey and tourist-loving Miami. The lead news story? "Four found murdered on yacht in Barbuda." Barbuda, pronounced like Bermuda, is not far from St. Martin. Lesser Antilles, like St. Martin. But, okay place. Until I heard about the murders. I quote, best as my memory and I can now, Antigua Radio.

"Four found murdered on yacht in Barbuda. Late on Sunday, the 63-foot Hinckley, Swan, *was boarded after her dinghy was found drifting close to shore. Four persons, rumored to be the skipper, the hostess and two passengers were found bound and gagged in the saloon. All four had been shot dead, and the boat set afire. A Scotland Yard detective, who was in Antigua on another matter, is said to have started investigating, together with members of the FBI who flew in on Monday. The manner*

in which the killings were carried out and the area in which they occurred, has led to speculation that this was a drug-related incident. No doubt further details will soon be revealed."

"I'm sure," I said to myself as I put the radio to bed. To off.

"Spedarrone," I thought. "Fat Tony."

The same news broadcast told of another small semi-submersible, fiberglass submarine found washed up on a reef off the island of Saba, almost a ton of cocaine in the bilge. And the final cheery news item related to the fire-bombing of a cinema on the island of Anguilla, the little cinema burned to the ground.

Do I sail southwest to Venezuela, or do I set sail against contrary winds toward chilly Newfoundland. I wondered. Arrive too late to help Luther Van Ogtrop's granddaughter. And it is none, none, none, none of my business I decided, as I crawled into my bunk, then lying awake, thinking: I love Laura.

I love Conswella. Swell, swell, swell. I bet she is beautiful, I thought.

Tough to love two people. There was a song about that. The lady singer was in love with two men. Don't care here. But who sang that song?

Don't care.

I was off to never-never land now. Venezuela tomorrow?

Are you ready Boogie to Go? *"Yes," she said.*

I'm with her, I said to myself, then reminding myself that I was also in love with Judy, the waitress.

(I was about as much together that evening, watching the moon through the hatch, as anyone might have been with all of the events that were swirling around. And four Red Stripes didn't help. And it wasn't four.)

53

Wanted for Murder

PHIL RIZZUTO was finally elected to Cooperstown's Baseball's Hall of Fame in 1993 by The Old Timer's Committee, thirty-seven years after his retirement as shortstop of The New York Yankees. It was not clear to me on August 6, 1993, that the "Scooter" would have enough votes to gain Cooperstown entry the same month, but it was clear in the mind of the old man who dismounted his motorcycle, a de-mothballed 1949 Harley, outside my front door at Finnsheep Farm that night; remembering a bet and a promise he had made forty years before; a bet and a promise and a man and an ex-baseball player all long disappeared from my thoughts.

We talked for just the half hour; the two dogs with their sixth sense, sitting on the floor next to him wagging their tails. He nervous; anxious to go.

I told him he did not have to keep his promise and eat his hat.

He told me that he was on the run.

We didn't talk about treasures.

He had just turned seventy-seven.

Someone was after him. It had begun in earnest years ago. He had moved frequently and assumed two different aliases. The U.S. Government ignored his requests for protection. He was afraid that time was running out rapidly for him. Traveling around in an old Conestoga wagon with his friend. Always on the move.

He was wanted for "murder."

I insisted that he stay, that he would be safe at Finnsheep Farm.

He declined.

It was only the second time that I had seen him in all my fifty-one years.

He stayed for just the half hour, and then he left.

"I'm about to be rich."

"I thought you were rich; already rich," I said.

He winked at me and smiled as he exited, the dogs

licking his trousers.

"Finally, this time it will be for real," he said, taking a final drag on his Camel.

I did not see him again. And will not. That I learned last November when the trawler, Glory Be, *was discovered drifting, southeast of Newfoundland - 400 miles out at sea.*

54

"Where Is Everybody"

AFTER LAURA left and I headed to St. Martin last September, my mind kept wandering. Thoughts of Conswella. Strange how you can feel so close to someone that you've never met. I had a lot of confidence in her. Her passage through the North Sea must have been a horror. When news of how severe that storm was finally reached me, I thought that her chances for survival were not good. Nevertheless, she made it through.

I could not get the telephone call of September 11, out of my mind. The call from Fat Tony's mouthpiece. Tony Spedarrone. I figured that much out. But, why would he have any interest in and knowledge of a woman solo sailor from Austria? And I wondered how he could possibly know what Conswella was after? How? He knew something. He knew enough to know that Conswella was about to embark on a search. And, he knew that I had knowledge of that, and that I had influence over her, so he thought. No one had influence over Conswella Van Ogtrop. Certainly not I.

When I had spoken with her by radio from *Boogie to Go* on September 12, the following afternoon, to warn her, I asked if the name Tony Spedarrone meant anything to her, and told her of the phone call and my grave concern. She just chuckled and waved it off. "You are getting paranoid," she said. But I didn't get it. At all. And I couldn't approach Fat Tony. Even if I had wanted to. He was "a wanted man," off island, and had been for some time, my sources told me when I landed, "since he got out on bail." No scheduled return date. Meanwhile his casino, The Maho, was doing a land office business and his two Cigarette speedboats were sitting on moorings accumulating pelican shit on top and weeds and algae below. Who knows, maybe he is gone for good, I thought. "Call her off or your boat sinks." Nice phone call.

I wished Laura were there. We had had some great sails along the New England coast together, but never further south. I decided to be content to sit on my boat, putter and make sure that no one tried to sink *Boogie to*

Go again. Venezuela could wait.

One evening in the spring of last year was weird. Or maybe I'm just weird. The "supervision program" instituted by the Dutch to oversee the local, native government in Sint Maarten, to tighten things up a bit and squeeze out some of the corruption, was due to expire in six months, the end of the initially announced eighteen-month period. But, when Holland suddenly announced that the supervision program would be extended, the Antillians were less than happy about it. They were bullshit. I walked into the Turtle Bar about 6:00 P.M. for a couple of pops and a cheap dinner of ribs and rice. The place has about a dozen tables in addition to the bar. Six of the tables were taken by twenty to twenty-five Caucasians in camouflage army fatigues. I couldn't believe my eyes. I sat down at the bar and asked what the scoop was. Judy leaned her head forward and whispered, "Dutch Marines. Here on maneuvers." Now, I'd been coming to the island for some time, and had never before seen anything like that. Looked like a friendly show of potential force to me. A gentle reminder that the Dutch call the major shots. I didn't like it. Those high, lush, green mountains just the other side of the lagoon, across the bay from where I sat looked like great potential guerrilla hideouts to me. No one could find you up there. I didn't think it would come to that on the tiny island. But, I didn't like what I saw and heard.

I decided to mind my own business on that subject and spent the rest of that Easter week hunting for specimens to add to my butterfly collection. Some good spots in the hills near Grand Case, twenty minutes away. Did you know Monarch butterflies are poisonous? Only if you eat them. I think I told you that already. Maybe saute a batch for Laura. Just kidding. Sick.

55

In Love Again

THAT BUTTERFLY chase last year was a zero. Didn't even see one. I think I'm going to sit down and write now. Maybe ramble a bit. It's nearly the end of January already. About one month since I started to pull all of this together on paper. I hope the rest of 1994 does not fly by as fast as this month has. Maybe I do, on second thought. But fly by uneventfully. Good God.

Sometimes, I am two people. The rational one and the irrational one. Like Buzzie. And sometimes I ask the rational one to comment on the irrational one. Like last summer, and thinking about it today. Like so.

"Where is #1 child these days?"

"Off island with her Dad."

"What is the special tonight?"

She placed both elbows on the bar, hands on her cheeks, leaning forward, beautiful, sparkling, mesmerizing green eyes riveted to my red ones, "Something right up your alley, Chuck."

"Really," I said. "Tell me, Judy."

"Road Kill Platter with a side of baked beans."

"Sounds splendid," I said. "Cat or dog?"

"All cat."

"Persian?" I asked.

"You will never know."

"I'm sure of that, but will it give me nine lives if I clean my plate?"

"You bet," Judy said, bolting erect, "and you will need every one of them."

I looked at her. Her eyes were driving me in love. Again. "Oh, no," my rational friend whispered. "Oh, yes," I said to my rational.

I thought. "I absolutely love Judy." (Oh, no.) It was not just her eyes, though indescribable they are. Her sense of humor, gait, hair. Banter. Awareness. Right there. Pretty. Attractive. (Oh, no.) I am still head over heels in love with her.

"How long have you known her?" my inner obnoxious, rational friend asked, as Judy pulled away from the bar and began filling beer mugs and mixing rum cokes and margaritas, not taking a second to look at me.

"A week," I mumbled, looking around, hunching my shoulders, trying to sink my non-existent cheeks deep down into the bar stool cushion.

"You're nuts," my rational other said.

"I know," I said to myself, moving my lips and mouth only slightly.

Well, I didn't order the Road Kill Platter with the side of beans. But, I did ask Judy to marry me in the morning. "It would be criminal," she said. I guess it would be. Judy is married. Happily. And there are three other problems. Three, at least. Child #1 (Hanna), #2 and #3. Ages 7, 3 and 1. I fall in love at least once a month. What is the deal? Don't say anything to me, Mr. Rational. But, I decided one thing then; that when I cast off, if I ever did, Judy would be with me. Oh no. Oh, yes. "I'm madly in love with Judy," I mumbled in my beer.

"You told us that. What about Laura? What about Conswella? You love her, sight unseen, right?"

"Yes, I do."

"And Laura?"

"I love Laura."

"Now, wait a minute. You love Laura, unseen Conswella Van Ogtrop and little known Judy, Judy who?"

"That's right. That's right."

Actually I had fried clams instead of the Road Kill Platter. Plus an order, double, of dill carrots, to remind me of Buzzie and improve my night vision.

There is something going on in my head now. Is that okay? All right. Yes. All right. Settle down. All right. Yes.

All right. Something going on in your head. No kidding.

I thought of the Papaguyas. The wind which swirls down off the mountains of the Yucatan and Venezuela, smacking those vessels within ten miles of shore with a wallop that can only be understood by those who have felt it. Been through it. I want to run down the Caribbean, down through the windward islands of the Lesser Antilles - St. Vincent, Grenada, the whole stick. And haul down to the southwest to Caracas, jibe, and experience the Papaguya exhilaration with Judy. Run before the wind at eight knots, lie on deck with the sun and wind in her hair, me touching her gently; her cheeks,her shoulders, brushing the hair back from her face.

"Oh, no," the bastard rational other just said.

I am thinking of Buzzie. Again. And his death-defying, according to him, awful marriage to Jubilee Chosen. "Do you keep her in a closet?" I had asked him on the few occasions that I really got to talk to him after we left Swarthmore in 1964.

"Should. But I don't," he always said.

"What's the problem with her?" I would ask.

"Where should I start?" he always said. "Fooled me. From time zero. After my money. Always right."

"But you never had any money, Buzzie," I would say.

"She thought differently. She thought Elmont & Thornton. Investment and insurance money. Blowfish." He would turn to me and smile.

"Blowfish," I said. "That is a good one."

Running before the wind. It is the second best point of sail. After a broad reach. I am going to spend the rest of my life running before the wind. No close-hauled for me. Is that okay, Mr. Rational? He says for me to go for it. To do it. To do it for the rest of my life. I will.

I used to love to go to the Turtle for a pop. When Judy was on duty. Wednesdays, Fridays and Sundays.

(Excuse me. Hector is roaring up and down the driveway on our new tractor. Christ. Get the kid into school. I'll be right back.).

Back. I just thought of something while I was chasing after and then chastising Hector. Most of it is relevant. I think so. Some, anyway. Maybe. Maybe none of it actually. So what. It will make good practice reading for Hector. There he goes again. Here I go.

Swarthmore College, April 1964. Dorm E. Suite 6.

"What you want to be when you grow up, Buzzie?"

"I am grown up."

"You're not."

"Fuck you, Chuck."

"Fuck you, Elmont."

"Don't call me Elmont."

"Fuck you, Elmont."

"When we get out of here, I don't expect to ever see you again, Wingate," he said.

"You may."

"May not," he said. "Won't."

"You're nuts."

"Count on it."

"I do."

"Fuck you."

"Fuck you, too."

We both smiled, pulled our blankets over our heads. Sleep. Life with Buzzie.

And also.

"Get up and sit down." That's good. My third grade teacher, "Miss Get Up and Sit Down." No wonder we are all two slices short of a loaf. Simon and Garfunkel had it right. "When I think of all the crap I learned in high school, it is a wonder I can still think at all." And Thomas Edison - whose early schoolhouse schooling ended when his teacher concluded that his inattentiveness rendered him not worth keeping in school (shades of Dunkerque and Buzzie) - had it right when he said the problem with the educational system is that students were listening to teachers who didn't know the brown stuff from Shinola Shoe Polish.

Edison didn't say it that way. Not exactly. But, what he meant was that the untold scores of tidy and untidy subjects sitting submissively at their desks were learning from someone who had done nothing, in the vast majority of cases, but learn to teach and then teach. Experiences? Yawn.

If you can, *do*. If you can't, *teach*.

Best of all "do and then teach."

My, oh my. Tell me about it. Right and wrong. Answer fast, or you're toad tickle. Get it straight, fast. No time to contemplate or mull it over, and no space for the creative brain. "An interesting idea, Tommy, but let's get back to basics." Basics? Yes, basics. Basics? Basic what? Basic conformity. Don't tell anybody that truth may be a function of time, particularly scientific truths. Kids couldn't handle it? Wrong. Teachers couldn't handle it, let alone begin to know how to teach it. "Be sure to stay inside the lines when you color, Tommy."

Albert Einstein's early teachers described him as a hopelessly impractical dreamer. I wonder if he ever thought about inventing "no-stick, gum-shoe soles." Like Buzzie.

Imagination, creativity, mulling it over, time to think about it. No place here. Get it right. The first time. Clock's ticking. Teacher talking. Drop down, drop out. The system is so screwed up, it's like shit hitting a waterwheel at high speed. Duck, don't fight it. No place for the crazy, with the crazy ideas. Put him in the coatroom. Let him out for lunch. The kid is nuts. A danger to the classroom. He draws okay. He gets his homework done okay and on time. But the kid is nuts. Far out questions. Transfer him to another class. A teacher doesn't need this stuff.

Those are just a few reasons I like home schooling. For some kids. (Edison's mother home-schooled little Thomas on their white, front porch in Port Huron after he got bounced). Judy uses it with Hanna. Maybe I should home school Hector. Really encourage him to be different. Maybe he is a budding Edison or Einstein. If he is, it is all quite well disguised at this stage. Maybe a budding Lucifer. Just kidding, Hector. Just testing your reading comprehension.

I thought of Edison's views eleven years ago as I waited in vain for a call from Buzzie, hoping that it was all a hoax, that he was indeed alive and well, that the telegram from Santa Fe was just the latest in his long and increasingly looney line of capers. And I wondered, as I had over the years before, whether he was crazy or a genius (defined here simply, as one who sees the follies of one's own times), or maybe both. He must have been a treat for the teacher to have in class when he was a kid. I remember him telling me about the time in third grade when he put a noose around his neck and then got two kids to lift him up and hook the back of his belt on the coat hook in the coatroom, his feet two feet off the floor, his eyes rolled back in his head, tongue out and to the side as his teacher scuffled in and then let loose with a blood curdling scream; Buzzie then yelling, "She is trying to hang me, she is trying to hang me," the teachers in adjoining classrooms running to see Buzzie in the air, noose over his head, his teacher with her hands on the noose, trying to get it off his head. According to Buzzie, it was two weeks later, with his teacher suspended, that he confessed to his parents that he was "just kidding." That was the second of five schools Buzzie attended between third and tenth grade, when his father somehow managed to get him admitted to Westminster. But, he also, I should add, did things like build a working cloud chamber at the age of fourteen, which he personally took to MIT where the professors were astounded, Buzzie flunking every exam in his high school physics course back home at the same time.

Buzzie attempting to bail himself out with a letter of commendation from the MIT Physics Department, a letter which his teacher at Westminster decided had been written by Buzzie himself, which it would have been, if necessary, but in this case it wasn't. The letter was legit. Oh, Buzzie. Love him or hate him. Who could hate him?

Love/hate relationships I have never understood.

Maybe like I never understood until after I had begun to set things down on paper earlier this month that Hector could understand English, spoken English. Not perfectly, but far, far better than I ever imagined. And I think I have a love/hate relationship with the little bastard, though he is not so little anymore.

It was that way with Laura also. Not me and Laura. Our relationship never really hit intense extremes. But rather Laura and Hector. She would be all over him one minute and then praising and hugging him the next. He would cast this look at her and then at me as if wondering if she had a bolt loose. There were times she got after him which I felt were entirely unfounded. About little things, like not eating enough or not finishing his breakfast, and mistakes in his practice spelling and writing. It wasn't all the time and truly it wasn't that often, but it was often enough to cause me to tell her to mind her own business on more than one occasion. Her response was usually to bake him a pie or brownies. All a bit weird. But she was weird in some respects. For sure.

I really can't say that I have a love/hate relationship with Hector. That is much too strong. My feelings for him are not strong one way or another. I feel no closeness to him other than viewing him as a sort of project, to see if I can help him in his move from illiterate to somewhat educated. And, as I have said earlier, he is a good worker and quite a help to me both at the farm and on the boat. Most of the time. (He will not be reading this part, for sure.)

I did have, speaking of weird, a weird thought cross my mind. One evening last year, I had just come in from the field, from haying, and sat down at the kitchen table with a beer. Laura was in the downstairs shower, I could hear it running. Then I heard her turn it off. "Hector, are you there?" she hollered. "Could you bring me a towel?"

I glanced toward the hallway and saw Hector go to the closet at the far end, oblivious to me, as Laura stood halfway out of the bathroom. He brought the towel to her and just stood there watching as she began to dry herself. Her eyes were fixed on his the entire time. "I need you to help me with something," she said, holding the towel at her side, standing no more than two feet from him, directly in front of him.

"Okay," he said. Or "O-key!"

She took him by the hand and marched him into the bathroom. And closed the door. Weird.

"I wanted him to check my hair for ticks," Laura said when I confronted her a bit later.

"I don't think it is real smart to parade around naked in front of a ten-year-old boy," I said.

Laura looked at me with a smirk and said, "I was *not* parading around naked. And for your information, he is almost eleven."

"Okay, okay," I said, "but use a little more discretion."

She stormed out of the kitchen. I must admit that we were in the midst of the worst tick season I had ever seen at the farm. Ticks everywhere, and the three of us, Laura, I and Hector, frequently did check each other's hair for them. But not while naked!

I don't know why I just thought of that except that I did. From time to time, little things like that pop into my head.

It seems to have been that way since Laura's death.

56

Random Thoughts

I AM NOT SURE I even want to write anything about this, but I guess I will, since my pen is now moving across the page at a spirited clip, propelled this freezing January Maine night by a large vodka martini, and guided by a slew of random thoughts, my imagination, observations and memory.

"Oh, God, no," my rational other just said.

Get away from me, you interfering interloper. Okay, now he is gone. My heart, left brain and weirdness (a gift from the Buzzer) may now take over. Completely. Yes. All right. Settle down. Okay, I'm settled. Take over Mr. Irrational, Charles Wingate. Thank you. I will.

Right now, I am thinking of everything that happened. I just chucked my pen out the window into a heated "sheep tea" puddle. To see if it would float, out of ink. It does. Cheap pen. Thought it would at least last for one hundred pages. No chance. Just bought it last week. Maybe a month ago. I guess that's not bad.

Yes, I do have time on my hands. Snow is coming down. Big time. I'm just watching and waiting to see what, if anything happens next. I hope, nothing. Let 1994 continue to be a calm, uneventful year.

In a slip near to mine in Sint Maarten was a sloop, about 28-30 feet. *Avontuur* was its name; a nice little sail-boat, and aptly named. Not something I would own but all in all probably not a bad little sailing vessel if you're not hitting the open ocean. The cockpit is huge. Good cockpit to fill with water and sink the boat in an off-shore, prolonged gale, like *Boogie to Go*. Good cockpit to down a case of Heineken in with one or two of your closest friends. Like Basil on *Othello*. The *Avontuur* is owned by a Dutchman; very likeable guy. As he went out one day early last fall, he is about sixty, I guess, he put his engine in forward and bounced off the concrete dock, his eyes like a little boy's; a man-boy who sheepishly tried to ease his boat out without making a mistake that people might see and laugh about. Why should anyone, let alone a grown man of sixty, be concerned about what anyone says about him, his words or his actions, if he is trying his best, is not offending anyone, and is being himself? I think it is sad.

Sadder was the fact that the nice Dutchman owner, sailor of *Avontuur*, got into real trouble on his three-day cruise; a planned, relaxing three-day weekend with his wife and their friends, another Dutch couple. When he limped backed into the lagoon, he was alone and looking like a ghost. His wife and friends having fled the boat like rats when the steering crapped out, the rudder fell off, and the roller-furling jammed; the Sunday sailor Dutchman having spent $4,000 the month before to have new hydraulic steering installed, a new Pro-Furl roller-furling jib hung on, and the rudder post inspected. The man to limp into his Simpson's Bay slip, alone.

Just thinking. Shapes are funny. People shapes. There are probably very few people shaped like a pear who enjoy being that way. Except for Poley. Poley "Bartlett." Well, Bartlett wasn't his real name, but it seemed to fit; that's what people called him, and he liked it. Poley surely was born with genes that contributed toward his pear shape, but he actually worked at it. He would exercise his arms and feet only. And he would sit at the Turtle Bar hour after hour, cheeks hanging over the sides of the stool like oversized round boat bumpers, his torso narrowing as it rose from waist to gnat-size shoulders. On top of the shoulders was a skinny neck, like Buzzie's, supporting an oversized head with a jungle of unkempt, uncut, curly brown hair and one good eye and one eye which seemed to always be straining to look for an oncoming truck from the rear. Like Fury Ipdown. But, maybe I'll write about him later. I'm thinking about something else.

I was just thinking about little Hanna, Judy's #1 child. "*The* child," according to Judy.

"Calvert School," said Judy, last year. "Know it?" I did know it. The same Judy I fell in love with the moment I met her at the Turtle Pier Bar & Restaurant across the road from Queen Julianna Airport in Sint Maarten. The same Judy who once almost served me the special, "Road Kill Platter," and said I would need all of the nine lives offered by the cat meat in the main course. The same Judy whom my rational other told me to forget about because I was too old and she was married and had three kids. The same rational other that I told to go find someone else to counsel.

But, I did know about the Calvert School. The home schooling program for kids. And Judy told me that her seven-year-old Hanna was being schooled on their boat in the Calvert Program, Judy finding it a tedious process, Hanna telling her that she wasn't interested. I taught for a few, actually two years and wrote a course for Calvert years ago. And when I gleefully told Judy that I like to teach kids and would be happy to work with Hanna, get her mother off the hook, Judy thrust her pen and paper across the Turtle Bar and said, "Put it in writing."

"What are you doing down here, living on this old boat, by yourself, no shoes on, the boat so messy with all of these papers around?" asked precocious Hanna, walking through the main cabin of *Boogie to Go*, straightening papers and piles, picking up stuff, looking at the morass of mess.

"Time to work on arithmetic," I said, "sit down."

"You have to answer my questions, first," she said, "then I may cooperate."

"Sit down," I said.

"No."

That was my first encounter with teaching the Calvert School Program to little Hanna. Two weeks later, she began reading notes I had made to myself and monitoring my short wave talks as I sat on *Boogie*, sipping a cold one with Judy, her mother. Eventually, she "showed" me that *John Wilkes Booth didn't kill Abe Lincoln*. That's correct.

I thought of Mr. Aki Igamuche yesterday. I don't really know why.

Not because of whom he killed or didn't kill, nor of who or whom he was, or who or whom he wasn't.

Nor because of "Family, Country, Love and Honor," that which may have made him so driven. If indeed he was driven. For sure, he was. But, I don't know. I only know what I've heard. And, I often listen but don't hear. That's what Laura used to tell me. Ears and eyes of cotton and clay. Or vice versa. I still love her.

I' m not sure really what to believe about the man. At this time. And I really don't care. I don't think so.

I've got my own problems.

If I can believe everything I've heard, and I do, most of it, the Japanese man killed my uncle. And also killed a woman. In London.

I thought of that yesterday because of other reasons. Because I go about my chores at Finnsheep Farm now, many times or most of the time, not knowing where the next problem will come from; knowing, rather, convinced that one or more will certainly arise, and trying to forget. Lots of things.

From what I've been told, Igamuche had problems coming out of his ears. Most of them self-made. The problems. Not the ears. Personally, I'm inclined to believe he is dead. Actually, I have little doubt as to that. No. I know he is dead. On an intellectual level, I do. The same feeling I had when I received the Buzzie bullfight death telegram from Santa Fe in 1983. But, it is not the intellectual or rational level that I am concerned about. It's the irrational and the gut feelings which make me extremely uneasy.

I've always had a problem with that.

According to my RATIONAL OTHER, anyway.

57

Where to Begin?

Twenty Feet Down

I DON'T KNOW where to begin. A lot happened quickly after I gave Hanna that first Calvert School lesson last year.

Let me begin by writing about the dig, as it was told to me; then a death in Newfoundland which shocked me, beyond comprehension; then the contents of a woman's knapsack, after Buzzie's knapsack.

Then, off to the island of Saba. On paper only this time. Good God. Saba.

Good Lord, I must be crazy. "You got that right," says my rational other.

Shut up.

"There was only one problem," she said. And here I attempt to duplicate her own words. And his.

"The burial sight was below sea level at anything but dead low tide. So, to start digging at dead low tide, the only time you could, you also had to finish digging on the same dead low tide, because as soon as the tide began to come back in, all your efforts would be wasted; the hole would quickly fill with sand and water. And that was something I was not fully ready for. To not be able to dig over a period of time; hours or days, if necessary. It had to be done all at once, start *and* finish on the same dead low tide, unless I could devise a way to prevent the hole from filling. I doubt that I could have done anything without him." She looked at him, motioning for him to pick up the story.

"It was a real brain-teaser. I liked it. I liked it," he said.

She interrupted and looked at him, then at me, gave just a hint of a smile and said, "It helped that he can see in the dark." He crossed his eyes and laughed. "He started to cut down trees, saw them up and . . ." He reached into his knapsack and withdrew a folding axe with a hollow steel handle. He unscrewed the end of the handle and pulled forth a saw, a folding saw with shark-like teeth. She just shook her head. "Men," she said.

"A real brain teaser, but actually pretty simple," he

said. "We cut the trees into logs and split the logs into planks three feet long and five to six inches wide."

"Don't forget the sap buckets," she said, a distinct smile now forming in the corner of her mouth.

"I won't," he said. "The second day, I began to set taps in some trees. The sap had just started an unusual fall run. I put nail taps in ten trees and connected them all by one-half-inch polypropylene tubing to an army collapsible canvas bucket on the tenth tree. Then I told each tree in turn to start peeing into the tubing or I would cut it down next."

She started a full-fledged laugh.

I looked at him, then her. I looked away and chuckled, smiled to myself. This is too much, I thought. But the best, and worst, were yet to come.

"They began to pee," he said.

"I'll bet they did," I said, looking at him with a twinkle in my eye.

"I mixed the sap with crushed seaweed and toothpaste. With a pile of planks and the waterproofer ready, we could start. Except for the pumping system.

"Wait a minute," I said. "Toothpaste? What waterproofer?"

"The waterproofer. Non-sticking."

"Same stuff you used for the shoe soles?" I asked.

"Same exact."

I shook my head. "Where'd you get the toothpaste?"

"Knapsack," he said, poking it with his finger.

"Same place you got the folding axe with the shark tooth saw," I said looking at her.

"Same exact," he said.

"How much toothpaste did you have in there?"

"Couple dozen tubes. Left more on *Ocean Loon*. A whole gross on Desert Loon."

I shook my head again and said jokingly, "Any special brand?" She started to smile again.

"My own concoction," he said.

"Sorry," I said. "Sorry to interrupt."

He looked at me. "Think I'm nuts, do you, Chuckie?"

"Still," I said.

"Well. We'd dig at low tide. Dead low. When the tide started to come, we'd cover the hole with the planks and waterproofer. Sealed it up real tight. First time, we got down three feet before we had to cover it over. Then six feet, then nine."

"How'd you get in and out of the hole that deep?" I asked.

"Plank platform steps across alternate sides of the hole," he said.

"Of course."

"That's when I thought we might have the wrong spot," he said. "When we hit fifteen feet,"

She had no doubts though. "None whatsoever," she said.

"What's with the pumping system you mentioned before?" I asked.

"Planks and waterproofer not one hundred percent as we got deeper. When we would open her up to start digging at the next low tide there would be some water in there. Not a lot, but some. I took the polypropylene tubing and cut it up into six equal lengths; one end of each went into the bottom of the hole, the other out the top and down the shore, out, until the ends were lower than the lowest part of the water in the hole. Then I sucked until I got water and dropped the ends.

"Siphon," I said.

She puffed out her cheeks and held her breath until her face reddened. She exhaled, smiled and patted him on the back.

"Like a blowfish," I said.

The three of us burst out laughing.

"We'll get to her in a moment," he said. "Blowfish."

I want to pause here because our conversation turned deadly serious at that point as both of them described what happened when they were twenty feet down in the hole. Caught off guard by two men and a woman. I looked at her shoulder as she talked. I looked at his chest. I thanked God that they were alive.

58

Death at Gull Island Point

IT CAME without warning. The razor sharp arrow point plunged into her shoulder. She dropped the cypress wood box and cried out in pain, the arrow's shaft with its red crest, feathers and nock protruding from the front of her shoulder, the steel broad head hunting point sticking out ugly from the back. He did not hear her cry out, twenty feet above him next to the top of the hole. Nowhere to run she thought, stumbling down onto the first platform step, three feet down, the protruding arrow catching on the side of the hole's opening as she jumped in, the caught arrow twisting in her shoulder, sending a stabbing, horrifying pain the length of her arm, the arm paralyzing, her head bowed, teeth and eyes grimacing in pain. She hollered down. He stopped his work and looked up. He began to climb toward her.

The two men, guns drawn, approached behind the woman whose hands and fingers clenched the compound bow with its cam wheel, limbs, cable and bow-string at the ready; the three of them now within twenty-five feet of the hole and the cypress box where it had been dropped.

The impaled woman continued to crouch on the wood platform, three feet down. The man continued to climb toward her.

The woman with the machine-like bow motioned the two men to the cypress box. The two men quickly opened it, stood up, stepped back and smiled. "Let's go," said the rotund man, cigar clenched in his teeth, oily black hair plastered straight back.

"All right," said the other man, the dim wit.

The two men took the box and began to run up the knoll, as best they could, the fat one waddling and puffing. The woman with the compound bow let them get some distance, for she could travel the knoll much faster than they. They disappeared over the crest of the knoll like wild pigs. The woman with the bow watched them disappear, then shouted toward the hole as she withdrew a fresh hunting arrow from the quiver on her side and placed the arrow's nock around the bow string, the shaft on the handle's rest.

The woman with the bow approached the hole, threw a glass jar containing warm water and lye into the hole, drew back her bow string, loading the bow to its maximum pound pull, and gritted her teeth as the man climbed past the woman on the wood step between him and the top of the hole; and as he stuck his head out and saw who the woman with the bow was and she saw who the man in the hole was, they both froze momentarily, she sighting the length of the arrow drawn back, its nock in the bow string and ready to explode; her eyes fixed on his and his on hers. And her finger tab let go the bow string as he unfroze, and the broad head hunting point flew toward his chest as he brought the folding, now opened, axe around from the right with the full length and strength of his arm, like a side-arm pitcher. The axe hurtled through the air, tumbling over once, before splitting her skull in two.

The men with the box were halfway back from Gull Island Point to the Old Route 10 before the arrows were both removed by Conswella Van Ogtrop; from her own shoulder and then from his chest. He knew he would die. She knew neither of them could.

When they reached the road and uncovered their vehicle, the men opened and counted the contents of the box. $19 million in bank notes. Damp but intact.

And the woman with the compound hunting bow could have shared in the find. But her grudge toward the woman in the hole, a grudge of untold proportions toward a woman she had never met had taken hold. And she paid for it with her life. A life that had its origins with a woman aboard the side wheel steamer, S.S. *Claxdow* in 1872, more than 120 years before. It's origins with the woman named Sara Kellog who survived the wreck of the *Claxdow*. A woman who was given half a map by a man who only physically survived that wreck. A man by the name of Dunkerque Chamonix, the great-great-grandfather of the woman in the hole, Conswella Van Ogtrop.

Conswella Van Ogtrop, victim of an arrow let fly by Sara Kellog's great-great-granddaughter. The forty-eight-year-old woman with green eyes, blue contact lenses and clear-lensed spectacles. The librarian, soap and candle-maker who murdered Luther Van Ogtrop and the parrot Guyane. The woman who married Buzzie Thornton as "Jubilee Chosen" and manipulated the Japanese man, Aki Igamuche. The woman herself now dead. My confidante. Laura Reo.

The two men, huffing and puffing did not wait for the woman and did not bother to break camp as they trudged right through it and on, two miles to the old Route 10 where they drove their parked Land Rover out of the woods and on to Route 10, and did not look back as they drove east, then northeast, then north through Trepassey, Portugal Cove South, Cappahayden, Bay Bulls and on to St. John's, 164 kilometers, 98 miles away. They abandoned the Land Rover outside St. John's and flew by waiting plane to a landing strip in the Adirondack Mountains of New York State, hundreds of miles to the southwest where they refueled, money no object.

Less than twenty-four hours after running off with the cypress box in the September twilight at Gull Island Point on the southern tip of Newfoundland at 46° 51.22′ north latitude, 53° 28.13′ west longitude and 28° Fahrenheit, the two men were sitting in a power boat, a Cigarette, as it roared away from the island of St. Martin, in the dead of night, drinking beer, laughing and playing poker for $1,000 a hand, Billy Waddie at the wheel.

Less than two weeks later, on September 28, 1993, a stainless steel vessel that looked like a whale with masts and upside down sails, and with a reconditioned World War II Browning submachine gun mounted on deck covered with a rubberized canvas bag passed under the open draw bridge at Simpson's Bay Lagoon, less than two miles from the spot where pelicans had the month before been busy whitewashing two powerboats, Cigarettes, at anchor. And the whale with masts and upside down sails and submachine gun headed across the lagoon. The captain, his chest still heavily taped from the ordeal at Gull Island Point, dropped anchor, cracked a beer and looked around. He scanned the slips at the marina to the west. He spotted an old sailing ketch in a slip with an old friend sitting in the cockpit sipping a cold one and reading, nestled in a bosun's chair. The captain of the whale *Ocean Loon* lowered his dinghy and rowed over to *Boogie to Go*. He came alongside, sunglasses covering his eyes and taped to his ears, a sombrero with chin strap on his head and a woman in the dinghy's stern.

"Permission requested to come aboard," he hollered, feigning a half salute. "Permission granted," I said.

"Meet my 'following sea,'" she said as she bowed toward him. Buzzie Thornton and Conswella Van Ogtrop climbed aboard *Boogie to Go*.

"Just was trying to help," he said, speaking as if we had seen each other only yesterday.

"White Fly Beak," I said.

"All beaks have a point, even mine," he said. "And sea gulls are white, and they do fly, just like me. Gull and point. That and a Texaco road map was really all I needed. Conswella told me about you cracking GIPUSOLLILANNTD afterward."

"Gull Island Point," I said to myself. "From a parrot. And a diary."

It was only later that day that Buzzie Thornton casually mentioned that he also had "happened to have" gotten hold of the exact coordinates. "From papers in a suitcase thrown from a window," he said with a grin, then jumping up and down, laughing hysterically. At that point I was so confused by everything that I declined his offer to elaborate.

It was just good to see him. Alive.

And meet Conswella. Of course. She was all that I had imagined. And more.

59

No Longer a Blowfish

THE CONTENTS of her knapsack told more about the woman than Buzzie could have dreamed. He knew she was a schemer and a money-grubbing opportunist shortly after he married her. He did not know that her greed knew no bounds. That the $200,000 life insurance policy which she insisted upon adamantly during the divorce proceedings in 1980 would not be enough. He had reluctantly agreed to the life insurance, and crazy Buzzie only later wondering if she would truly go so far as to kill him to collect, to try and kill him or have him killed. "The blowfish might," he had thought. Hence it was easy in Buzzie's mind, his career well over at Elmont & Thornton, gladly, to send the telegram from Santa Fe, New Mexico, in 1983, declaring his death. And, in his wildest thoughts, many they were, he never thought that his once ballooned-up ex-wife, the former Jubilee Chosen, would continue to pursue, for ten more years, Buzzie's own little mystery search. "Not enough brains nor brawn," he had thought, dismissing the notion. But he didn't know the other Jubilee Chosen, the one I came to know, and, yes, to love. Love, quite a lot.

But when he and Conswella reflected on the contents of Laura's knapsack, little more than a day out of Mutton Bay aboard *Ocean Loon*, his chest and her shoulder heavily taped, a course set directly for the island of St. Martin, in the Caribbean, two thousand miles away from Newfoundland, a northeast gale building at their backs, he realized how badly he had underestimated the mysterious Jubilee Chosen, his wife of fifteen years.

The greed was well underestimated to be sure. And the determination, the cunning. "No longer a blowfish," he said to Conswella as she checked their course and she wondered about her own boat, the old pilot cutter *Weitra* which had brought her down the Elbe to Cuxhaven, Germany, to and across the North Sea and then the Atlantic Ocean to St. John's, Newfoundland, and then Mutton Bay to the South, west of Cape Race. It seemed all so distant to her now.

"The Caribbean or bust," Buzzie Thornton had yelled above the howling wind, raising a Rolling Rock from the companionway. "Smile," he said to Conswella as she plotted their course, "Smile."

"You're crazy," she said, a by then less rare half-smile creasing her lips. "I do not smile. Never. Not since . . ." She stopped.

Buzzie yelled, "Conswella," crossing his eyes as she turned to look at him, Buzzie's crossed eyes just south of the Rolling Rock can he held perched on his head, in the crease of his pink sombrero.

"What?" she hollered, first not looking at him and then looking at him and his stupid head with the crossed eyes and beer can on top, Buzzie beginning to hop around and dance in the companionway. He was driving her to insanity she thought and maybe to laughter. "What?" she hollered again.

"You do not smile since when?" he asked. The wind abated for a moment.

"Not since my father left me. When I was seven."

"I see," said Buzzie, and "You sail with me, you laugh, okay?"

"I try," she said. "Maybe."

"You try," he said.

"I will."

"Yes?"

"Yes."

"Good."

She smiled. "Okay," she said, eyes gleaming.

In the former Mrs. Elmont Thornton's knapsack, the knapsack of Laura Reo, the woman who had married Buzzie Thornton calling herself Jubilee Chosen, Buzzie and Conswella found some interesting things. And Buzzie thought back to his honeymoon on the island of St. Martin years ago, accommodations arranged by me, neither Jubilee nor Buzzie having visited the island before, and a honeymoon following a wedding which I did not attend because I was hunkered down in a faraway bunker. But a honeymoon which introduced the two love birds to the island, and introduced Jubilee to the casinos and the endless possibilities for her in them. And then the twice-a-year, month-long vacation returns to the island where Jubilee would spend her nights in the casinos and Buzzie would spend his nights dreaming, sleeping or thinking up capers and stunts, while his wife was cavorting with Fat Tony Spedarrone. Fat Tony and his Cuban cigar. Fat Tony the slob. Jubilee the schemer. Jubilee the money hungry. Jubilee who would steal Buzzie's thoughts about the mystery of Dunkerque Chamonix. Thoughts which needed more documentation and facts, she had decided.

And the woman would hook up with Fat Tony and then Billy Waddie and then, years later, Aki Igamuche. And the woman whose real name was not Jubilee Chosen would hook up with me. Me, the trusting fool.

And I would fall in love with her.

Hector's really getting into my writing now. He keeps asking if this or that is really true. "Unfortunately, yes."

"Mr. Thornton loco?"

I laughed, "Everybody thought so."

"Mr. Ipdown?"

"Sometimes," I said.

Hector smiled.

"Mr. Igamuche?"

"A tragic figure, I gather. And, yes, I think from all I heard that he was also crazy. Besides being a killer."

"What tragic?" asked Hector.

"Good question," I said, "I'm not sure how to define it."

"Sad," said Hector. He put his head down, turned his back to me and began walking toward the turkey coop, a sack of grower pellets held over his shoulder with his hook.

60

Saba or Bust

WHAT LITTLE common sense I had either increased or totally disappeared when I was around Buzzie. As I watched him hoist anchor, set a course for Saba, 33 miles from St. Martin to the southwest on a heading of 220° magnetic on the first day of October last year, I stood on the deck of *Ocean Loon* and wondered which was the case now; then concluded common sense had totally left me; that if I had any at all I would jump ship right then and let Buzzie and Conswella, the two Dunkerque legacies, pursue their insane mission alone. But I didn't, of course. I looked at Conswella. She shrugged her shoulders, smiled at Buzzie and said in my general direction, "Leave if you want." I stayed. Fool that I am. The two of them never thought for a second that they would do anything other than press on. Talk about obsessions. But, then again, I wasn't at Gull Island Point. And I am not related to Dunkerque Chamonix. Thank the good Lord.

Antigua radio that morning told of the Dutch government's additional and absentia indictments of Fat Tony Spedarrone for murder, the Barbuda yacht murders, for more gun smuggling, drug running, money laundering, and now the fire-bombing of the little cinema on Anguilla added to that list; and of Billy Waddie for more corruption, skimming, kickbacks and the like. Fat Tony the casino operator. Billy Waddie, the upstanding native Antillian ex-governor of Sint Maarten, popularly-elected. Both men missing. Evidently disappearing in Fat Tony's Cigarette speedboats, *Big Boy* and *Baby*. *Baby* and *Big Boy*.

Tough to hide if you look like Fat Tony, particularly in a Cigarette, I thought to myself.

As Buzzie steered *Ocean Loon* across the lagoon towards the drawbridge leading to the open waters of the Caribbean Sea, I looked at my watch. Two hours before the bridge would open. "What are we going to do for two hours?" I asked Buzzie. "Might just as well have stayed at anchor until the bridge opens," I said.

Buzzie hollered, "Cat's ass," and tightened the chin strap on his pink sombrero. Conswella smiled. Buzzie and Conswella went forward. He removed two long stainless steel bolts from the mast-step and proceeded to lower the main mast, hinged at the deck, so that it then lay flat fore and aft on *Ocean Loon*. He did the same with the second mast. I watched in amazement. He went below and cranked up the retractable keel, as if it were a centerboard. He emptied two port and starboard ballast tanks of water by opening seacocks with check valves. *Ocean Loon* rose a foot in the water.

I just shook my head and then, strangely, began to think about Dunkerque Chamonix's diary entries in 1865 when he went to Ford's Theater, the night President Lincoln was shot; and then the letters "AJNODHRNE-SWON" which Dunkerque had carefully penned on thirteen separate, consecutive pages. "The two are connected," I said to myself, not knowing why. "The two are connected," I hollered to Buzzie.

"Now for the power," he said, starting what sounded like a jet engine.

"Holy Christ," I shouted. "What we got for power?"

"Twin 1962 rebuilt and modified G.M. Corvette engines," he said with a wave of his arm, in the general direction of Detroit, I guess. "Four four-barrel Holly carburetors on super-chargers. Eleven hundred horses." And then, "Hang on, me hearties. Don't pee in your pants."

He threw the transmission into gear and jammed the throttle forward. I lunged to grab hold of the rail as the now mastless, stainless steel whale-like missile shot forward in the water like a bullet. *Ocean Loon* flew through the water, planing at fifty knots, under the unopened drawbridge and out the other side, Buzzie at the controls whooping and hollering, dancing up and down, sombrero on his head, oversized sunglasses taped to his ears with the silver duct tape. He waved at the Simpson's Bay Bridge superintendent hanging out the window high above, eyes bulging, looking like he was seeing a ghost, Conswella doubled up with laughter, and I clenching the rail for dear life, my mouth agape.

"Hi, ho, Silver," hollered Buzzie above the roar of the 1,100 horsepower. "Saba or bust. Remember the Alamo. Remember the HMS *Truro*. And the S.S. *Claxdow*. Three cheers for Dunkerque Chamonix."

I peeked back over my shoulder through *Ocean Loon*'s enormous wake, boats around us pitching wildly from side to side as if an underwater ordinance had exploded, a crowd gathering on and next to the Simpson's Bay Bridge, a cadre of Dutch marines quickly joining ranks.

"Look out Fat Tony," I said to myself. "Crazy Buzzie is on the loose."

But, I thought then that my fifty-one years had been great. That I had experienced more than two or three people ever experienced in collective lifetimes. And that my chances of seeing my fifty-second birthday might now be less than those of Abe Lincoln rising from the dead.

61

"Diamont Rots, Here We Come"

I LOOKED AT THE back of Buzzie's sombrero covered head bobbing up and down at *Ocean Loon*'s wheel as we roared toward the island of Saba, the waters of the Caribbean Sea ahead dead calm and beautiful in hues of green and blue. I thought back to a conversation I had had with Laura only weeks before, back at Finnsheep Farm.

"I miss Laura," I said aloud.

"She sounds so sweet. Like a woman you should have married," hollered Conswella, above the roar of the engines.

"Absolutely," said Buzzie.

To the conversation with Laura.

"I think it is very magnanimous of you to help someone you have never met, Chuck. But really," Laura had said, "don't you think you are taking this a bit too far?"

"I don't think so," I said.

"Would you be doing as much for me as you have been doing for Miss Van Ogtrop if I were her?" Yes, I thought.

"Of course, Laura, of course," I said, and "do I detect a bit of jealousy here?" I asked, smiling at her.

"Really, Chuck. I don't even know the woman and neither do you." And I really didn't then, except for how Luther had described her to me in 1988, and the impressions I got from our brief, but frequent, short wave conversations; I at Finnsheep Farm, she aboard *Weitra*.

"I know, I know," I said.

"Let her finish her foolish mission if she wants. But for God's sake, stay out of it, Chuck. She should be on her own at this point."

I scratched my head. "She is on her own, she is on board a small sailboat, alone, somewhere in the North Atlantic."

"Well, forget her, you can't help her now."

"I'm not," I said quizzically.

"You try to raise her every night on the short wave,

don't you?"

"Yes, but . . ."

"No buts. She is all you think about and all you talk about. Forget the bitch."

I recoiled and stared at Laura, who was now on her way upstairs. "Bitch?" I said.

"That's right, bitch," Laura hollered back down the stairs before slamming the door.

"That's not the Laura Reo I know," I said to myself.

Talk about jealousy, I thought, knowing only now that it was more than that.

I cleared my head of thoughts of Laura and looked ahead on the horizon; Saba, a virtual rockpile, rising almost 4,000 feet out of the water. Conswella was checking the charts. "The cliffs, the cliffs," she said, mouth next to my ear, "there is nowhere to land."

I thought again of how much I missed Laura, but didn't utter another word about that.

"South Side Landing, here," I hollered, pointing to it on the chart set on Conswella's lap, "or Ladder Landing here on the southwest side. The only two anchorages."

"I doubt if they are going to be sitting in a yacht anchorage. Sitting there in their Cigarette boats, drinking beer, waiting to be nailed by us or the authorities," hollered Buzzie, knee centering the wheel, hands and arms pulling two feet of duct tape off a roll.

"You're right," I said. I knew the waters around Saba quite well. It doesn't get a lot of visiting yachts. The waters surrounding the high, very steep island are frequently too rough to anchor, anywhere. But I love to go to Saba, its two tiny towns on the Dutch island reminding one instantly of Holland. Clean white houses; small, almost all with beautiful gardens. This visit, however, was not one I was looking forward to with pleasure.

"You are just going to have to circle the island, but stay off; stand off; the surf hits the cliffs like nothing you've ever seen, Buzzie," I said, slamming my fist into my palm and then bursting fist and palm apart.

"We'll find the bastards." Buzzie reached for his ukulele.

"If they're here," I said. "You might. There are hideaways in the cliffs, but they are hard to find, and dangerous as hell to go in."

"Get the knapsack, Conswella," Buzzie yelled to Conswella. "Get the Blowfish sack."

"Here, my good warrior," she said, handing Laura's or Jubilee's knapsack, brought with them from Gull Island Point, to Captain Buzzie.

"Very good warrior," he hollered. "A most sensible one, too." Conswella laughed and whacked him on the backside.

I looked across at her and yelled, "Sensible? Senseless would be a better word."

"Good, better, best. Sensible, insensible, sane, saneless, senseless," hollered the Buzzer, raising his ukulele high in the air, looking down at the compass and then forward to the World War II Browning submachine gun.

"The reports I had said you never laughed or smiled," I yelled to Conswella.

"Sometimes, now, I do," she said, a serious look returning to her face.

"Thank you, Blowfish," Buzzie screamed, pulling a

notebook from the knapsack with one hand, holding a Red Stripe in the other, steering *Ocean Loon*'s wheel again with his knee on the spokes. I looked at him and wished I had brought the camera. The pink sombrero with chin strap and sunglasses taped to his ears with silver duct tape were what really got me going.

But we were not headed into a laughing matter.

If we found Fat Tony Spedarrone and his accomplices, we could, probably, very easily, come out losers. Dead. They were not men to be fooled with. I thought again about the four murders on the yacht in Barbuda, the fire-bombed cinema, the mini-drug subs, believing that Fat Tony was behind it all, that he may have even done the killings himself. With him on the run, a long jail sentence or worse hanging over his head, he would be twice as dangerous, nothing to lose. To say nothing of Billy Waddie; and I thought of his hand dipping into my grocery bag in front of the Sandy Ground Church of God. "There is a time to live and a time to die." Ouch.

Buzzie studied the notebook. "Right on," he hollered. "Cat's ass. What a dumb blowfish. Date, time and place to meet and divide the booty. Saba. Diamont Rots. 1100 hours GMT. Today is the day. Diamont Rots, here we come."

"Diamont Rots?" I shouted, bolting from my seat. "That's all reef, a ship graveyard, cliffs eight hundred feet straight up. We can't go in there, Buzzie. It's crazy."

Conswella stared at me and went below, mouthing, "*You* are crazy."

"That's me. Crazy," yelled Buzzie. "We're goin' in. This is it, Dunkerque, we're almost home. It's for you." And, looking below toward Conswella, "For your great-great-granddaughter."

It's all over, I thought to myself.

We rounded the southern side of Saba, wind screaming in our ears, and roared our way up the western side, surf spraying 100 and 200 feet up the face of the cliffs, past Ladder Landing and on up toward Diamont Rots, and what I knew now might well be certain death. One way or another.

Conswella took *Ocean Loon*'s wheel as Buzzie removed the waterproof canvas cover and then began to oil the deck-mounted submachine gun. "Kind of cute, isn't it?" he screamed, squirting oil at me, as I looked up at the top of Mt. Scenery, 3,900 feet in the air, the peak of Saba.

I can't put my finger on it. It is difficult for me to think of any specifics. But I now feel more than ever that something strange is going on here at the farm. I began to feel that way upon returning from St. Martin after the Saba episode, sort of the conclusion to the whole mess. Maybe my feelings actually began shortly after Laura's death. Or before. I can't be sure. Maybe it is something to do with Hector. But again, I can't put my finger on any specifics there. There is a feeling I have of deep-seated, changed behavior on his part. More in his eyes than anything he has said or done. And maybe I am just imagining things. That surely is possible after all that has happened. Maybe I am crazy. "Mr. Thornton crazy? Mr. Ipdown? Mr. Igamuche?" Actually, I chuckle a bit to myself when I think back to Hector asking me those questions. Less so when he repeatedly asks me about "the old pocket watch," which I have permanently locked away.

I am very uneasy right now.

But I am going to write some more.

About Diamont Rots, Baby *and* Big Boy.

Why does Hector sleep with Laura's towel? I wasn't going to write that, but I just did. Let's see his reaction when he reads that. Just kidding you, Hector. But, I will be glad when you are in school. You budding Einstein, you. Lucifer clone.

62

Ocean Loon, Baby and *Big Boy*

MY HEAD snapped back like a whip as Buzzie pushed the throttle all the way forward, the stainless steel bow rising in the air, pointing skyward, sun glistening off the water, dripping and blowing aft from the hull, *Ocean Loon* rocketing ahead like a sea-going missile gone wild, spray from the sides of the hull towering high in the air to port and starboard, totally obscuring my vision.

We bounced over the reefs, cleared the last one, no more than one hundred yards from the towering cliffs of Diamont Rots as Buzzie pulled the throttle all the way back and threw the engines into neutral, *Ocean Loon* settling down into the calm waters between reefs and cliffs like a cork.

"Lord Almighty," I said, sweat dripping from my brow.

I looked at Conswella. She was laughing again.

Buzzie was studying the cliffs in front of us. "See anything?" he asked.

"Nope," I said, "let's went."

"There," said Conswella, pointing at about 2 o'clock off our starboard bow.

"I do believe so," said the Buzzer, easing the silver projectile forward. "I do declare."

Only partially visible to the eye and visible only at close range, inside the reefs of Diamont Rots on the northwestern side of the island of Saba, we spotted an opening in the cliffs. We slowly made our way to and then into the opening, traveling at no more than a knot or so. Once inside, we just looked at each other. The cave was less than 20 feet wide and 10 feet high at the opening. But, inside, it opened to a vast expanse more than 100 feet high and as far ahead as the eye could see into the darkness. We inched ahead in *Ocean Loon*.

"Looks totally desolate," I said. Neither Buzzie nor Conswella answered. "Deserted," I said.

"There is a boat tied up ahead," said Buzzie, leaning

forward, squinting his eyes, sunglasses now perched at the end of his nose.

I stared ahead into the darkness, the only sound a low hum from the idle speed of *Ocean Loon*'s engines. "I don't see a thing," I said.

"I do believe so," said the Buzzer again, continuing to ease the silver projectile forward. "I do declare."

"Shh," said Conswella.

"Carrots," said Buzzie softly, turning to me and smiling. "I told you to go heavy on the carrots. Look at me, my eyes are like spotlights."

I tried a half-smile, but it wouldn't come, and I tensed to avoid peeing in my pants.

And sure enough, a minute later, a boat appeared in the darkness, a boat tied to heavy cleats attached to a rock ledge. "A Cigarette," I said to myself.

Buzzie cut the engines and *Ocean Loon* drifted alongside the Cigarette, freshly painted. I could smell the new paint and read the lettering, also newly drawn, on the side. We tied *Ocean Loon* to *Baby*, and my two shipmates climbed aboard.

"Careful. Careful," I said as Buzzie and Conswella searched the boat. I watched and kept one eye moving about the cave as far as my eye could see, which wasn't very far. Buzzie ripped open *Baby*'s engine compartment and smacked the side of a spare fuel tank with the ring on his hand, the tank full. He smacked the second spare tank. It responded with a ping. Buzzie disconnected the tank, leaped with it from *Baby* to *Ocean Loon*, unscrewed the tank cap and looked in at $19 million in sterling notes and a gold pocket watch with a shattered glass face. "My word," he said.

Conswella smiled. I was silent.

We cast off the docklines tying us to the Cigarette, *Baby*, as Buzzie started *Ocean Loon*'s engines. He turned the steel whale on a dime and headed her out toward the opening in the cave. "Take over," he said to Conswella as he moved away from the ship's wheel. "Slow and easy, dead ahead." I sat staring at the sterling notes.

Buzzie Thornton. Crazy, ugly Buzzie went forward on deck, once again shot some oil from a can over the deck-mounted, Browning submachine gun, and then proceeded to blow *Baby* to Kingdom Come. The cave sounded like a series of bombs exploding in rapid staccato succession. Conswella and I covered our ears as Buzzie continued to fire way, swinging his body and gun side to side. *Baby* hung from its docklines, the Cigarette completely under water within a minute. Another volley directed at the docklines and all that remained of *Baby* were bubbles on the calm cave water's surface. "Christ," I said, "that was stupid." Buzzie looked at me and saluted.

Buzzie re-covered the gun with the waterproof canvas bag and retook *Ocean Loon*'s wheel. None of us said a word. Ten feet from the cave's opening and the safe little lagoon outside, a steel door shot out from the left side of the cave, traveled the twenty feet to the other side of the cave's opening in a split second and slammed shut with a thud that instantly brought to mind the lid of a coffin being slammed closed. With me in it.

Did I think it was all over for me? Are you kidding? My first reaction when I saw that steel door shoot across the opening, the exit to freedom, though we still had the reefs to get back over, was the coffin image. And then a feeling of being in a dream. These things don't happen in real life, I thought. And then, how and why did I get myself into the whole mess? I knew, had known for more than thirty years that Buzzie was two slices short of a loaf. Why didn't I mind my own business? Of course, none of that mattered at that moment. I thought of Boogie to Go *sitting back waiting for me in my slip in Simpson's Bay. And then I thought about the bridge from a nice relaxing life at Finnsheep Farm to getting involved with one of the most notorious crooks and, indeed, probably killers in the Caribbean, Fat Tony Spedarrone. I thought of Jubilee Chosen, Laura Reo, Guyane the parrot, Luther Van Ogtrop, Dunkerque Chamonix and the whole weird mess. But, interestingly, despite a fate I felt certain of, I didn't panic.*

It was now pitch black. And for what seemed like an eternity, not a sound could be heard save a gentle lapping of the water against *Ocean Loon*'s smooth hull. Without warning, a searchlight blasted on from the top of the cave, its beam capturing the three of us and *Ocean Loon* like three clowns on a vaudeville stage. There was an exchange of words and three men appeared out of the darkness, toting automatic rifles, and jumped onto the deck of *Ocean Loon*. The last man to jump on board, huffing and puffing, I recognized immediately from newspaper photos. Fat Tony Spedarrone. It was only after that that I recognized the second man as the man who had called my name as I stood outside the Sandy Ground Church of God, Billy Waddie. The first man aboard, a dim wit, held his gun directly at us and said nothing until Spedarrone was in place on deck. Then, looking at me, he mumbled, without a smile, "You must be Shit Toes." I still didn't say a word.

Billy Waddie looked at me and said, "You don't listen too good, do you Wingate?" I still didn't say a word.

Fat Tony, still huffing and puffing, said to his dim-witted henchman, "Tie the bastards up. All three of them." He then lifted his rifle butt and smashed it into the side of Buzzie Thornton's head. Buzzie dropped to the deck unconscious. I wanted to kill Spedarrone instantly. But, again I didn't move or say a word.

"Pretty fucking stupid," said Fat Tony. "Pretty fucking stupid." I glanced at him. He was looking right at me. A scar down his arm ran from shoulder to wrist, the old wound looking as if it had been made with an errant jig saw and sewn up with rope. It was gruesome. His eyes were red and puffy, his face bloated and thick, oily black hair plastered down, combed straight back. The belly hanging over his yellow pants peeked out from the bottom of a green and orange shirt open to the navel. His feet were shoeless; huge, oversized purple toes sticking out, toenails long enough to pick his nose. A Cuban cigar was clenched in his teeth.

"Here?" asked the henchman.

"Same as Barbuda," said Fat Tony. "Tie 'em all up. Shoot 'em in the back of the head and leave 'em."

"Can't do it," said Billy Waddie, looking befuddled as he scanned the highly confusing control panel of *Ocean Loon*. "We need this boat. Look at yours." He nodded toward where a few stray bubbles rose to the surface, marking *Baby*'s final resting place.

"We'll take the other one," said Spedarrone.

"*Big Boy*?" asked the very dumb-looking henchman dim wit. I thought his IQ probably hovered around the freezing point on the Fahrenheit scale, at most.

"No, the fucking *Queen Mary*," said Fat Tony raising the butt of his rifle as if to strike the boob in the head. Then, "Just do it. Waste them right here. Right now."

I looked at Buzzie, semiconscious, lying in a heap in the cockpit next to me. I glanced at Conswella who was cool as "an iced-down quail," as Luther, her grandfather, had described her.

"Line up, on your knees, hands in back, next to each other," said the henchman, poking Conswella, then me, then Buzzie with his rifle barrel.

"You're forgetting something," said Conswella, stepping forward and looking Spedarrone straight in the eye.

"What's that sweetheart?"

"The money," she said, the spare fuel tank and its contents now out of sight.

Fat Tony looked over to where *Baby* had sunk and then back at Conswella.

"Not a problem," she said, "we found it, all of it, and removed it before we sank the boat."

Fat Tony looked at Billy Waddie who was staring at Conswella. "Shit," he said, looking at Waddie and then the henchman.

"We've got to get out of here," said Waddie. "Now."

"Not without the money," said Spedarrone.

"Not without the money," said the henchman.

"Shut up," said Spedarrone.

A gun shot resounded throughout the cave, a shattering of glass, and the cave was pitch black, again, the beam of light overhead reduced to rubble.

"Guns in water," hollered a voice which was impossible to source because of the triple and quadruple echoes. "Guns in water, fat man. All three of you, Schnell (fast)." Spedarrone, Waddie and dumbo froze.

A searchlight suddenly blared from a far side of the cave, momentarily freezing the three thugs in place. "There," yelled Spedarrone, pointing in the direction of the searchlight. "Blow him away."

As the three men swung their rifles in the direction of the light framing them and throwing their shadows against the side of the cave, a voice hollered out, "Tombe Mort. Tombe Mort. Tombe Mort."

Conswella Van Ogtrop instantly dropped flat in the cockpit of *Ocean Loon*, pulling me down by the arms as she went, the two of us landing on top of Buzzie as he lay prone. The sound of automatic weapons fire filled the cave, but the searchlight stayed on. I heard the thud of bullets impacting flesh and ricocheting off *Ocean Loon*'s inch-thick stainless steel hull.

Out of the corner of my eye, I saw Fat Tony pitch into the water, his gun flying, followed by a "ther-rump" and water rising into the air as if an over-sized cannonball had been dropped. Billy Waddie was right after him, his blood running into the cockpit. I turned my head slightly and saw the henchman, head literally blown apart, lying face down, hands and arms and legs and feet twisted eerily in all directions.

"You okay?" I asked Conswella, her eyes no more than

two inches from mine. She didn't answer me. "You okay, Buzzie?" I asked.

"Never better," he said, lifting his head, eyes crossed and sombrero cocked to one side.

Conswella Van Ogtrop was the first to rise. She looked in the direction of a man walking across the rocks toward *Ocean Loon*, a gun in his hand and a black hood with cut-outs for eyes, nose and mouth over his faceless head.

"Dein Gedächtnis hilfst ihr wohl." Your memory saved you, the man said as he stepped on deck.

Buzzie and I just stared at the bizarre figure before us.

Frederick Van Ogtrop threw his arms around his daughter and held her. She started to cry. And he began to cry then, too.

63

Camouflage Uniforms and Laced-Up Black Boots

WE SAT IN the cockpit of *Boogie to Go*, drinking beer, all but Frederick Van Ogtrop. He sipped on a Ting, king of Caribbean orange crushes. Buzzie plucked away at his ukulele and sang, horribly, "Take Me Home," a John Denver song. Conswella spoke quietly with her father. Hector worked on his boat chores.

"What's next?" hollered Buzzie, doing the two-step, plucking at the uke's strings.

"Nothing, I hope," I said. "Why don't you take a long, quiet vacation, in Austria, with Conswella and Frederick? Climb the Alps, roam the meadows, read books, relax."

"I am relaxed," he said, crossing his eyes and grabbing at his groin. Conswella looked at him and rolled her eyes.

Conswella asked her father again to come home to Austria with her, to the homeland he had left twenty-six years before for his ill-fated helicopter mission.

"I cannot," he said, "there is still unfinished business here for me. My friend comes tomorrow." And with that he hugged his daughter and took his leave. I would see the man only once, fleetingly, again, the man with the burned-off face.

Frederick Van Ogtrop thought back to his wrecked movie theater, wrecked the first time by Fat Tony's extortion mob. He thought of his naive call to the officials, the two local Antillian authorities in the office of then Sint Maarten Governor, Billy Waddie. They said they could do nothing. There was no proof. "Maybe you wreck the place, yourself, eh?" they had laughed. He had gone directly to the Dutch Council, pleading his case. They looked at him solemnly and told him to leave, to get his movie theater back in operation within five days or they would see to it that the Anguillan authorities transferred his license to someone else, to one Mr. Tony Spedarrone.

Frederick Van Ogtrop thought of the Dutch marines on maneuvers coming into his movie house, sitting down without buying tickets, saying they had free passes from the Governor of Sint Maarten, never showing their passes and taking seats from paying customers from whom Frederick Van Ogtrop needed the meager receipts to pay his expenses, pay off Fat Tony, to keep his little business alive; and maybe save a little for an operation, operations, someday, which might allow him to walk in public with dignity and self-respect.

And then he thought of the fire-bombing. His little cinema, all he had to his name, destroyed.

He hated the Dutch now. When they could have and should have helped him, they turned their backs on him. He had heard of their tendencies twenty-six years before when he sat at the bar of the old tavern in Cuxhaven, the night before his departure for Vietnam with the International Red Cross; the night he drank with the owner who had rebuilt his burned-out tavern with his own hands after the war, the Haar Auf Der Hund destroyed by the drunken Dutch on July Fourth, 1945.

Frederick Van Ogtrop went to Queen Julianna Airport the day after our return from Saba to meet the plane carrying his "friend." Frederick to meet Frederick again.

Frederick Van Ogtrop and Frederick Wenzel went to the Sandy Ground Church of God that night. They met with the group of assembled patriots and they distributed guns. Joe Priest was there, leader of the Alliance Party. "Movin' On," was their slogan. "Movin' On," they all said.

The next morning, with the sun peeking over the top of the lush green mountains to the east, across Simpson's Bay Lagoon, fifty Antillians fanned out in the hills, taking up their positions; Joe Priest, Frederick Van Ogtrop and Frederick Wenzel in the lead. A native Antillian, an

Austrian, and a German. Three men who hated the Dutch.

I was sitting on deck washing clothes in a rubber bucket when I heard a loud "whoosh," looked up and saw a projectile in the air over the hills. "Jesus Christ," I said. The projectile arched high over the lagoon and came screaming down onto Simpson's Bay Bridge, blowing the drawbridge in half at the center, effectively cutting St. Martin in two, save the long roundabout route by auto up through Marigot on the French side.

"It's happening," I thought to myself. "Can't be." But it was.

In the slip next to mine, Jack on *Storm Ruler* began running around on deck, screaming at anyone and everyone in sight to help him protect his boat, just before his normally submissive wife hit him in the back of the head with a dinghy oar, and the old but fertile, yawning dog from Philipsburg took a poop through the open deck hatch. I burst into short-lived laughter.

I heard the sound truck, it's blaring horn, coming from Cole Bay, down the airport road. "What have the Dutch done for us? Nothing. Nothing. They take our land, our property. It time to take our island back. Now."

Three more"whooshes" and puffs of smoke from the mountains across the lagoon. One shell took out the control tower at Queen Julianna Airport, less than three kilometers, two miles, from where I sat on *Boogie to Go*'s deck. The second mortar shot landed in the lagoon. The third leveled the upper story of The Royal Palm Beach Club, a hotel, time-share, built and owned by a Dutchman. I heard terrible screams.

It was no more than twenty minutes from the first mortar shot that I watched as truck after truck of Dutch marines in camouflage uniforms and laced-up black boots rolled down the Cole Bay Road past the marina.

And then I saw Frederick Van Ogtrop for the last time as he hurled a grenade from the bushes beside the road. A dozen Dutch marine machine guns then to riddle his body with bullets.

64

"Hello, Buzzard"

"HERE COMES trouble," said Buzzie Thornton four days later. We all watched as a diminutive man dressed in dark suit and tie in ninety degree heat limped down the dock in the direction of *Boogie to Go,* cheeks bulging like a squirrel's, the man burping and running his fingers through his funny-looking hair as he came toward us. "Trouble, trouble, trouble." But Buzzie was smiling.

"Hello, Buzzard," bellowed the man, mopping his brow with a wadded, soiled handkerchief pulled from his rear pant pocket.

"That's me," said Buzzie, helping the man aboard, I looking at the two of them and then Conswella with a look of complete perplexity on my face.

"The arsehole?" asked the man, looking at Buzzie with one eye, the other eye rolled back in its socket searching the heavens, and the man pointing at me.

"Same exact one," said Buzzie, smiling.

The man began to laugh, then held out his hand to me. I still didn't recognize him from our only meeting, the brief and unpleasant one as he made an obnoxious fool of himself twenty-nine years before in the room that Buzzie and I shared at Swarthmore College. "Fury Ipdown," he said, shaking my hand, then laughing, "Want to shoot 'em up?" Then I remembered. Buzzie was now alternately dancing up and down and playing his ukulele again, laughing uncontrollably. Conswella was just shaking her head, smiling.

Well, that was when I found out a few things. Buzzie related as to how he and Fury Ipdown had been in touch "more than once" after the purchase of Elmont & Thornton by Ipdown in 1982, the purchase which brought with it perpetual rights to the $19 million which had disappeared 111 years before. There was only one catch. Buzzie had disappeared in 1980, and without his signature, the sale of Elmont & Thornton was not technically valid. After Buzzie's "death telegram" in 1983 sent *by Buzzie, the two men met on several occasions, unbeknownst to me certainly or anyone else. "Thought I was ashes, Chuckie, didn't you?" Buzzie said to me. Yes, I did. Everybody did. Except Fury Ipdown. And except Buzzie's Conestoga wagon companion traveler. His Pecos River fishing partner.*

Fury Ipdown counted the $19 million with Buzzie, while Conswella and I watched. "A deal is a deal," said Ipdown to Buzzie when they had finished counting.

"None for me," said Buzzie. "What would I do with it?"

"A third, a third, a third," said Fury Ipdown. "Conswella, Dunkerque's great-great-granddaughter, one-third. Me, Fury Ipdown, great-great-grandson of Jersey Ipdown, Dunkerque's best friend AND partner, one-third. And you Buzzard, Dunkerque's great, great messed-up grandnephew, the other third. Without you and the diary you found, no one would have a shilling."

"No interest," said Elmont Buzzie Thornton IV. "Give it to Chuckie here."

And he really didn't have any interest.

He looked at me and smiled. "We might still be looking if my fishing partner and Desert Loon traveling companion hadn't thrown the suitcase of computer print-outs and papers with the twelve numbers, the longitude and latitude coordinates, from the window of the Japanese man's bedroom, to Fury and me as we rode in, in the train's club car, sipping martinis," hollered Buzzie.

"Hear, hear," said Fury. "Don't forget his visits with old Dunkerque in the steeple in 1940 either."

Camels, Phil Rizzuto and Harley Indians with side-cars, I thought to myself.

"God bless him," I said, then: "Who gets this?" I asked, holding up the old, gold pocket watch with its shattered face.

65

Loyalty in the White House

THE FOLLOWING morning, Judy brought Hanna over for one of her now daily Calvert School lessons, and Buzzie and Conswella got ready to head back to Newfoundland, to pick up *Weitra*, Conswella's boat, still anchored, hopefully, in Mutton Bay. We all sat around in the cockpit of *Boogie to Go* having coffee and tea, Hanna forward on deck working, intermittently at best, on the assignment for the day, United States Presidents. She listened while I told Judy again about Dunkerque Chamonix's entries in his diary in 1865, when at age eighteen, he went to Ford's Theater and wrote that he had seen a man fire two pistol shots into President Lincoln's box at close range, and then thrust the gun into the hand of a second man standing next to him, pushing that man through the curtains and into the box; the first man then to bump into Dunkerque, according to the diary entries, and drop a watch, the glass face shattering next to Dunkerque Chamonix; the man to run away, the boy to pick-up the broken watch and exit the theater. I, very skeptical about the then eighteen-year-old boy's recorded tale.

Hanna emptied her bag of colored plastic letters on deck and, looking at the list of presidents in the Calvert School assignment, spelled out "Abraham Lincoln," with the letters. She motioned me forward to look. "Good," I said, then, "next."

Buzzie opened his bag and pulled forth the gold pocket watch with the shattered face, the watch stashed with the $19 million by Jersey Ipdown for his friend Dunkerque Chamonix in 1871. He handed it to me and I turned it over to read the inscription on the back, engraved. "A.J."

I thought back to the diary and the two sequences of letters, "GIPUSOLLILANNTD," or Gull Island Point, in 1871 and "AJNODHRNESWON," in 1865. I looked at Buzzie and slowly repeated the mysterious letters "AJNODHRNESWON." He looked at me quizzically and then smiled as I nodded my head toward little Hanna.

I brought Hanna and her bag of plastic letters to the cockpit. I sat her down and pulled out thirteen plastic letters, AJNODHRNESWON, from the bag.

"Next," I said again. Hanna fiddled with the letters, lining them up correctly. "Right," I said, "Good."

ANDREW JOHNSON.

"Doesn't look good for him" I said.

"Do you think he is worried?" cracked Buzzie, crossing his eyes.

"I doubt it," I said.

"I know what you are thinking, Wingate," Buzzie said, opening his thermos and dumping out a handful of sliced, raw carrots, not looking at me, handing a slice to Conswella, Judy, Hanna, Fury Ipdown and then me, reluctantly; Hector looking over his shoulder at us from his perch on the bowsprit.

"What's that?" I asked, "what am I thinking, Elmont IV?"

"Who you are going to tell about recovery of the treasure?" asked Judy, innocent, imploring, sparkling eyes fixed on Buzzie, then turned to me.

"Exactly," said Buzzie. "You took the words out of Chuckie's mouth. And, add that my old friend is now thinking about how to break the news about loyalty in the White House in 1865, the poor John Wilkes Booth and his broken leg, an innocent man dead because of Vice President Andrew Johnson. If anyone could believe that stuff."

"There is not one thing in Chamonix's diary or anything else we have all come to learn about our beloved old man that has a hint of falsehood, a hint of anything but fact," said Fury Ipdown, applying a cotton swab to the hair plugs on the top of his forehead, and letting forth with a long burp.

"Right you are, gimpy," said Buzzie.

"Can we have some of this money, Mommy?", asked seven-year-old Hanna, plying her fingers through the bills now in one of my old sail bags.

"Of course not," said Judy, "get your hand out of there."

"Give her a fistful," said Buzzie. Judy grabbed her daughter and sat back, looking at Buzzie Thornton who, I could tell, was about to hold court.

"The watch," said Buzzie, "and the original diary," holding both of them up in his two hands. "The copy of this diary, Wingate, given to you by me for safe-keeping in 1980, thirteen years ago; where is it?"

"Stowed below," I said. "Safe-keeping."

"Unsafe keep it," said Buzzie. "Please get it for me now."

I looked at Buzzie. He was not smiling. I looked at Fury Ipdown. He was glaring at me. I looked at Conswella. She was studying a chart of the Atlantic Ocean. I looked at Judy. Her eyes, those eyes, were fixed on mine and told me to forget about Laura. I looked at Hanna. She had her hand back in the "money bag."

I retrieved my copy of Dunkerque Chamonix's diary from the hanging locker below and gave it to Buzzie.

Buzzie Thornton took the winch handle from its

holder and smashed Andrew Johnson's gold pocket watch into crumpled metal gears and springs. He ripped every page out of Dunkerque Chamonix's diary and the copy he had given to me years before. He put all of the pages into his sombrero and stirred the mess with the winch handle, and then dumped the filled hat overboard, poking a hole in the top of the sombrero's straw.

"Now for the watch," he said.

Hector looked at me. A can of varnish in one hand and a paint brush in his other hand.

"No," I shouted. "I want it."

"Here, Pancho, take it," said Buzzie tossing it in my direction.

"That's it," he said, watching the pieces of paper, the pages, float away with the out-going tide, the sombrero bobbing on the surface. "Tomorrow, we dump all the money into the sea," he said. "Out where no one will ever find it."

Fury Ipdown, Conswella, Judy and I looked at Buzzie. "What?" I said.

"Well, maybe not all of it," said Buzzie, satisfied that he had gotten a rise out of all of us. "Just kidding."

Fury Ipdown burped, Hanna laughed, Conswella smiled. I touched Judy lightly on the shoulder. Fury Ipdown burped again and took on a grave look. "Where is Igamuche?" he said, half aloud and half to Buzzie. And then, again, "Where is Mr. Aki Igamuche?" He tugged on his sleeve and, looking at all of us, shivered.

"Who?" I asked.

I then watched, first in astonishment and then in anger, as Hector threw the can of varnish into the water and slammed his hook into the wood mast not fifteen feet away, staring directly at me.

And then I sat and listened for the next hour as Fury Ipdown proceeded to tell me, "Everything I know," about Mr. Aki Igamuche.

And that is it. All my story. All I know. Rather, all I knew when I boarded my plane with Hector and headed back to Finnsheep Farm in Maine via San Juan, Boston and Portland on the morning of October 12 last year, 1993, two-and-one-half months before I began to set down my recollections and the facts. Set them to paper. Beginning to do so on New Year's Day, January 1 of this year, 1994. The year of Our Lord. Praise The Lord.

Postscript (Original)

January 28, 1994

FILLING IN THE pieces now, less than a week after I finished telling, writing of all the bizarre happenings. I write now for Hector. And for me.

When Elmont Thornton's Pecos River fishing partner and Desert Loon traveling companion, Airman First Class, bombardier aboard *Bock's Car* on August 9, 1945, was found murdered last November - his decomposed hands tied, a sword with hand-scrolling run through his back, old scorched sandals dangling from his feet, the skeleton face down in a dried pool of blood aboard the *Glory Be*, drifting 400 miles out at sea, alone and apparently murdered more than two months before, not long after he had slipped from his bed in Room 113 of Grasslands Hospital in White Plains, New York, and made his way to JFK Airport, Boston and St. John's, Newfoundland to find Aki Igamuche - I was not surprised. Buzzie had convinced me in St. Martin that the threat to Didier's life was probably real.

He never believed that Phil Rizzuto would be elected to the Hall of Fame. And he had bet me so, promising to eat his hat if he were wrong. God Bless him. May Uncle Didier Mollard rest in peace. He was seventy-eight.

No trace of Aki Igamuche has been found. He is presumed to have become separated from the *Glory Be* and drowned in the Atlantic Ocean. After savagely killing the man he held responsible for murder. The 30,000 dead, including Igamuche's mother, father and sister, in the city of Nagasaki.

Aki Igamuche was wanted by Scotland Yard for the murder of Mandalay Mandarin, granddaughter of General Robert Creighton, twenty years before; and by the FBI. For the murder of Didier Mollard, embezzlement from the firm of Elmont & Thornton and involvement in cocaine smuggling from Colombia to Dominica and Miami. Igamuche was sixty-two at the time of his disappearance.

Fury Ipdown, now sixty-four years old, sold Elmont & Thornton to a private investor group from Philadelphia last December. He returned to England where he now lives outside Gloucestershire in the Cotswalds, seventy-five miles north of London on the old family seat, where his great-great-grandfather, Jersey Ipdown, was born in 1847 and buried in 1872, the year the *Claxdow* went down.

Conswella Van Ogtrop, thirty-four, returned to Germany aboard her old Bristol Channel pilot cutter, *Weitra*, solo, as would be expected. She purchased the old tavern in Cuxhaven, Haar Auf Der Hund, from the estate of Frederick Wenzel.

Frederick Wenzel died with Frederick Van Ogtrop, Conswella's father, in the uprising against the Dutch on the island of St. Martin last fall.

Elmont Buzzie Thornton IV tends bar and is in charge of entertainment at the Haar Auf Der Hund in Cuxhaven. At fifty-two, he attends the University of Hamburg by day, working toward degrees in oceanography and astronomy. "Cat's ass," he says.

I am still in Maine at Finnsheep Farm with my animals, crops and butterfly collection. And Hector. The budding Einstein, at times now seeming on track to become an early drop-out.

The body of Laura Reo, a.k.a. Jubilee Chosen, was transported from Gull Island Point, Newfoundland, to her birthplace in Boston where she is buried in Mount Auburn Cemetery, fifty feet from the bodies of her great-great-grandfather and grandmother; Elijah Kellog, author of *Child of the Island Glen*, and his wife Sara Kellog. Laura Reo was forty-eight at the time of her death, five years after she had visited Luther Van Ogtrop and left the man and his parrot Guyane to die from lethal lye fumes. Her small farm in Maine was sold at auction.

I plan to continue to visit St. Martin and sail *Boogie to Go* in the Caribbean during winter months. Judy is still home-schooling Hanna. She is still married. But, I will look her up.

And the history books will continue to list John Wilkes Booth as President Abraham Lincoln's assassin. There is no longer a shred of evidence that exists to even remotely suggest otherwise, save my writing here. And the watch. Locked away with my butterfly collection. Mine, the only basement door key.

But Hanna knows.

Just as Buzzie Thornton, Fury Ipdown and I now know to whom the $19 million which vanished from the HMS *Truro* in 1871 rightfully belonged at the time of its disappearance.

The boxes of old ledgers and insurance policies at Elmont & Thornton told us that before they were transported to the roof of 10 Hanover Street; to then be shredded page by page and sent in the air, to float east in the direction of Wall Street and the New York Stock Exchange; the man on the roof jumping up and down, clapping his hands or paws; dressed, once more, head to toe in a full-body, rabbit suit, complete with giant ears and, between the ears on the top of his head, a new, now purple and gold sombrero.

Postscript Two

March 11, 1994

LOOKING BACK at what I have written, I feel very stupid. The signs were all over the place. I did not see any of them. At times, I was looking, at least subconsciously. But I failed to see. And, at times, when I was listening, I did not hear. Not anything. Old story with me, Charles Wingate.

Today is March 11, 1994. Not long since January 28 when I thought I had finished writing of the people and events. "Filling in the pieces." My "Postscript (Original)." From Dunkerque Chamonix to Elmont Buzzie Thornton IV to Conswella to Fury Ipdown. Uncle Didier Mollard and Laura Reo and Jubilee Chosen.

I write now with great difficulty. Most of my wounds have healed, though I have a scar which runs from the back of my left shoulder and down to my elbow. Marks from the 328 stitches. And nerve damage in the arm prevents me from holding a pen very well or for very long. But, I consider myself lucky. Lucky to be alive. The emotional scars will take longer to heal.

I have never liked hospitals and am glad to be home, back at the farm now, three weeks after I lunged for the security alarm button next to the sink and then collapsed to the floor. The last thing I remember, the sound of the alarm horn blasting from the peak of the barn, both dogs dead in the driveway. I didn't hear nor see the police cars and ambulance when they arrived, no more than ten minutes later, I'm told. I find that hard to believe since they had to come from twelve miles away.

It's lonely here, but maybe I should be thankful for that. And I am less concerned now, right now, for Fury Ipdown and even Conswella than I am for Buzzie. He is crazy and does not take precautions. Ipdown and Conswella are aware of the risks and will conduct themselves accordingly. I'm not concerned for myself. The four of us are the only ones who know all, or most all, of the pieces. Collectively we do, if not individually. But, oddly, after all that has happened, there is little hard evidence. About anything. *Now that the watch is gone.*

I feel betrayed. And, I believe, with more than ample justification. But I am not bitter, and I really don't blame anyone but myself. I looked but did not see. I listened but did not hear. So, so stupid. Laura and my rational other would agree I'm sure.

The dogs always seemed to spend as much time barking as not. Hector didn't bat an eyelash when I took his queen, whispered "check," and the dogs began to howl. I was sure I heard a car coming up the driveway. It was almost 11:00 P.M., late for me.

"Who the hell is that, at this hour?" I said. Hector stared at his queen.

"I hear nothing," he said. He then glared at me.

"What's wrong?" I asked.

"You," he said. I thought he was talking about my

capturing his queen.

There was no knock at the door after the dogs went silent. I heard it being opened, and stood up. I began to walk down the hallway, Hector close behind me.

I turned the corner and stopped dead, incredulous at first and then telling myself not to panic. He just stood there, staring at me through his thick glasses and then past me to Hector. Thoughts of the phone calls with silence on the other end and letters to Hector with no return address flashed through my mind.

All at once I knew.

Hector's steel hook caught me on the left shoulder as I turned to him. I felt it rip down my arm and saw the rage on his face as the intruder now behind me brought the stainless steel wire over my head to my neck. Somehow, I managed to slip to my knees, pulling my head back and down with my body, rolling on the floor, and then staggering to the alarm button. I thought of Uncle Didier Mollard and the wire through his neck and then the sword through his back.

Neither Hector nor his father have been apprehended. He is a cunning bastard. And I am concerned for Buzzie.

Strangely, I feel very sad for Hector.

As I do for his mother.

Laura Reo.

Author's Final Note

THE FOLLOWING is an edited, partial transcript of an interview with FBI Director William Sessions conducted by the Associated Press's Wanda Roberge and Elizabeth Vargas of NBC on June 6, 1994, two months after the April disappearance of Charles Wingate.

ROBERGE: "Mr. Director, can you tell us whether you have any leads into the disappearance of Charles Wingate?"

SESSIONS: "We know only that he flew from Boston to Frankfurt on April 10, and that he rented a car at the airport there."

VARGAS: "What about Mr. Igamuche and the boy whom Mr. Wingate claimed in his manuscript was Igamuche's and Ms. Reo's son?"

SESSIONS: "As you know, there has been a world-wide alert for Aki Igamuche since long before the attack in February on Mr. Wingate at his home in Maine. As we have said before, we believe that Mr. Igamuche and the boy left the country under assumed names on February 28, aboard a flight from Chicago to

Tokyo."

ROBERGE: "Have the Japanese authorities been cooperative in terms of the search?"

SESSIONS: "No comment."

VARGAS: "What does that mean?"

SESSIONS: "I don't think that the issue is high on their priority list."

ROBERGE: "Why not? The man killed at least two people that you know of and tried to kill a third."

SESSIONS: "Right."

VARGAS: "Is that it? On that?"

SESSIONS: "Right."

ROBERGE: "Right." (sarcasm)

VARGAS: "Has the FBI done any investigating with regard to the other issues in Mr. Wingate's manuscript?"

SESSIONS: "Such as?"

VARGAS: "Such as the $20 million which disappeared in 1871 and supposedly was recovered by Mr. Thornton and Ms. Van Ogtrop. And, such as whether there is any validity to Wingate's implication that Lincoln was murdered by Vice President Andrew Johnson, not John Wilkes Booth?"

SESSIONS: "$19 million disappeared in 1871. Not $20 million. $1 million, according to the Royal Bank of Canada's records, was never missing from the ship's safe."

ROBERGE: "Big deal. What about the $19 million then?"

SESSIONS: "A 20-foot pit was apparently dug on Gull Island Point on St. Mary's Bay in Newfoundland within the past year or two. While the tides have filled the hole, the St. John's authorities have found numerous wood planks, cut not very long ago, as deep as 20 feet, at the spot Mr. Wingate wrote of, as well as a number of empty toothpaste tubes, 76 meters from the old oak tree he wrote of. Whether any money was recovered by anyone there, we do not know."

VARGAS: "Why don't you know? Has anyone contacted the man named Elmont Thornton IV, or Ms. Conswella Van Ogtrop? Supposedly they recovered the money and split it in thirds with Mr. Ipdown."

SESSIONS: "Right."

ROBERGE: "Right what?"

SESSIONS: "Scotland Yard has spoken with Mr. Ipdown. Berlin authorities and the police in Cuxhaven, Germany have spoken with Thornton and Van Ogtrop."

VARGAS: "And?"

SESSIONS: "They claim, each of them, to know nothing about any missing and found money."

ROBERGE: "Oh."

VARGAS: "What about Lincoln's assassination?"

SESSIONS: "What about it?"

VARGAS: "Is there any way to determine if there is any validity to Wingate's claim about Andrew Johnson?"

SESSIONS: "Not a shred of evidence exists to support Wingate's writing in that regard. And we don't spend our time tracking made-up stories."

ROBERGE: "How do you know he made it up? Why would he do that?"

VARGAS: "It doesn't appear that anything else in his manuscript was fabricated."

SESSIONS: "We don't know."

ROBERGE: "How much evidence do you have then that Mr. Igamuche murdered the woman, Ms. Mandarin, in London and the man, Mr. Didier Mollard, at sea?"

SESSIONS: "A great deal."

VARGAS: "What about the mini-subs and the cocaine running operation?"

SESSIONS: "What about it?"

ROBERGE: "Do you have solid evidence that Mr. Igamuche was involved in that?"

SESSIONS: "The computer records of the firm of Elmont & Thornton for the past several years implicate the man in far-flung embezzlement, beyond a shadow of a doubt. And we have confirmed that very significant portions of the embezzled money were funneled to and through two casinos on the island of St. Martin, and from there to the Bank of Colombia in Bogota. We have substantial evidence that the funds went from the bank to individuals who produced the mini-submarines that were caught, nine of them to date, each loaded with a half to a full ton of cocaine."

VARGAS: "The whole story is bizarre."

SESSIONS: "Indeed."
ROBERGE: "Mr. Director, we at Associated Press have done a little research on our own. Actually, Elizabeth here at NBC and I have been doing a little snooping on our own."
SESSIONS: "How nice."
VARGAS: "We think that Mr. Igamuche was initially out to avenge the deaths of his brothers and his parents as well as his sister."
SESSIONS: "In Mandalay in 1942. Nagasaki in 1945."
ROBERGE: "Correct."
VARGAS: "But we think there is more."
SESSIONS: "Of course. He apparently supplemented revenge with greed."
ROBERGE: "More than that."
VARGAS: "Yes."
SESSIONS: "How so?"
VARGAS: "We believe that he had a copy of the diary kept by Dunkerque Chamonix in the 1800s."
SESSIONS: "Interesting. But that's of little interest to us at the FBI, and we have no proof there ever was a diary. And if there was, how would he have gotten hold of it?"
ROBERGE: "Possibly Ms. Reo, a.k.a. Jubilee Chosen, made a copy of it, at least some pages; either before or after it was found, discovered, by her ex-husband, Mr. Elmont Thornton."
VARGAS: "Or, possibly, the boy Hector or Ms. Reo copied Mr. Wingate's copy."
SESSIONS: "Interesting speculation. But what is your point? Your question of me?"

ROBERGE: "The thirteen letters. AJNODHRNESWON. Igamuche wanted to, needed to get the gold pocket watch."

SESSIONS: "Excuse me. I'm obviously missing something here. What is your question?"

VARGAS: "No question, Mr. Sessions. Only an answer. Mr. Aki Igamuche's mother's mother, his, Igamuche's grandmother was American born. Mrs. Nishikata. Ada Booth Nishikata."

SESSIONS: "Very nice."

VARGAS: "Her father's first name was John, Igamuche's blood great-grandfather."

ROBERGE: "Family, Country, Love and Honor."

VARGAS: "John Wilkes Booth."

WCH III

Designed by A. L. Morris

Composed and printed by Knowlton & McLeary

Farmington, Maine

Bound by New Hampshire Bindery

Concord, New Hampshire